Cathy Maxwell

THE MARRIAGE RING

AVON

An Imprint of HarperCollinsPublishers

This is a work of fiction. Names, characters, places, and incidents are products of the author's imagination or are used fictitiously and are not to be construed as real. Any resemblance to actual events, locales, organizations, or persons, living or dead, is entirely coincidental.

AVON BOOKS
An Imprint of HarperCollins*Publishers*
10 East 53rd Street
New York, New York 10022-5299

Copyright © 2010 by Cathy Maxwell, Inc.
ISBN 978-0-06-177192-7
www.avonromance.com

First Avon Books paperback printing: March 2010

Avon Trademark Reg. U.S. Pat. Off. and in Other Countries, Marca Registrada, Hecho en U.S.A.
HarperCollins® is a registered trademark of HarperCollins Publishers.

Printed in the U.S.A.

10   9

To Chelsea and Daniel Maerzluft

Love is all that matters.
May yours grow and grow and grow.

THE
MARRIAGE
RING

Chapter One

London
March 1810

A God-fearing man kept his base instincts under control, if he valued his pride—and Richard Lynsted was very, very proud. Even still, the blood coursing through his veins was male and right now, it wasn't listening to brain or reason.

She *was* the most beautiful woman he'd laid eyes on.

For once, the extravagant praise heaped on an actress was accurate. If anything, what they said

about the "Scottish Songbird" Grace MacEachin might even have been subdued.

The male population of the crowd filling the theater had grown antsy during the long *Macbeth*. At one point an argument had started between one of the actors on the stage and a heckler who'd summed up the crowd's feelings by announcing they had come to see "Gracie." The only way Shakespeare could have held their interest is if Macbeth had grown "ripe, plump breasts and shining black curls."

And now, at last, *she* was on the stage, making her entrance in the light farce *The Quaker*. She played a small role—the tempting sister of some character or other such nonsense, the part that didn't wear drab brown but a rosy pink with a very low-cut bodice. At some point she would sing, presumably after the Quaker had chased her around the scenery. Richard wasn't a fan of farce . . . although he didn't mind ogling Miss MacEachin's ample breasts.

He wasn't alone. The audience stomped and clapped its welcome, necks craning for a better look. What women who had stayed for her performance became equally animated. Fans flipped open and started fluttering as lips hid behind them to express to compatriots what they *really* thought of her looks.

Miss MacEachin started to speak her part—

"I lovvve you, Gracie," a male voice from the overcrowded two-shilling gallery interrupted.

"Yes, we looovvve you," the fashionable young bucks on the front row mimicked.

Happy laughter agreed and then everyone began repeating her name. "Gra-cie, Gra-cie, Gra-cie." The syllables came out faster and faster as they clapped the beat, effectively cutting off anything the actress had to say.

Richard stood in the shadows of the private box, his arms crossed, sizing her up.

Miss MacEachin had that deceptive quality called presence that made her seem both at ease and in control. She held up her hand, begging for a silence her admirers were not ready to give.

The other actors and actresses on stage were not so patient. One actor began shouting his lines.

"*Sing,*" someone in the boxes opposite Richard's yelled out and the demand easily swept the audience, who began chanting, "Sing, sing, sing."

The actor again tried his line and ended up with a head of cabbage being thrown at him. He dodged it but then began a new game—chasing the actors off the stage with a new barrage of vegetables or whatever else was close at hand.

The actors and actress scrambled to the safety of the wings, including Miss MacEachin. Only a few months before, this same theater had been the scene of riots over a hike in the price of tickets. They respected what a London crowd could do.

"Gra-cie, Gra-cie, Gra-cie." The chant went up again, the sound growing louder, more insistent—

Miss MacEachin came stumbling onto the stage, obviously pushed there by one of her colleagues. Her audience roared their approval.

She quickly recovered her poise, tugging up her bodice to keep herself intact. Richard wondered if she could feel every male in the crowd undressing her with his eyes.

Then again, she must like it. Why else would a woman stoop so low as to become an actress?

Miss MacEachin's gaze went directly to his box in search of her good friend Fiona, the Duchess of Holburn. The box belonged to her husband, who was also Richard's cousin. The lovely Fiona, a woman Richard didn't know well because his side of the family didn't mix with Holburn's, was both countrywoman and friend to Miss MacEachin. Clearly she had been expecting to see Fiona in the box this evening.

Fiona *had* been there. In one of those happenstances of fate, Richard's path had crossed his cousin's. Fiona had insisted Richard join their party, which had included their Spanish friend, the *barón de Valencia*.

Holburn and Richard rarely appeared anywhere together, especially in public. They were of the same age and had attended the same schools, but while the duke was well liked, Richard was not. He knew that. He lived with it.

However, marriage had obviously made Holburn mellow because he had seconded the invitation—and what choice had Richard save to accept it?

Of course, he'd been concerned. How was he to confront Miss MacEachin and speak his mind with Fiona close at hand? Then, to his surprise, the duke, duchess, and the Spaniard had left the box abruptly after the *Macbeth*.

Richard had assumed they would return for Miss MacEachin's performance. However, the curtain rose and there had been no sign of them.

A polite knock on the door interrupted his thoughts. A porter handed Richard a note. It was from Holburn. There had been an emergency and it was imperative they leave with Andres, the Spaniard. Fiona had added a postscript prettily begging Richard to personally deliver an apology for her absence to Miss MacEachin and her promise to call on her friend as soon as she was able.

Meanwhile, on the stage, Miss MacEachin was saying a few words to the conductor, who nodded and passed the word on to the musicians. His baton went up and they played opening strains to a lovely ballad, "Barbara Allen."

Miss MacEachin sang, her voice clear and pure.

However, the crowd was not satisfied. They had not come for sweetly sung music and their thoughts were summed up by an obviously inebriated wigged gent who stood up in his chair on the front row and yelled, "Here now, something lively. Didn't come here for ballads. I want to watch your titties bounce."

His comment startled the crowd, who quickly recovered and burst into laughter.

The bucks down the row from the gent began shouting, "Titties!" And a new chant was born.

Blushing furiously, Miss MacEachin tried to go on with the song but found she couldn't. She looked offstage as if for help, and discovered none was forthcoming. With one man's crudity, she'd become fair game. It was the way of the world. People turned mean.

Any other woman would have cried quarter and run off the stage. Not Miss MacEachin. To Richard's fascination, her whole manner changed. Her back straightened. Her chin lifted in pride and her eyes took on the unholy light of battle.

She marched to the edge of the stage where the wigged man stood in his seat, waving his arm and encouraging his cheer. He was a pudgy thing, dressed in white knee breeches and a cerulean blue coat that was a size too small for him. His lips were small and pouty and his nose the size of a pig's snout.

The cheering crowd went silent in eager anticipation of what Miss MacEachin was about to do.

The gent didn't immediately realize he was shouting alone. He glanced around and only then noticed Miss MacEachin on the stage above him. She tapped an impatient foot, her hands on her hips. This was the sort of woman Richard had suspected her to be. Bold, unabashed.

Her wigged admirer smiled. "Love you, Gracie," he slurred with a happy hiccup.

"Then come up here," she suggested. "You can't watch my titties bounce from that seat." She had a magical accent. Some Scots sounded guttural or too flat in their tone. Hers had the lilt of music.

The audience loved her suggestion. They cat-called and urged the man to go up onstage.

He was only too eager to comply. He looked for steps, walking in first one direction and then in another.

"I'm waiting," Miss MacEachin chastised.

"Where's the stairs?" her gent begged.

"Who needs stairs?" was her reply. "Climb up on the stage right here."

The gent eyed the climb, a bit daunted.

Miss MacEachin bent down, giving an eyeful of her ample cleavage. "Hurry. Everyone is waiting," she said. "*I'm* waiting."

Voices from those around him chimed in now, telling him to climb upon the stage and placing his pride on the line. He made his first attempt to hoist himself up onto the stage and failed. He failed a second and third time, too. By now the audience was enjoying itself at his expense. Their laughter grew louder alongside his frustration.

And then, with the help of a push to his fanny from one of the bucks sitting beside him, he made his way up onto the stage. He balanced there at the edge on his knees, waving his arms and encouraging the crowd to clap for him.

Miss MacEachin brought an end to his antics by waiting for him to start to climb to his feet and giving his rump a good swift kick with her foot. The man went flying into the front row, his wig sailing off into the second.

The theater went wild with laughter.

"*That* is for not having the sense to listen to me when I sing," Miss MacEachin informed him. "And for the rest of you, I have this song to share."

She didn't wait for music but launched into a defiant, lusty little song about how a woman should always put a man in his place. The chorus was,

"Hi diddle, hi diddle, hey!" By the time she was finished singing, her audience, including her disgraced admirer, was lustily singing it with her.

Miss MacEachin didn't linger. She made a quick curtsey, waved to the two-shilling seats and the boxes and ran offstage.

Now Richard understood why all the men had gathered here. She was as beautiful as she was bold . . . but she also had talent. There was far more to her than creamy skin and ebony curls.

The theater's pillars and crystal chandeliers shook with applause. Flowers flew through the air to land on the stage. "One *more* song, Gracie," became the refrain. "*One* more."

But Miss MacEachin was not accommodating. The bouquet-covered stage remained empty.

Many men, including the fancy bucks on the front row, rose from their seats and headed for the nearest exits. Richard knew what they were about. The frenzy of entries in London's betting books over which man would be the first to bed her had become the stuff of legend. From what Richard had heard, well over two hundred vied for the honor. The race was on. Every buck, every beau, every Corinthian schemed to lavish her with jewels, money, and promises to claim her for his lover.

But as Richard left the box to join the stream of men queuing up outside the stage door, he knew there was a difference between them.

He wasn't there to bed Miss MacEachin.

He was there to destroy her.

Chapter Two

"*G*o back out onto that stage and *sing another song*," John Drayson, the stage manager ordered. He was a dark-haired man with distinguished gray at the temples. Many women found him attractive. Grace didn't. He lacked sincerity and had a touch of the bully in his demeanor. "Listen to them," Drayson continued. "They are mad for you."

Grace shook her head. She was trembling she was so angry. "Mad for me? They didn't hear a word I sang."

"Oh, yes they did! They heard that last song clear as a bell. Tomorrow, that 'hi diddle hey' refrain will be on everyone's lips. Go out there,

Gracie. Give them more of what they want," he ordered, taking her arm to steer her back onstage.

Grace dug in her heels, but before she could answer such an outrageous command, Chester, one of the stagehands, interrupted. "Excuse me, Miss MacEachin," he said, his arms full of bouquets he'd pick up off the stage. "What do you want me to do with these?"

"Burn them," Grace instructed, yanking her arm free of Drayson's hold. She'd had enough. She needed privacy, a place to think and evaluate the public humiliation she'd just experienced on the stage. Some women might covet such attention. She did not. She started for the stairs leading down to the dressing rooms.

"Collect them all. Take them to her dressing room," Drayson countermanded as he fell into step behind her.

With an impatient sound, Grace moved away with every intention of outdistancing him, but as she walked past the other actors waiting in the wings, she overheard one of the other new actors, Mr. Holland, opine, "So, we have a new Grand Doxy of London."

Grace came to a halt.

The "Grand Doxy of London" was a name the actors had for the actress who would become the next big rage in London. It was not a compliment Grace wanted. It meant the woman had more looks than talent and would soon be sought after as a mistress by London's most powerful men. It was assumed she would accept this protection.

The actresses surrounding Mr. Holland, especially the ones who had been so *un*helpful since Grace had been promoted from a dancer to one of their company two weeks ago, sniggered over the comment.

"Shut your mouth, Holland," Drayson snapped, taking Grace's arm before she could comment. He guided her forward. "Don't listen to him. That cabbage should have hit him in the head and spared us all from his nonsense."

But Grace knew Mr. Holland spoke aloud what was whispered everywhere she went. Wagers were being placed in betting books all over the city linking her name with a host of rakes, scoundrels, and idiots. Claiming her had become a game. Men seemed to rush at her from every direction when she was in the theater, including Mr. Holland, whose advances she'd spurned earlier that afternoon. So, his surly comment shouldn't have surprised her. There was no man more dangerous than a rejected one.

But Holland was the least of her worries. She'd

been informed the notorious Lord Stone was placing the highest wagers. The stories she'd heard of him were unsettling.

Grace had taken action to avoid offending him and all the rest. She was refusing all callers save for Fiona. Rumor had it that Stone had offered a hefty purse to the watchman and several of the porters and stagehands for access to her. Fortunately, she was well liked in that quarter and his bribe had been rebuffed—for now.

If the attitude of Mr. Holland and her fellow players was an indication, it was only a matter of time before someone would sell her out.

Thank the Lord that Fiona had *not* been in her box tonight. Grace had left word with the watchman to let the Duchess of Holburn pass, but was now so glad Fiona had stayed away.

"My temper found the best of me," Grace murmured, now mortified at the way she'd set that wigged man in his place in front of everyone in the theater.

"Your temper knows how to put on a show," Drayson answered. "Go out there again, Gracie," he coaxed. "Sing another one. They are still waiting. Can't you hear them stomping their feet?"

How could she not? The floorboards trembled with the clamor.

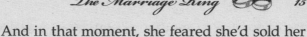

And in that moment, she feared she'd sold her soul.

Fiona had tried to warn her. When they'd first come to London, Fiona had taken work as a seamstress, but Grace had wanted more. In spite of her friend's warnings, Grace had pursued the stage . . .

"Don't call me Gracie," she answered. "I'm Grace. Grace, Grace, *Grace*." She grabbed the stair rail and went charging down the narrow, winding steps leading to the dressing rooms.

Drayson was right on her heels.

He caught up with her at the foot of the stairs, grabbing her arm and whirling her to face him.

"Grace, listen to me. We are giving you your own place on the bill. And I want you to continue wearing this costume. We'll put people out in the audience to rile them all up. There won't be an empty seat in the house—"

"*No*," Grace said, attempting to shake off his arm. "I'll not parade myself around."

He gave her arm a vicious shake. They were alone here. Everyone else was still upstairs dealing with the muddled mess the show had become.

"Now, listen here, we lost a lot of money during the riots and you can make it up. You are becoming famous in London. Every day more people hear about you—"

Chester, his arms still full of flowers, poked his head down and over the railing. "Miss MacEachin, they are lined up outside and howling to see you. Mr. Kemble said for you to come greet them."

"She'll be right there," Drayson answered.

"Very good, sir." Chester left to pass the word.

"I won't go out there," Grace said.

"You have no choice, if you value your place in this company."

"Then I *quit* my place in this company," Grace answered. She shoved him out of her way with her shoulder and charged toward her room. With her growing popularity, Drayson had given her a private dressing room, another thing the actresses could hold against her. She now ran in there to hide, slamming the door behind her.

At last she could breathe.

So there it was: she was out of work.

It was just as well. She hated London, and she'd wanted to leave anyway. She and Fiona had thought to find their fortune here. Fiona had succeeded. She'd married Holburn, but Grace had not been so fortunate. She'd thought she could handle the stage, this way of life. She couldn't. After all was said and done, she was Scot.

The wave of homesickness for the Highlands almost brought her to her knees.

She wanted to go home.

Grace dug out a valise from a corner of the room and began throwing clothes into it, slowly at first and then with increasing urgency.

When she'd run away from Inverness five years ago, she'd thought of never returning. For the past month, it had been all she could think about. She'd started to wonder if things truly had been how she'd imagined them or if, perhaps, she'd overreacted, made more of what was happening than should matter. Funny how life's twists and the tricks it played had finally brought her to her senses. She wanted to go back—and she wanted to make amends.

Sitting at her dressing table, she began washing off the paints she'd used, silently vowing to never use them again. The woman in the reflection appeared apprehensive. Grace reminded herself she had enough money to see her through to the end of the month, but old worries died hard.

How different her life would have been if her father's path had never crossed that of the Lynsted twins. They had accused her father, a vicar at St. Ann's Church, of stealing funds from the estate of Dame Mary Ewing, the widow of a well-known soldier who'd made a fortune during his service in the Indies. On their testimony, he had been sentenced to a penal colony for ten long years, years during which Grace and her mother had gone

from being important members of Inverness society to outcasts living hand-to-mouth as best they could.

She set aside the washcloth, not wanting to think about her mother. The woman was dead to her.

But her father . . . he'd done nothing wrong save disappoint her mother. And Grace hadn't the maturity to understand all that was happening between them. She'd blamed him for her mother abandoning her. The poor man. He'd suffered so much, and upon returning home hadn't even had his wife to comfort him . . . or his daughter.

But now she had a chance to right not only an old wrong but to prove her loyalty to her father. Perhaps her running away five years ago was God's hand bringing her to London so that she could demand justice for her father and her family name.

Who else but the Almighty could have led her to learn that the Duke of Holburn's uncles, Lord Brandt and Lord Maven, the family members no one liked and avoided, were also none other than the villainous Lynsted twins?

Grace had put it together when she'd met the twins while out shopping with Fiona. Their stern demeanors, slashing black brows, and hooked noses were etched into her childhood nightmares. She'd recognized them immediately and since that day had plotted ways to find justice for her father.

She'd not told Fiona or Holburn about what she'd planned to do. Blackmail was a touchy thing. Fiona might not understand Grace's motives.

Their lordships were now very wealthy, probably from a fortune that built on Dame Mary's once sizeable estate. Meanwhile, her gentle, educated, kind father was nothing more than a caretaker, living off charity in a tiny cottage on St. Ann's grounds. He'd never left Inverness. She didn't know why, but he'd stayed . . . without benefit of family or friends.

Her father deserved a portion of that fortune.

Grace had threatened to take her charges against them to a magistrate if they did not pay twenty-five thousand pounds for her silence. She didn't worry about whether or not the magistrate believed her story. The twins were self-made men and society frowned on that sort of thing. Rumor had it their own father, Holburn's grandfather, had disinherited them. No one knew why, but it spoke volumes against them.

For all Grace knew, there was a host of crimes they were guilty of and she was doing the world a favor by making them pay up.

She wondered what her father would say when she reappeared in his life with enough money to make him comfortable and begged forgiveness for the hurtful words she'd hurled at him five years ago. The image gave her peace—

A knock sounded on the door. Before she could answer, it opened and Drayson stepped inside.

Grace rose from her seat. "I did not invite you in, Mr. Drayson."

"We need to speak," he answered, closing the door behind him. "You will not quit this company."

"I have said all I am going to say, Mr. Drayson," Grace answered, reaching behind her for the hand-sized dirk in its leather sheath she had placed there. "I appreciate the opportunity to be part of such a fine company, but I regret I must leave."

He shook his head. "No, you won't." He moved toward her.

Grace found the knife. Keeping her hand hidden behind her, she slid the dirk from its sheath. "Whatever you have to say can be saved for the morning," she informed him. "I'm tired. I wish to go home."

"You know, there is quite a bounty on your head, Miss MacEachin. And many men wish to claim it."

"I don't know what you are talking about," she

lied, the dirk now in her hand. She grasped the handle, ready to fight. She was a petite woman, no more than five foot three. He would try brute strength. They all did. He'd be surprised.

"You do. You know very well. And you may put on airs and keep your distance, but you've been had before, Grace. Probably by more than one man. It's there in the way you walk, the way you talk to us. I've seen the way you look at each of us. You know men."

Suddenly, he lunged for her.

She whipped the knife around and plunged it into his forearm without so much as a blink of an eye.

He yelped in pain and fell back a step. "*You she-bitch.*" He pulled the knife out of his arm. Looking at it in the candlelight, he tossed it aside and picked up one of her scarves to wrap around the wound.

Grace wanted to leave but he stood between her and the door. Her only hope was to run for it.

She dashed toward the door. He stuck out a foot and tripped her. She landed heavily on the ground. With a shake of her head, she scrambled to her feet and would have made it to the door except he took hold of her hair and yanked her back.

The wind left her as he threw her against the wall. "Stabbing me is going to cost you dearly," he said and laughed, the sound angry and mean.

Grace reached out, blindly searching for something else to protect herself with, but he was on her in a blink. He shoved her against the wall, pinning her there with his body weight. His lips slobbered over her cheek, her ear. He squeezed her breast so hard she cried out.

"This is what happens when you flaunt yourself," he said against her ear. "And the best part of all is that I will claim those wagers, *after* you're here tomorrow and singing exactly as I say."

His hand was fumbling with the buttons of his breeches. Grace attempted to lift her knee, to kick him or hit him in any place she possibly could. He shoved his knee between her legs, blocking the move.

He pressed his open mouth against hers. She sealed her lips shut, fighting back with everything she had, but he was too strong. She'd had her one chance with her knife and she'd failed—

Mr. Drayson's body came off of hers. Unprepared for such sudden freedom, she lost her balance and slid down the wall to the floor. She looked up, dazed, not knowing what Mr. Drayson was going to do next, until she realized he was being held in midair by the scruff of the neck, his feet dancing as they tried to touch the floor.

And holding him up was the tallest, biggest man Grace had ever set eyes on.

His dark hair almost brushed the low ceiling of her dressing room and his brow was furrowed with righteous anger. His nose was long and straight, his jaw square. He wore black evening attire under a black, caped greatcoat, the cut so severe it gave him a parson's air.

No one would call him a handsome man. His features were too bold for that word.

Grace wasn't the only one taken aback by him. Mr. Drayson whimpered as if he was looking into the face of the devil.

"What's going on here?" the man demanded, giving Mr. Drayson a shake.

" 'Twas between myself and her," Mr. Drayson managed to say. He reached down to button his breeches up.

"She didn't appear to be a willing participant," the stranger said.

Grace shook her head, whether out of agreement or fear she didn't know—and then realized her dirk lay on the floor close at hand. She grabbed it and leaned against the wall, holding the weapon in front of her.

"Who are you to be coming in here anyway?" Mr. Drayson demanded, finding his bluster.

"I am the man who will throw you through the wall if I ever see you treat another woman that way again," the stranger answered. He dropped Mr. Drayson to the floor.

The stage manager came to his feet. He shrugged his coat back up on his shoulders. "You don't know what you saw. That lass is a whore. Why do you think she was given the opportunity to sing? She serviced me and she serviced me well. Nor am I the only one."

Grace was on her feet in a blink and charging toward Mr. Drayson. She would rip the tongue from his head—

The stranger stepped in front of her. He easily caught both her wrists. He looked over his shoulder at Mr. Grayson. "I'd advise you to leave now, sir. I don't believe I can hold her off much longer."

"I was leaving anyway," Mr. Grayson answered. He curled his lip. "*Whore*," he said as his parting epithet.

Grace shook her fists in fury trying to escape the stranger's grasp. "I'm going to bury my knife in your heart," she promised him.

"And I never want to see you in my theater again," Mr. Drayson answered. He turned and realized the stranger had left the door open and a good number of the theater's company stood there with raised brows and wide eyes.

"Be gone," Mr. Drayson ordered. They quickly dispersed and he stomped out.

That there had been witnesses to what was happening to her and no one had offered to protect her infuriated Grace.

She wrested her arms from the stranger and charged into the hall. "You were listening?" she shouted to the ones who still lingered there. "You knew what was going on in here but didn't offer to help?"

Marching back into the room, she slammed the door. It made such a satisfying sound she was tempted to do it again and again. She was that crazed.

All her life she'd been the one everyone gossiped about—first because of her father's ruin and then later because of her looks, which had condemned her to too much male attention, especially of the wrong sort.

Her eye caught the tip of the knife she still held. How easy would it be to gouge her own face? To destroy what few blessings God had given her? And how freeing the thought was—

The knife was taken from her hands.

She looked up, startled. She'd been so lost in her anguish, she'd forgotten she wasn't alone. She now reached for the knife. "That's *mine*."

He held it away from her. "I'll keep it for the moment. I don't want you to hurt someone with it."

"You don't know what I'm thinking."

A sharpness came to his eyes, a moment of quick understanding, and she realized he had known. She shook her head. Impossible. No one knew the dark thoughts that haunted her.

"You are afraid I'll hurt you," she declared, hiding any vulnerability behind bravado. "And I might if you don't give it back to me."

He laughed, the sound not particularly nice. "You're a kitten. I'm not afraid of you with a knife." He tossed the knife onto her dressing table, almost as if he dared her to go after it.

"Who are you?" Grace demanded. She'd never set eyes on him and yet there was something familiar about his features.

"What? No thank-you for intervening and tossing that scoundrel out of your room?" He had a deep voice, a melodic one. "Or perhaps my interruption was not appreciated? Perhaps that was the sort of play you two enjoyed?"

Grace reached up to slap him, even as she was mortified to her soul that she should appear so ungrateful. She caught herself in time. Lowered her hand. "You are right, I am less than gracious. I do appreciate your coming to my rescue."

She ran a distracted hand through her hair and realized only then it was falling around her shoulders. In the short span of violence, the pins had come undone in her struggles and Mr. Drayson had ripped her sleeve to expose half her breast.

Embarrassed, she pulled the fabric up to cover herself. Anger gave way to fear. The stage manager had come very close to raping her. She'd been raped once and had promised herself it would not happen again. Mr. Drayson's attack left her vulnerable and feeling very foolish.

Tears choked her throat. She held them back. She never cried in front of anyone. She had too much pride.

"Thank you," she managed to say. "I mean that truly. I fear what would have happened."

"There is always a price to pay for women like you who live on the outside of society."

Women like her . . .

Once again branded. Her good will toward him evaporated and she gave him a hard look, truly seeing him for the first time and noting the harsh lines around his mouth. This man didn't trust anyone.

She could respect that. She felt the same way.

"Again, I thank you," she said stiffly. "Now, if you will excuse me, I need to pack."

"I have a note for you," he replied, pulling a folded piece of paper from the inside pocket of his black greatcoat. "It is from the Duchess of Holburn."

Grace grabbed the note and opened it, turning so he could watch her reading it. She immediately recognized Fiona's handwriting. Her friend apologized because she could not stay. A situation had arisen with a friend and she had to accompany her husband, but wanted Grace to know just how uniquely talented and gifted she was.

Dear Fiona. Grace folded the note and pressed it between her palms. She faced the gentleman. "Thank you for delivering this. The duchess is very close to my heart. I shall value her friendship always."

"You sound as if you will not be able to convey that message to her yourself?" he observed.

Grace frowned. This man paid close attention to her, but it wasn't the sort she usually earned from his sex. She sensed he didn't like her.

"For all of your great height and breadth, you are not a dullard, are you?" she said. "You pick up on every nuance . . . or is that something you are doing only for me?"

He smiled, his eyes going hard. She knew then

her instincts were right—this man was not to be trusted.

"You're not a dullard either, Miss MacEachin," he said. "Let me introduce myself. That might explain a great deal. My name is Lynsted. I'm the Honorable Richard Lynsted, Lord Brandt's son and heir. You and I have a few matters to discuss. Especially about your attempt to blackmail my father."

Now Grace understood why he had appeared familiar to her.

So, *this* was the son.

She smiled, certain of herself now. "I beg to differ with you, Mr. Lynsted. Is it blackmail to speak the truth?"

Chapter Three

*R*ichard's guard went up. Before his eyes Miss MacEachin transformed from a distraught, shaken creature who had struggled to fend off an attack to a calculating Scot.

His father and uncle had always warned him about the Scots. They were ruthless and manipulative—two apt descriptions of the infamous Grace MacEachin.

Well, she'd just met her match.

"There is no truth in your charges," he replied briskly. "And if you continue your threats, we shall be forced to take you before the magistrate."

"By all means, *please* take this before a magistrate," she urged him. "In fact, that is what I've told your father and uncle I would do. I will be more than happy to have my day in court and speak my piece to the public and the papers. Although I'm surprised Lord Maven and Lord Brandt are so anxious to have me do so. What I have to say would tarnish their sterling reputations—"

She broke off as if struck by a new thought. "They don't know you are here, do they?" she said slowly, reasoning aloud. "You've come on your own . . . because, believe me, your father and uncle do not want what I have to say anywhere near the papers and gossip mongers."

She was right.

Miss MacEachin had seen through his threat.

This afternoon Richard had found his father uncharacteristically deep into his cups. He rarely drank and to see him in a drunken state in the middle of the day had been alarming.

When he'd asked what was wrong, his father had confessed how Miss MacEachin was black-mailing him by accusing them of a crime they hadn't committed. He and his brother had never embezzled money from anyone. Ever.

Richard believed him. His father never lied to him. Besides, both he and uncle were the most morally righteous men Richard knew.

He was also flattered that his father had, for once, confided in him. The twins were very close.

Richard was the outsider. They rarely requested his advice or sought his counsel. He wanted very much to resolve this matter for his father. He longed to prove his loyalty.

"Have they told you exactly what charges I make against them?" she wondered. "Did they tell you they ruined my father when they stole money from an elderly woman's estate and then pinned the blame on him?"

"My father and uncle would never do such a thing. Anyone knowing them would find it impossible to imagine."

"Truly?" She crossed to her dressing table and picked up a leather sheath. She slid her knife into it. "Her name was Dame Mary Ewing. She was very ill and her only son was serving our country far away. She trusted my father to handle her accounts. He had the bad wisdom to place them in the hands of your father and uncle. They stole it and accused him of the theft. He was sentenced on their testimony."

"Ah, sentenced in a court of law," Richard agreed. "And by jury of his peers, I presume. I can sympathize with your desire to prove your father innocent, Miss MacEachin but falsely accusing other men is not the way to go, especially after he was *convicted* of the crime."

She didn't like his rational logic. Her chin came up. "I know about you. I've done my best to learn everything about your family."

"And what do you know about me?" he challenged, intrigued in spite of himself by every facet of this woman.

The truth was, Miss MacEachin was even more lovely up close—but what caught him by surprise was her sense of purpose, her intelligence. Her obvious education. She spoke well and moved with a natural grace one wouldn't expect of the lower classes.

"I know you are a snob." She smiled at him as if she'd known what he was thinking.

"I am not," Richard said, not liking the word.

"It's your reputation." She shrugged as if helpless to change her opinion. "You are also known as a fine legal mind, although to the dismay of your mentors, you don't practice law. The Honorable Richard Lynsted," she said as if reading his name in the air. "Graduated with high honors from Christ Church College and then took your training and study of the law at Lincoln's Inn. But you turned your back on it. Instead, you manage your father and uncle's business and to great advantage. You've made them very rich and although you keep to yourself, there are those who have noticed your financial acumen. Do you like that word, Mr. Lynsted? Acumen? It means you have a natural gift, an understanding, a perception for something." She paused and then said softly, "*I* have an acumen."

She moved toward him. Her bodice barely clung to her left breast. Moments before she'd been modest and tried to keep it up. Now, she didn't care, and he had a damned time keeping his eyes off that curve of flesh.

Miss MacEachin stopped in front of him, standing so close their toes touched . . . and her impudent, immodest, alluring breast was less than an inch from his chest.

She smiled up at him. "My acumen is that I know men. I've always known them from the moment I first started to bud." She drew a deep breath, the movement lifting her breast and looking down from this angle he could see the edge of her nipple. The scent of roses filled the air.

"Do you know they say you never laugh?" she asked him, her voice husky. She knew what she was doing. She ridiculed him, but not with words.

Richard prided himself on his control, but God had also made him a man. The sight brought the blood rushing to his groin—and she knew it.

With a dismissive laugh, she backed away from

him, raising her bodice. Teasing him with not only her body but with her confidence.

In that moment, Richard could have hated her. He chose not to. Here was his enemy and it would behoove him to look deeper.

Her manner sobered. "Your father and uncle are guilty. They are too moral, too upright, too unforgiving. That's the way men are when they are guilty. I also know that they left London decades ago disinherited by their father. The twins had a violent streak that their father would not condone."

"You are speaking nonsense," Richard said.

Her gaze studied him a moment. "You really don't know, do you? You should. It would explain society's attitude towards them."

"My father and uncle are very well respected—"

"What *nonsense*," she declared.

"There is jealousy because they are so successful—"

"There is suspicion because of the murder."

Richard shook his head, his anger like bile in his throat. "The stable lad's death was an accident. For decades they've lived with those rumors. That's why they are concerned about your insinuations."

"Yes, because they are *true*," she flashed back.

"You have *no* proof."

"I do!"

"Then what is it?" he demanded.

Once again they stood almost toe-to-toe but this time there was no attraction. Only animosity. She could have been stark naked and he wouldn't have cared.

"Where did they earn the start of their fortune?" she wondered.

"They invested."

"In what? Ships, funds, businesses?"

Richard almost laughed. "They invested in the *Wind's Mistress*. She was the beginning of our shipping company."

"And where, after they'd been cut off from the old duke, did they find money for such an investment? They purchased that ship outright."

She had been doing her investigating. But Richard knew the answer. "They started with several small investments until they accrued the funds for the ship."

"Is that what they told you?" she asked, her tone insinuating she thought him a fool.

"Yes."

"And I suppose they've also told you they've never been to Scotland?"

He really didn't like her. "They have." His father had reiterated as much only that afternoon.

"They are lying."

"If you were a man, I'd call you out for saying that."

"Why don't you do something better?" she challenged. "Why don't you come to Scotland with me and hear my father's story? If you don't believe him, you can walk away. But you won't. You'll hear the truth if you are the man they say you are."

"You don't know me," Richard shot back. "Nor do I answer to you."

"Poor Richard Lynsted," she mocked, "always behind his ledgers and locked up with his accounts."

Her mark hit home. He did spend hours each day poring over the accounts he managed. The businesses had taken on a life of their own. He'd been very successful and made lots of money, but was increasingly finding himself imprisoned by that success.

"Who told you that?" he said, annoyed that she knew so much about him.

She smiled, an expression much like that of a cat who'd found the cream. "Whispers. Rumors."

"Lies," he added.

"Truly?" she wondered, daring him to answer. "*Yes.*"

Miss MacEachin laughed. "Then what difference would it make for you to come to Scotland

and hear my father's story? Or are you afraid of the truth?"

"What do you gain from my doing so?"

"Justice." The lines of her mouth flattened. "This isn't about money, although I believe my father deserves something for the suffering the twins have caused him. They destroyed his reputation, his marriage . . ." She paused as if catching herself from revealing more.

Richard filled in the space. "Are you and your father close?"

"No." She crossed her arms as if suddenly cold and then reached for a shawl draped over a packed valise on a chair. Tossing it around her shoulders, she covered herself. "We haven't been." She raised her gaze to his. "We could be." She paused and then added, "I owe him this."

So, it really wasn't about money.

The understanding shifted the situation for Richard. He ran a hand through his hair, realized that when he'd entered the room and grabbed the scoundrel attacking her, he'd lost his hat in the fray. He spied it on the floor by the door and reached down to pick it up. As he did so, he came to a decision. "I'll go with you to Scotland. Of course, I have work here—"

"Work that is more important than the truth, Mr. Lynsted?"

God, she was like a conscience.

"We can travel fast," she assured him as if realizing she should have held her tongue. "With good weather, the post can make the trip to Inverness in four to five days. You listen to my father's story and leave. To hear the truth will take a little more than a week of your life."

"I could ride alone faster."

"But my father won't trust you. He won't tell you all."

Richard frowned. "You just said you were estranged. Does that mean he'll speak the truth in front of you? Perhaps you are the one who has been lied to."

Her shoulders tightened. She hugged the shawl closer. "Perhaps," she conceded. She stood for a moment in indecision and then confessed, "I want to go home."

"So, I take you home, listen to your father, and whether I believe his story or not, you cease making these unfounded accusations."

"They aren't unfounded, but yes, I will agree to those terms."

"And money?" he asked pointedly. "Did you not want a healthy sum from my father and uncle?"

Her brow knit together as she considered the matter. "If my story is true, then yes, I believe my father is owed something, do you not?"

"If it is true, there should be recompense."

"Just so," she agreed, smiling. "I am not lying, Mr. Lynsted. And I know it appears I am attempting to blackmail your father, but I truly want what is just and rightly my father's. He lost everything he had in paying back Dame Ewing's estate and still owes more. Time has passed but my father has a heavy conscience."

She held out her hand for him as if wanting to shake. "So, it is agreed?"

Richard eyed her hand suspiciously. He'd shaken many a man's hand during a business transaction but never a woman's. "That's not necessary."

"Yes, it is," she insisted. "We have an agreement. A handshake will bind us, or at least that's the way we Scots look at it. You can't trust a man who won't shake your hand."

"Some would say you can't trust a Scot," Richard murmured.

She laughed, the sound as musical as her singing. "Don't believe everything they say about the Scots," she advised him. "So, do you take my hand?"

"Very well." Richard took her hand in his own gloved one. Hers felt small next to his but there was strength there, too . . . and something else. It was almost as if sparks shot from the tips of her bare fingers and up through his arm, even in spite of his gloves. He could feel her warmth, her spirit.

His initial reaction was to release her fingers immediately and yet he had to hold on. He *wanted* to hold on.

And he wanted to kiss her, too. The desire primitive and demanding.

This was not like him.

He released her hand, his action abrupt.

Miss MacEachin noticed. She was too clever not to. Her smile grew tight.

"When shall we leave?" he asked to cover the sudden silence.

"Tomorrow?" She shrugged. "The man you threw out of my dressing room was the stage manager. I'd already quit, but I'm certain after you showing him the door, I am definitely not welcome back now."

"Tomorrow?" Richard tested the idea, and discovered the first stirring of excitement over the idea of adventure.

She was right. He did spend too much time with his ledgers and accounts. His initial enthusiasm for making money and brokering new deals had lost its appeal years ago. Now, his work had become a chore, a daily drudge to be endured. He'd recently taken up the sport of boxing and had found the physical exertion the only way he could cope with a growing restlessness.

"Tomorrow would be good," he heard himself say.

She rewarded him with another one of her smiles. "Excellent. What time should we leave?"

"Early morning. Say around eight?"

"I'll be ready. Will we go by coach? I can pay my own way—"

"My family has a coach. We might as well be comfortable."

She appeared ready to argue, and then thought better of it. "I'll see you on the morrow at eight then." She began gathering her things. The shawl fell open and she remembered her torn bodice. She heaved a heavy sigh. "Please, I have another favor to ask. Would you wait for me to change and then escort me to the stage door? Mr. Drayson has a nasty temper and I have no desire to run into him again."

"Of course," Richard said. "Shall I wait in the hall?" he asked, realizing as he said it how silly that sounded. "Of course I should wait in the hall," he mumbled, rushing out the door before he added to his awkwardness.

Grace was charmed. Richard Lynsted was not what she'd expected. Yes, he was stuffy, but so was his sire. However, unlike his father, there was an honesty and a bit of naiveté about him.

She slipped behind the dressing screen in the corner of the room and changed from the torn costume into a blue sprigged day dress with a demure bodice trimmed in lace. After repinning her hair, she set a gold velvet cap at a flirty angle over her curls, and threw her cape over her shoulders.

Grace was not displeased with her agreement. All she wanted for her father was the chance to tell his story, a chance for justice to be served.

Would Mr. Lynsted give him a fair hearing? She thought so. After all, the man had shaken her hand. She pulled her gloves on.

Nor was she afraid of him. One thing Grace had confidence in was her ability to handle men. She could keep him in his place for the space of the ride to Scotland.

Before picking up her valise, she took a moment to strap her dirk in its sheath to her wrist. A woman couldn't be too careful.

Mr. Lynsted waited outside her door. He'd been leaning against the wall, his head nearly brushing the ceiling. He straightened as she came out of her room. His gaze traveled over her, but he looked away before she could tell if he approved of her more modest attire or not. She'd assumed he would and was surprised she was a bit annoyed he hadn't offered a compliment.

Perhaps Mr. Lynsted would present a challenge as well. It had been a long time since Grace had met a man who ignored her. The trip to Scotland might prove entertaining.

"Let me carry your luggage," he said.

"I'm fine. I carry it all the time."

"I'll carry it," he repeated in a voice that brooked no disobedience. Grace let him have it.

She led him up the stairs. As she'd anticipated, Mr. Drayson lingered backstage, waiting for her. As she came up the stairs, he moved forward, saw Mr. Lynsted, and then hastily retreated.

Grace didn't wait for an invitation but tucked her hand in the crook of the big man's arm. She liked standing next to him. She liked big men. They made her feel protected.

Chester had never delivered the flowers to her room. Instead, they had been dumped in a rubbish bin by the backstage door. They filled the bin to overflowing.

Other than Mr. Drayson and a few stagehands, the theater was empty, the other actors and actresses having left while she'd been arguing with Mr. Lynsted.

Walter, the watchman, nodded to her. "Hear

you are leaving, Miss Grace." He was Scottish, too, and they'd formed a fast bond.

Grace released her hand from Mr. Lynsted's arm and gave the watchman a peck on the cheek. "I'm going home, Walter. I'm returning to Scotland, where I belong."

"God go with you, lass," he said.

"And be with you," she answered. "And, Walter, thank you for all of your help these past weeks."

"I wish I could have done more."

"You did enough." Grace opened the backstage door and went out into the night.

The alley behind the theater was deserted. The only light was that of a half moon and the lamp by the stage door. She usually left at this hour and had no difficulties. She turned to Mr. Lynsted. "I'll take my valise now."

He looked up and down the alley. "How are you going home?"

"I walk. It's not far from here. My valise?"

Mr. Lynsted held on to it. "London is not safe at this hour of the night. Not for you. Don't you have a maid or someone who can accompany you?"

"I don't have a maid. I don't need anyone to help me dress."

"You should have a companion," he assured her, giving another glance toward the street.

"My Scot's nature is too frugal to spend money on such silliness, Mr. Lynsted. Now, I appreciate your help leaving the theatre but I must go home and pack for the morrow. Please hand my valise to me."

"I'll walk you home," he answered, taking her arm without invitation and sweeping down the alley toward the street.

Grace didn't mind. In truth, she was glad for the company and this way he could see where she lived for when he came to pick her up in the morning.

The March air was heavy and damp. This wasn't her favorite month. It seemed to rain all the time.

The street beyond the alley was dark. Grace noticed the globe on the lamppost was broken. "I can't believe that is out again. They only recently repaired it."

Mr. Lynsted grumbled something about "lamp-lighters not being worth a shilling," and Grace laughed.

"Why do I sense you are one of those people who sees danger everywhere?" she suggested, making conversation.

He frowned at her. "What do you mean?"

"What I said. Some people, like myself, aren't afraid of the dark. We don't believe in beasties and ghosties and, well, so far, at four and twenty, I've managed to keep myself safe. Whereas you are more cautious."

"Caution is a wise thing," Mr. Lynsted answered with his usual brisk tone of decision. "Keeps one safe from angry stage managers and an overeager public."

"*Touché*," she said. "Although it doesn't seem fair I must live my life expecting the worst because I am female."

"The world is not fair, Miss MacEachin," he said with a grim smile. "But then, you already knew that."

"Yes, I did," she admitted soberly. He was exactly right. "Now I am searching for my own fairness."

She hadn't meant to sound so sad . . . and yet, the loneliness had escaped her.

In the dark, she could feel his sharp, questioning glance. She'd have to guard her tongue. Mr. Lynsted had a barrister's quick mind. He'd read something into everything she said if she wasn't careful.

And probably use it against her.

"Here we are," she said. "My building is only two doors down. I'll meet you on this corner in the morning. You can hand over my valise."

"You don't trust me to see you safely to your door?" he said with a hint of disapproval.

She kept her voice light as she replied, "You warned me to be cautious." She reached for the handle of her valise to take if from him, when two shadowy figures unfolded from the bushes and came at her.

Chapter Four

*R*ichard didn't think; he reacted. He'd dreamed of someday clearing a line of men with "his mor-leys" but had yet to test his mettle—and now, here he was.

He stepped in front of Miss MacEachin, lift-ing an arm to block the nearest man's attack. Clenching his fist, he punched the man in his soft, paunchy gut.

With a grunt of pain, the man doubled over.

Richard's lawyer's heart almost burst with pride—until the other attacker delivered a blow to his kidney.

Fortunately, Richard was a big man and the hit a puny one. His attacker's fist bounced off with little damage, but gave Richard the opportunity to pick the fellow up by his shirtneck and the hip of his breeches. He was a runt of a man with a foul mouth. Richard didn't think twice about tossing him back into the bushes from whence he came.

The first man regained his strength. He took a swing at Richard, who easily warded off the blow with his arm. However, before Richard could strike back, Miss MacEachin decided to enter the fray.

Most women would have screamed and gone running off or at least had the sense to duck out of the way.

Not the Scottish songbird.

She jumped in front of Richard, brandishing her sharp little knife at their assailant as if she would carve out his heart. What she did do was ruin Richard's clean shot at their attacker's jaw.

And, of course, the bloke used his longer arms to grab her at the elbow and swing her around as a shield against Richard.

What the man didn't anticipate was that she'd use the knife. She buried it in his thigh.

"God's balls in heaven," the man roared and then screamed as Miss MacEachin pulled the knife out. *"Here, take her.* I'm not being paid that much to grab 'er." He shoved her toward Richard with enough force she fell into his arms, her breasts against his chest.

Richard was stunned by the contact of her soft roundness against his hard strength. *Breasts*. He'd never had them so close before—and that second of stupefied hesitation was enough to allow the man to go running off down the street into the night. His companion had recovered from his interview with the bushes and limped off in the opposite direction.

Miss MacEachin shoved Richard away. *"They are escaping."* She started after the one she'd stabbed but quit after a few steps. "He's gone. *Damn*."

In Richard's world, women didn't swear. And he knew he was to blame for not capturing their attackers. In fact, it was a true blow to his pride that while he had acquitted himself well with his fists, Miss MacEachin and her little knife had sent the scoundrels running for their lives.

She made an exasperated sound. "We should have caught them." He heard the accusation in her voice. She meant *he* should have caught them.

Righting the valise she'd dropped to the ground, she opened it and pawed through her tumble of clothing until she found a kerchief. She used it to clean the knife's blade with little more concern than if she'd gutted a fish.

"We had the better of them," she grumbled. "Then again, perhaps you didn't want me to catch them."

"What does that mean?" he demanded, reaching for his temper. Temper he liked; feeling she was right, he didn't.

She closed the bag and rose to her feet. "It means you didn't try very hard to stop them.

"What?" The word exploded out of him. He recovered. "Miss MacEachin, I defended you."

"Yes, but not as well as you might have," she said, delivering the insult with blunt practicality. She picked up the bag and started walking. "Then again, if we follow the trail of blood from that one I stabbed in the thigh, we both know where he would lead us."

"And where would that be?" Richard demanded, falling into step beside her.

"To your front door step," Miss MacEachin informed him.

Richard's feet rooted to the ground. "What did you say?" he challenged, not certain he had heard her correctly.

Miss MacEachin turned and coolly responded, "I said, the trail of blood would lead to your doorstep."

His blood boiled. "That's an *outrageous* accusation."

She raised her brows, not offering apology.

Richard stomped up to her. "First, I *did* defend you. You're the one who let them escape by interfering. Second, my father and I would never be a party to such an attack. We have no reason to be—"

"I believe you do. Your father and uncle do not want what I have to say to become public."

"You are *infuriating*," Richard replied, stifling the urge to howl his outrage like the man she stabbed had. "How often do I need to repeat that my father and uncle would never involve themselves in such a scheme? And let me point out, I am so certain of it, I am traveling with you to the ends of the earth to interview your father. I shall be gratified to hear your apology."

She snorted her opinion in the most unladylike way. "There will be no apology—"

"And *third*," he continued as if she hadn't spoken, "you have so many enemies it could be any number of men who had attacked you. Those men could have been hired by that stage manager I had to pull off you earlier—" He paused. "Hmmmm, I don't believe I was ineffective then, was I? Or perhaps those two lads who came after you were working for one of those who have placed wagers all over town on who will bed you?"

She drew short breaths, one after the other, and he knew his barb had hit home.

"Oh, wait," he had to add, "*you* never have any difficulties walking home. I forgot. My apologies. You've become the most infamous courtesan in London, but you walk the streets without concerns."

"I never had a concern until *tonight*," she answered, as if accusing him.

Richard shrugged. "Considering your reputation, I'm surprised there aren't brigades of men hiding in your bushes."

She stormed up to him, raising her hand as if to slap him for his effrontery, but then seemed to realize she was too petite to do much damage. Instead, she glared up at him with a look that would have done the meanest governess proud.

Fortunately, Richard was past the age of being cowed by stern-eyed women.

And he was rather proud of himself for giving her tit for tat. How dare she accuse his father of planning an attack on her—

She kicked him in the shin.

The action startled him more than caused pain. "*Hey*," he said, offended.

"I am *not* a whore. Not a courtesan. Not whatever names you men dream up to label women like spice jars in a cabinet. Do you hear me?" she ordered. "I don't sleep with men. I'm my own person. I'm independent and ask *nothing*"—she spit the word out—"from *any* of you. So don't you ever make an accusation like that toward me again or I'll carve your heart out—no, wait. You don't have a heart. You are a Lynsted. Holburn is the only good one of your ilk. But speak like that to me again and I'll take my dirk and carve something, and let me assure you, Mr. Lynsted, *you will not like it*."

Her threats didn't bother him.

Letting him know she found him lacking when compared to his cousin the Duke of Holburn? That comment hit him square in the face.

Not that he shouldn't be accustomed to it. He'd spent a lifetime being compared to his cousin. Holburn was everything Richard wasn't. He was handsome, a normal size, always comfortable in social settings, intelligent, included in every event . . . popular.

Whereas, Richard was a great clumsy oaf who really did feel more comfortable with his ledger sheets than at a garden party or in a ballroom. He normally didn't speak his mind as freely as he had this past hour with anyone let alone with a woman. He was too reserved . . . and his father's son.

People didn't like his branch of the family. Richard wasn't certain why, but he'd always sensed others' disapproval. He'd assumed it was because of his father and uncle's strict sense of what was right and wrong—beliefs he shared . . . but what if there was something else behind it?

Immediately, he rejected the idea. Miss MacEachin's ridiculous accusations had put the suggestion into his head. His father and uncle would not hire brigands.

Well, his father wouldn't.

Richard wasn't really too certain about his uncle. Through his business dealings with the man, he'd seen him take a short cut or two of the sort that caused concern.

Miss MacEachin had turned and was walking away from him, her back ramrod straight.

He followed with grim determination. Something was afoot. Perhaps the stage manager *had* sent two brutes after her to exact revenge. Perhaps he was right and they'd been after what most men wanted from her.

Or . . . and he considered this gingerly, reminded of how panic-stricken his father had been this afternoon when he'd told Richard of her accusations . . . perhaps there was something to her story. Something his uncle had done that could destroy them all if it was revealed.

She marched to the door of a modest row house. Richard stopped on the walk and then came to his senses as he heard the key click in the lock in the door. "Wait, let me go in first."

"Why?" she asked, distrust coloring the word.

"Because if someone is waiting to attack you inside, I don't want you to accuse me of orchestrating it by watching you enter alone," he responded, gently pushing her aside and opening the door.

Richard opened the door to a pitch-black hallway. "Where do I go first?" he asked.

"Here, let me help," she murmured and, before he could protest, ducked under his arm, a black shadow carrying the honeysuckle and rose scent of her perfume.

There was the sound of glass against glass, a scrape, the flash of a match, and then the soft, warm glow of a lamp in a side room. She came out into the hall carrying a candle she must have lit off the lamp. "So, where shall you search first? The bedroom, to see who is hiding under my bed?"

Her sarcasm was like a nail to the back of his head. "I'm sorry for wanting to keep you alive," he shot back, mimicking her tone. He picked up her valise and carried it into the house. Setting it on the floor, he asked, "Do you have just this floor or is there an upstairs?"

"Another renter is on the floor above," she said. "Mrs. Nally and her cats. I have no fears from her." She laughed and said, "She has nine of them."

"Nine what?" Richard asked, distracted by her

leading him into a sitting room where the lamp was burning.

"Cats," she explained, but he didn't comment. Instead, he searched behind the settee and checked for strangers standing in the draperies.

The dressing room in the theater may have been a mess but Miss MacEachin's home was immaculate and rather charming. She clearly didn't own much and he suspected most of the furniture came with the lodgings. Clearly, she wasn't a frilly sort and seemed to admire clean, modern lines . . . much as he did.

"Next room." He kept his voice businesslike. He didn't want her to gain the idea he was enjoying himself. She'd kick his other shin.

She led him into a small dining room followed by a tour of her kitchen.

"Do you have anyone living with you?" he asked.

"Other than Mrs. Nally upstairs? No."

"You should have at least a maid," he responded. "A wise woman doesn't live alone in London."

"I said I was independent," she reiterated.

"Sometimes too much independence is dangerous," he murmured.

"So you keep telling me." She sounded bored.

The next room was the bedroom.

Richard's pulse kicked up a beat. Here, the scent

of her, a soft rose with that evocative undertone of spice, was very strong. And it didn't help that the room was dominated by the bed.

The coverlet was a blue and green stripe on top, at the head of the bed, were mounds and mounds of white, lacy pillows.

A person could sleep all day in comfort in a bed like that, or do "other" things.

Immediately his mind leaped to those "other" things.

He tried to close them out, but they were there, vivid, strong, hungry.

Richard prided himself on his control. Where other men turned into beasts, he continued to do what was right, to be a gentleman, to maintain wholesomeness.

Of course, that was before he'd felt her breasts against his chest. There was a beast inside him, and it was tired of being repressed, especially around a woman as vibrantly alive as Grace MacEachin.

He turned and walked out of the room.

She followed. "Mr. Lynsted, are you all right?"

"Fine."

"But you didn't check behind the doors or search the drapes as you did in the other rooms."

"What? So you could laugh at me some more?" he tossed over his shoulder as he walked through the sitting room and into the hall. At the door, he stopped. Not looking at her, he stated, "The place appears safe, but you should have a maid or companion here with you at all times—and if you tell me you have that bloody little knife to protect you, I shall break it in half."

"You are angry." She paused, considering him. "What did I do?"

"What have you *not* done?" he ground out. "I'll see you in the morning." He escaped into the damp, *cold* night air. It felt good against his skin and cleared the smell of her from his senses.

But what it didn't do was relieve the heft of his arousal pressing against his breeches. He'd just barely made it out of her rooms without her noticing. She'd have had a heyday if she had. There would have been no end to her merriment.

And he was going to travel to Scotland with her.

Richard focused on Abigail Montross, his betrothed for the past four years. She'd never once inspired this heady sense of lust Miss MacEachin seemed to conjure at will inside him.

He knew he shouldn't look back, but he did. He couldn't help himself.

Miss MacEachin stood in the doorway still holding her candle.

The woman didn't have the sense God gave a wren. "*Go inside.*"

Her head came up, tilting in that defiant angle he was coming to know very well. She did as ordered. He could hear the slam of the door from where he stood.

At last, Richard could draw a deep breath.

The stretch of the legs proved to be a good way to tame his lust. As he walked, he stacked all the reasons he didn't like Miss MacEachin in his mind. They might be cooped up in a coach for a few days, but he would stay away from her. He could easily. He was a man with high moral standards. The phrase would become his watchword. Miss MacEachin was a temptation, but he'd met temptation before and chose high . . . moral . . . standards—

Except, she really did have luscious breasts.

The moment the thought entered his head, Richard understood why some penitents scourged sin by whipping themselves. He wasn't in need of going that far. He just had to stop thinking about her breasts.

Or that inviting bed with its mounds of pillows.

"Highmoralstandards, highmoralstandards, highmoralstandards," he repeated until the tension eased, but the sense of excitement didn't, and he realized it wouldn't. Nor was it centered on Miss MacEachin.

He was leaving for an adventure.

Richard rarely traveled anywhere save for business. However, he was on his way to Scotland to clear his family name. That alone grounded him.

He could face Miss MacEachin's breasts and her bed because he was finally doing something to prove his worth to his father. At last, his father would see that Richard loved him. His father may be close to his twin, but certainly there was room for Richard there, too?

He would soon find out. As he came to the stoop of his father's house, he was surprised to see all the windows lit.

Marcus, the butler, opened the door. "Good evening, Master Richard."

If Marcus wondered as to why Richard, who rarely went out anywhere late at night, was returning home at this hour, he was too well trained to say so.

Letting a footman help him out of his greatcoat, Richard said to Marcus, "My father is still awake?"

"He's in the library with Lord Maven." Lord Maven was his uncle Stephen.

"Thank you," Richard said and walked down the black-and-white marble-tiled floor to the closed library door.

Richard knocked.

"Yes!" his father barked. "What is it, Marcus?"

"It's Richard, Father." So anxious was he to convey the events of this evening and his plans to travel to Scotland, he opened the door without waiting for an order to do so.

His father sat behind the huge mahogany desk that was his pride and joy. His uncle stood spinning a globe beside the hearth. The room smelled of leather, the smoke from the fire, and his father's sandalwood soap. There was no other light save for the firelight. The decanter in front of his father was almost empty. His father gripped a glass in his hand.

The twins both had dark hair and the elegant Holburn features. Richard favored his mother's family. His mother had been an heiress of ungainly height known more for her dowry than her looks. He thought her comely, although few others did.

His father and uncle visited the same tailor and the same boot maker. They always wore dark colors—black, gray, brown—and had the uncanny habit of wearing the same colors on the same day. Richard knew it wasn't planned in advance. Each just *sensed* what the other was thinking. And this extraordinary communication extended to other matters as well. They were hand-in-hand in most matters, although his uncle was often the more aggressive of the two.

One of the other few differences was that his uncle had never married.

Nor had he and Richard been close. It was presumed that Richard was his heir as well as his father's . . . but Richard sensed his uncle saw him as competition. Certainly, Richard viewed him that way.

"The two of you are up late," he observed.

"We are waiting for a shipping report," his uncle said.

It was not unusual for them to wait up if they thought a ship was coming in on the late tide. However, Richard didn't know of any ship expected to come into port this night. "What is the ship's name?"

His father closed his eyes. His uncle answered. "The *Willow*."

"I'm not familiar with it," Richard said.

"It's not ours. It's one we are thinking of investing in," his uncle explained.

Richard could advise them not to do so right now. They were already heavily invested in their fleet. The time had come to turn their attention to other matters. However, he knew to save his breath with his uncle.

"I've had a busy evening," he said instead.

"Really? Where have you been?" his father asked, opening his eyes as if appreciating the change of topic.

"The theater."

"Oh?" his uncle replied without interest. His attention was on his twin. "Gregory, don't you believe you have had enough?"

His father set down the now empty glass. He shrugged an answer, reached for the decanter, and then let his hand fall on the desk blotter.

He gave Richard a wan smile. "What did you see at the theater?" he asked, obviously making small talk.

"Grace MacEachin."

If he had announced that he'd signed a pact with the devil, their reactions couldn't have been more thunderstruck. His uncle turned so quickly to look at Richard, he almost knocked over the globe stand. His father stood and then sat, his face growing paler.

"Whatever for?" his uncle demanded.

"I want to help with this matter." Richard leaned an arm on the desk toward his father as he said, "I *can* help."

His father shook his head, his mouth open as if he wanted to speak and yet had no words. His uncle crossed to the desk to stand beside his twin. "What do *you* know about our business?"

"Father spoke to me this afternoon," Richard answered.

"Why, Gregory?" his uncle said under his breath.

"I was worried," his father explained. "I was weak. *You* weren't here."

"But *I* was," Richard said. "Don't worry, Uncle. I'm here to help."

"And what sort of help is that? Going to see that disgraceful woman . . . what lies did she tell you?" his uncle said.

"Nothing I believed. In fact, I've come up with a solution."

His father straightened. "What can be done?"

"I'm going to Scotland to confront her father," Richard said. "We leave on the morrow."

"Scotland?" his uncle repeated in disbelief.

"Yes, Inverness, where her father lives. I shall expose the man and his story for the sham that they are."

"That *cursed* woman." Richard's father stood, picked up the glass he'd set aside and threw it with all his might at the wall. The sound of shattering glass and the sweet, thick smell of brandy filled the air.

"Gregory," his uncle said, the word a warning.

Richard's father turned to his twin. For a second, they faced each other . . . and then his father's back straightened. He turned to Richard.

"No. You will not go *anywhere* with her. Do you understand? You will stay *here*."

Richard had spent a lifetime obeying his father's decrees. He'd done so out of duty and out of need for this man's approval.

And now, for the first time, he must disobey.

Something inside of him insisted he had to make the trip. He must.

"I'm sorry, Father. I must go."

Chapter Five

$\mathcal{H}$is father's head cocked to one side as if he wasn't certain he'd heard Richard correctly. His uncle stood very still.

Richard used his extraordinary height to his advantage as he attempted to explain himself.

"The only way we will contain these false allegations against the two of you is to confront them," he insisted. "Once Miss MacEachin and her father realize we refuse to be blackmailed, they will cease to be a nuisance or a threat. I'll be surprised if she doesn't change her story halfway down the road when she sees what lengths we will go for the truth."

"I don't want you involved in this," his father said, his tone harsh.

"I already am involved," Richard said quietly. "I've worked to help build our family fortune, but it isn't just about what's in my pocket or my inheritance." He wished his uncle wasn't in the room. He wished this conversation was just between he and his father. "This afternoon, Father, you told me about this woman and that you were afraid of her. You are right to be so. You've worked hard for your reputation, especially in the face of extreme prejudice and misunderstanding. I know how you feel. I've been the victim of it myself, but you needn't be afraid of her false accusations any longer. I shall expose her for the fraud she is."

His father shot a guilty look at his twin. He lowered his head. "I said I don't want you involved, Richard. This is not your affair."

"On the contrary," his uncle said, "I believe Richard should go."

Richard didn't know who was more stunned by this statement: himself or his father.

"He's not a part of this," his father said.

"Of course, he is." His uncle Stephen pulled his gaze away from his twin's and said, "Your father was upset this afternoon, as any honest man would be to be accused of such a vile crime. You know how rumors travel in London."

"All the more reason to confront MacEachin," Richard said, and his uncle nodded.

"It's a fool's errand," his father insisted. "They want money. We should just pay them. That will shut them up."

"And then the threat of their accusations will be hanging over our heads forever," his uncle said. "Besides, the hour grows late. I don't believe we'll receive a report from the *Willow*. The ship might not have found port." He said this pointedly, as if it meant something to his father. Richard wondered at the odd change of subject. Did they fear for their incomes?

"There is plenty of money in the accounts," Richard stated.

"Yes, yes, we know that," his uncle said. "Richard, you have been a paragon. You've made us two of the most wealthy men in England. We could offer money and not worry about this nonsense forever," he said, addressing his father, "but why should we, when Richard, who is so able at other matters, has offered to take care of the situation?"

His father still stared at his uncle as if uncertain . . . but then slowly seemed to understand. That look passed between them once again, leaving Richard out.

"There isn't another way?" his father asked.

"I wish there were. But I've come to believe Richard is right. He is already involved through his relationship to us. And out of necessity, he must be. If Miss MacEachin carries on enough, she can do irreparable damage to our reputations. We've worked hard for them, Gregory. Very hard. And we have more than a few enemies who would only be too happy to see us ruined."

"It's my family name at stake, too," Richard pointed out, but his words were overridden by his father.

"You've always underestimated him," he said to his twin as if Richard wasn't in the room.

"Yes, so you have accused me of doing several times over the years," Uncle Stephen answered. "However, he has earned my respect, especially after confronting the tart tonight. Tell me, Richard, what did she say when she met you? You are a big man. I'm surprised your presence alone wasn't enough to set her right."

"Miss MacEachin has more spirit than common sense," Richard reported. "To give you an example of her tenacity, she was attacked twice this evening and whereas other women would have gone off in a swoon, she is still ready to do battle."

"Attacked?" his father asked, his voice cracking.

"Yes," Richard said. "I came upon a scene in her dressing room where a fellow with the theater, the stage manager, was attacking her. She fought with all she had. I quickly ended the fight by throwing the man out. Then later, he must have had some of his cronies attempt to waylay her by her door. They weren't expecting to see me," he said, unable to keep the pride from his voice.

"Waylaid on the way home," his uncle repeated. He looked to his twin. "This tart lives an adventurous life. Imagine, attacked *twice* in one night."

His uncle's use of the word "tart," while in principle correct, annoyed Richard so he made a point of using her name. "Miss MacEachin has the looks that make men. . ." He paused, suddenly at a loss for words. How to explain her without making her look like a "tart"?

"Act like dogs chasing a bitch in heat?" his uncle suggested.

Richard didn't like the comparison. It might apply to himself as well.

His uncle read his silence correctly. "I beg pardon. That was earthy of me. I can be too blunt."

"But apt," his father jumped in. "I'd wager a hundred guineas it is the truth. She's in all the papers. They can't seem to print enough ink about her. The 'Scottish songbird.'" He rose from his desk and crossed to the liquor cabinet for another glass to pour himself another drink. "The Scottish songbird—how ridiculous!"

His uncle sighed heavily and then said to Richard, "My brother takes his reputation seriously."

"Each of us does," Richard answered. "And it is what I said to Miss MacEachin. She—" He paused, weighed what he was about to say and knew he must. Honesty forced him to speak in her defense. "It isn't that she wishes to blackmail. She truly believes her father's story, which is all the more reason for me to confront him. She even imagined the men who attacked her were hired by the two of you. I told her that didn't make sense. I was with her. Why would they attack me, too?"

"Exactly," his uncle agreed. He shook his head. "This has gone on too far. Richard, I am glad you are taking this bull by the horns. Or should I say the cow by the bell?" He laughed at his small joke, then added soberly, "I haven't been as supportive of you and your role in our businesses as I should have been. I felt you were too young. I know, I know, you are nine and twenty . . . but still, I am an uncle. It takes time for those closest to us to see the truth. But stepping forward for this . . . ? My nephew, you are impressing me.

His father gulped his newly poured drink, sitting silent behind his desk.

"I want you to take my new coach to Scotland," his uncle said with sudden decision. "It's well-sprung and fast on the roads. You won't find a better ride.

Besides, Dawson is from the North. There is no better coachman for knowing the side paths and shortcuts." Dawson was his uncle's driver and one of the best whips in London. Many had attempted to hire the man away from Uncle Stephen and been rebuffed. His loyalty was well known.

"Why, thank you," Richard said. Realizing he might not have sounded as appreciative as he was, he explained, "I've longed for a ride in the new coach but knew better than to ask."

"Nonsense, it is the least I can do. Isn't that right, Gregory?"

Richard's father lifted his gaze to his twins. Slowly, his shoulders straightened. He pushed the drink away. "That is right." He turned to Richard. "Take Herbert with you, too. You must look your best when you meet MacEachin." Herbert was the valet they shared. Miss MacEachin wasn't the only frugal one. Richard's father was notoriously tight and Richard prided himself on being of a frugal nature, too. Besides, he wasn't a fussy man and didn't require a valet's continuous services.

"Herbert is good with a gun," his father continued. "He can ride up with Dawson. In fact, I imagine he would enjoy the trip. He's been complaining about city life more than usual these last few weeks."

"That's true," Richard agreed.

"Gregory, I'll provide an extra coachman," his uncle protested. "Your valet can stay home.

His father frowned at his twin. "The valet is my contribution, brother. We both carry our equal weight. Always. Besides, I trust Herbert as you trust Dawson."

His uncle acted as if ready to argue and then, with a glance at his brother, must have thought differently, because he forced his lips into a smile. "As you say. Herbert and Dawson should be able to help you handle the tart—" He caught himself. "Miss MacEachin."

Richard *was* thankful Herbert would travel with him. His mind was having a hard time accepting this new, benevolent side to his uncle. The man came across as almost jovial, and that was suspicious considering the circumstances.

"What time do you leave in the morning?" his uncle asked.

"Early. Shortly before eight."

"I shall have Dawson and the team here at half past seven."

"Thank you," Richard answered because he thought he must. He stood. "Well, then I need to find my bed. Father, do you need help?"

His father had been pushing his brandy glass along the desk's leather blotter, his manner preoccupied. "No, I shall be fine." He glanced up at

Richard. "I'm not as deep into my cups as Stephen thinks."

His twin snorted his opinion.

"Do leave a note for your mother," his father instructed. Richard's mother spent a good deal of time in bed. She suffered from melancholy and had a taste for laudanum. They both knew she wouldn't be up before noon on the morrow, and even if she was, Richard doubted if she'd care about his leaving.

"I shall do so." Richard moved to the door. "Well, then, good night."

"Enjoy your adventure," his uncle said.

"I will," Richard answered. At the door, he paused. "By the way, Father, Uncle, this MacEachin, Miss MacEachin's father—*did* you know him?" His father had claimed to be unaware of him this afternoon, but the lawyer in Richard needed to ask one more time with his uncle present.

"I never laid eyes on the man," his father quickly said. "Never been to Scotland even."

"I was in Scotland," his uncle answered. "Up around Inverness on a fishing trip. That was ten, maybe even twelve years ago."

"The crime MacEachin is accusing you of would have happened around that time, wouldn't it?"

"Dear God, Richard, are you accusing your uncle?"

"No, Father. But I have to know the facts to expose the lies in MacEachin's story."

"He's right, Gregory," his uncle said. "Actually, I believe it would have had to happen a decade ago. After all, MacEachin was transported."

"And how do you know that?" Richard asked.

"Because Miss MacEachin told us in her letter," his uncle said. "Would you like to read it?"

"Yes, I would," Richard said.

"He's a good legal mind," his uncle said to his father. "We are fortunate for that. Give him the letter."

Richard didn't know why he was delving deeper. Perhaps because his uncle was too buoyant, too accommodating about the situation.

Or perhaps his extra suspicions were because Miss MacEachin was too beautiful and he wanted to believe the best of her.

His father pulled the letter from a desk drawer and offered it to Richard, who scanned it quickly. Miss MacEachin's forthright manner was very much in evidence. She stated her accusations and her reasons. She thought her father should receive some sort of compensation for what he'd suffered because of the twins and was bold enough to suggest a price of twenty-five thousand pounds.

"She believes his story," Richard said.

"It's unfortunate," his uncle agreed. "She could

not know her father well. He's lying and it may go badly for her."

His father didn't say anything.

"She says she wants the truth," Richard answered. "That's what I shall offer her. Good night."

He left the room, but he didn't leave the hallway.

Instead, he lingered not far from the library door, pretending to go through some mail on a table should his father, uncle, or a passing servant come this way. It was a habit he'd developed over the years, allowing him to eavesdrop. It was in this fashion he'd learned he was to be shipped off to school, of Holburn's father's death, of everything of importance in the family and his life.

"I feel good Dawson will be with him," his uncle said as if his father had asked a question.

"It is a pity everything couldn't have been laid to rest this night."

"But Richard's taking her to Scotland is even better. It removes her from town. From us."

There is silence. "He's my son."

His uncle made an impatient sound. "And my heir. Dawson will know how to handle everything. Will Herbert work with him?"

"Of course."

"Now come, let's see you to bed. You don't have a head for spirits."

Richard moved quickly down the hall and

climbed the stairs to his room. The twins hadn't said anything out of the ordinary . . . so why did he feel unsettled?

Herbert usually attended his father at night, so Richard set about throwing some clothes in a bag in anticipation of the trip. He planned on traveling light and didn't really want the burden of a valet but understood his father wished Herbert to keep an eye on him. He wondered when his father would finally trust him, or what he'd have to do to prove his loyalty and devotion to his sire.

A knock on the door interrupted his thoughts. Thinking it must be Herbert come to help him pack, Richard said, "I'm almost done packing, Herbert. See to yourself. I don't need your services tonight."

The door opened anyway and his uncle stepped inside. "I left Herbert with your father. Gregory should never drink. He doesn't handle it well."

"Fortunately, he doesn't do it often," Richard said, leery of his uncle's visit. They rarely talked alone.

"I sense you don't trust me," his uncle said flatly.

"Of course I do," Richard answered.

Uncle Stephen wagged a finger. "Shall I accuse you of lying? I think not. The truth is, nephew, you've impressed me this evening. I know my brother wishes only to protect you, but I admire what you did. Confronting the tart was a bold move and you called her bluff. You must know, I mean no harm to her."

"Of course not."

His uncle gave a relieved smile. "Good. Well, now the hour grows late and I should see to my bed." He lived two blocks away. "However, I do have one piece of advice. A word of caution from your bachelor uncle, if I may indulge myself?"

Richard nodded.

"Watch out, nephew, for the likes of this Miss MacEachin. The Lord has warned us of women who use their looks to prey upon a man. Remember the story of Samson, a strong, good man, who was destroyed by Delilah's charms. You are like Samson, Richard. A seeker of truth. Your heart is like his. You are good and assume the goodness of others. Beware the Delilah. Beware the woman who offers a man her body and steals his soul."

Richard would have laughed if he wasn't so uncomfortably aware of his attraction to Miss MacEachin. Delilah. The temptress. The label suited her. God had fashioned her for such a calling.

"You needn't worry, Uncle."

"I don't? Are you saying she isn't as lovely as the papers claim?"

"Oh, she is lovely," Richard to admit. "But she's

plotting to ruin my family. My loyalty is with my father." He chose those last words deliberately . . . because if there was some truth to her story, then he was certain his uncle was the one who stole the money. His uncle was the bolder of the twins.

"As it should be," his uncle said without any sign of taking offense. "And again, I am proud of you for taking the lead on this."

He started toward the door and then stopped. "By the way, how are matters between yourself and Abigail Montross? I fear I've failed to keep track."

"We sense no hurry."

His uncle shrugged. "Well, you may find what I was going to suggest a bit offensive but we are speaking man to man here?"

Richard nodded.

"You should have married by now, Richard. I don't know why you haven't—"

"There is no rush." Or desire. Their betrothal had been arranged by their fathers. It was the custom . . . but for some reason, Richard found he resented that fact.

"No one understands better than myself. Marriage is a chore. Fortunately, my brother's marriage saved me from the obligation. However, I do have a suggestion. Just a thought, actually. Since you are going to be traveling with Miss MacEachin

and since she doesn't worry, obviously, about her reputation, you might want to give her a poke. Prepare yourself for your wedding night."

Richard almost fell over at the suggestion coming from his straitlaced uncle, who always seemed slightly puzzled as to why God had bothered to create women.

"Ah now, I've shocked you," his uncle said.

"It's . . . unexpected." Richard was at a loss to explain further.

"Is it? We're both men. We understand needs. You have needs, don't you, Richard?"

Richard hesitated. "Of course," he said quietly.

"And I'd wager Miss MacEachin brings out those needs," his uncle guessed accurately. "Probably more so than Miss Montross."

Richard didn't answer. The conversation shamed him. He didn't want to think about using Miss MacEachin. The need to protect was very strong within him . . . and surprisingly, especially in relationship to her. Perhaps because he'd already fought twice this night in her defense . . .

"Play with her," his uncle advised, "but be wary. That's all I want to say. Remember Samson." He tapped on his temple as if wishing for Richard to ingrain his words in his memory. "After all, you are marrying this summer, and Abigail Montross will expect you to know what's up." He laughed at his own joke.

"I'll think on it, Uncle," Richard murmured, uncomfortable with this new side to his relative . . . and what more it could mean.

His uncle laughed. "You are a good lad and someday I'll dance at your wedding. Well, good night. Have a safe journey. I shall look forward to hearing your report."

"If weather is with us, I should return in two weeks time, maybe less," Richard promised.

"Good. We have that meeting with Hockingdale on the twenty-fifth. A pretty penny rests on our filling his ships with our cargo."

"Absolutely."

"By the way," his uncle said, hesitating by the door, "with that coach, you'll be home well before the end of the week. She's a sweet goer. Flies across the ground."

"I *am* looking forward to the ride."

"Yes, well, I'm anxious to hear your report upon your return. Good night, Richard."

His uncle left and Richard drew his first relaxed breath since the man had entered the room. What a strange conversation.

Richard walked to the window overlooking the street and watched his uncle leave the house.

· Something was amiss. His earlier disquiet returned. His father didn't overimbibe spirits. His uncle never ingratiated himself to Richard. Ever. And the advice to "poke" Miss MacEachin was at odds with his uncle's usual virulent stance against fornication when he spoke as a deacon of the church.

And the possibility that MacEachin's story could be true raised its ugly head.

Richard's mission for this trip changed. He needed to know the truth. Charges of embezzlement could ruin his father, their businesses . . . and himself by implication. Opinion was fickle. Everything he'd worked for these past years could be destroyed, and then what would he have left?

Nothing. His family's reputation was his.

Sleep didn't come quickly for that night. He dreaded what he might learn in Scotland and yet he would go. He was no coward.

And in the middle of his doubts and concerns, tossings and turnings was Grace MacEachin.

His uncle had seen right through him. He knew Richard was infatuated with the woman.

What Richard had to ensure is that Miss MacEachin never did.

Chapter Six

$\mathcal{P}$eople often didn't receive second chances in life. At least, that had been Grace's experience . . . and yet now she had one.

She was going home, and she was bringing with her an opportunity to clear her father's name. For a reason she didn't quite understand herself, she did believe once Mr. Lynsted heard her father's story, he would realize the great injustice done to him. In spite of being related to Lord Brandt, Mr. Lynsted struck her as a fair man. He'd demonstrated his character the night before, when he'd fended off Drayson and her attackers.

Grace was also looking forward to hearing the story from her father's lips. She'd heard the tale repeatedly from her mother but had yet to hear her father speak of it. Her mother had run away right after her father had returned from prison, creating more turmoil in Grace's life. Her mother had been her support, her one companion. Her leaving so abruptly had confused Grace. She'd blamed herself, blamed her father.

Grace looked back on that period of her life with shame. Granted, when she'd left, she'd been too young to understand all the nuances of what had been happening then or to realize that sometimes couples have problems that have nothing to do with the children or the outside world. Still, that didn't erase all of the hurtful charges she'd made against her father. Not only had his wife abandoned him . . . but his daughter had as well.

The time had come to make amends and clear her conscience. Then perhaps she could forgive herself for all that had happened.

Going to Inverness was the first step.

After that? Grace didn't know what she would do. She had hazy imaginings of taking care of her father. She could see him in her mind's eye, alone and bitter. She would change that. She'd take care of him, cook for him, and prove herself a loving daughter. What happened next to her would be in God's hands.

Grace hadn't spent much time packing. Other

than clothes, she had few material possessions. Everything she owned fit in her valise and one small trunk, and it wasn't heavy. She carried it out to the street and stood beside it, anxious for Mr. Lynsted's arrival.

She had taken extra care with her toilette. This was a new beginning for her and she wanted to set the right tone.

Her long-sleeved traveling dress was a heavy cotton in a cornflower blue and trimmed in off-white lace. The neckline, filled in with the same lace, was so prim and proper a parson's wife could have worn it.

Styling her hair had been a trial. She'd attempted a sophisticated chignon but her curls would not obey. Finally, she'd admitted defeat and gathered them up in a ribbon that matched her dress. The effect was more feminine than what she'd wished, but a woman's hair was what it was.

Grace finished her costume with her marine wool cape, gold velvet cap, and beige traveling gloves.

Her one vanity was her decision to wear kid slippers instead of good sturdy walking shoes. Grace couldn't help herself. She adored those soft leather shoes and had them in every color she could afford. They weren't practical but they were stylish.

Of course, there was nowhere to hide her dirk, which she usually tucked into her boot when she traveled. Her solution was to strap the knife to her leg just above the knee.

She'd given her key along with a letter to the landlord to Mrs. Nally, her neighbor. She'd included with the letter the final rent and that was it. There was nothing tying her to London.

Now, cooling her heels waiting for Mr. Lynsted, she admitted to herself she didn't know what to make of him . . . and that possibly part of her reason for taking so much care with her dress was to impress him.

She wanted him to respect her—and not just because he was Lord Brandt's son. She was attracted to him.

So many men in London were perfumed and pampered. In contrast, Mr. Lynsted's style was strongly masculine. Unapologetically so.

But there was something else that drew her. Something she'd not expected to find in Lord Brandt's son. Mr. Lynsted seemed kind. Gallant even.

He hadn't needed to walk her home last night, except it wasn't in his nature to let her go alone. He had the quaint notion of defending women. And he hadn't hesitated to fight with the thugs that had jumped them but had bravely placed himself in front of her.

Looking back over the incident, Grace could admit that he was right about her foolishness for joining in the battle, and yet she'd spent so many years fending for herself, she'd not expected his assistance.

Or his insistence in searching her house to see she was safe. At first she'd been suspicious. However, when she'd turned in for the night, she'd slept better because he chased all the dangerous possibilities away.

And now she was going to be spending the next few days with him.

It had been a long time since Grace had been attracted to a man. A fluttering of anticipation at the prospect of seeing him kept her on edge. She wanted to tell herself it was only nerves over the trip and what it signified. Some of that was true.

But a larger portion of it was that Mr. Lynsted was a well-built man whose muscles were his own and not the result of padding.

The day was damp and chilly but there was some hope for sun and a hint of spring in the air. A good day for travel. The mood on the street was lively. People bustled around after morning errands. An orange girl on the corner called out her wares while a gaggle of gossiping maids in mobcaps hurried toward the market street to do the shopping.

The whinny of a horse caught her attention.

Graced turned in the direction of the sound. Carts and wagons often went up and down her narrow street, but the horses pulling them were a dispirited, quiet lot. She noticed people on the corner halt mid-step and then move back on the curb, their necks craning to look down the intersecting street. Even the orange girl went silent, still holding a piece of fruit.

A moment later, the handsomest team of prancing grays Grace had ever seen came around the corner pulling a lacquered red coach with green spokes and yellow wheels. The brass fittings on the harnessing were so new and shiny they brightened the day. Sitting on the box were two coachmen dressed in black-and-gold-braided livery and wearing cocked hats on their heads.

Grace could only stare, too. She'd never seen a rig so well tricked out. No wonder people stopped and noticed.

And then the coach pulled right up in front of her.

The door opened.

Mr. Lynsted unfolded his big self and stepped out on the street. He was dressed for travel in buff-colored breeches and Hessian tall boots polished so shiny Grace could almost see her face in them. He wore the same black greatcoat of the night before draped over the shoulders of a very handsome hunter green jacket and brown vest.

All in all, especially standing in front of such a fine coach, he was the very model of a wealthy and fashionable gentleman.

"It's good to see you are punctual, Miss MacEachin," he said by way of greeting.

"Good morning to you, too, sir," she replied, reminding him of the civilities.

He had the good grace to appear momentarily embarrassed, but then he barged on. "This is Dawson," he said, introducing the driver, "and up with him in the box will be Herbert, my valet."

Herbert had climbed down and picked up her valise and trunk, wrinkling his nose in distaste as he did so. Grace wanted to snatch them back from him, noticing how shabby they were against the magnificence of the coach.

Instead, she put on her own mantle of hauteur and warned, "Be careful with that."

The valet raised an eyebrow.

She raised one right back.

"Yes, miss," he murmured, barely polite.

"Are you ready?" Mr. Lynsted asked, sounding impatient and slightly bored.

So. This was to be the tenor of the trip.

Grace experienced a stab of disappointment. The letdown was her own fault. She'd started to build Mr. Lynsted in her imagination into a better man than what he obviously was. She realized she'd begun to romanticize the trip. 'Twas her nature, a foolish side of her that life experience should have eradicated by now.

Apparently it hadn't.

No matter. She was made of stern stuff. They'd make this trip cold shoulder to cold shoulder.

"Of course I am," she said briskly and removing her cape from her shoulders, climbed into the cab.

The interior was close quarters, albeit comfortable ones. The leather of the seat was as deliciously soft as her kid slippers and there was a wooden bar on the other side of the coach to rest feet on in comfort like a footstool. Hooks were built in to the silk lined wall for hats and other personal items.

And then Mr. Lynsted climbed into the coach.

For the briefest moment, his gaze flicked over her and she sensed he was both surprised by her conservative dress and approving. Men always developed a certain intensity in their eyes when they liked what they saw and Mr. Lynsted was no different, although he quickly looked away.

His body took up more than its share of the

coach. He settled in, hanging his hat on a hook. Grace moved over, all too aware of his thigh resting alongside hers and how broad his shoulders were. The air filled with the spicy, crisp scent of his shaving soap. Grace approved. She didn't like the sweet, occasionally flowery scents many men wore. She liked a man to smell like a man.

"Excuse me," he murmured as if uncomfortably aware of her, too. He leaned into his corner but he couldn't move his legs. They were too long for the footrest to be of service.

"I'll angle this way and you can stretch out," she offered.

"I'm fine," he said, not looking at her. Instead, he reached up and knocked on the roof. "We're ready to go, Dawson."

There was a crack of a whip and the grating sound of wheels rolling over cobbles. They were off. Grace looked out the glass window at all the people staring as they drove by, envy in their eyes. At least she was leaving London in style.

"This is a nice rig," she said.

He grunted an answer and reached under the seat to pull out a thick black leather satchel. He opened it and pulled out several ledger books and a pair of spectacles. Ignoring her, he settled the spectacles on his nose, opened the ledger and began reading.

Grace watched him for a moment. The glasses surprised her. Most people she knew avoided their use out of vanity. Perhaps the reason Mr. Lynsted was so surly was because he felt self-conscious about spectacles.

She considered the matter as she watched the passing scenery. Inside an hour, the city gave way to countryside. All was very green because of the good rains they'd been having.

Besides, if he could ignore her, she could ignore him.

Or so she thought.

The dirk strapped to her leg began to irritate her. Using her cape as a cover for modesty's sake, not that Mr. Lynsted would have noticed, she unstrapped it and stashed it under the seat.

For a good three hours, Grace was a dutiful traveling companion. She contemplated the passing scenery, daydreamed the scene when she would see her father again, and then grew silly with boredom and composed limericks in her head about Mr. Lynsted. She hadn't brought a book. She didn't own any. Nor did she have any needlework. She'd been working for her living, not indulging herself in pleasure pursuits.

But her temper was alive and well.

He was deliberately treating her poorly, his behavior contrary to what it had been last night.

He was setting her in her place and she wasn't pleased.

"I like your spectacles," she said, deciding to interject herself into his life.

He flicked over a ledger page. At some point, he'd taken pen and ink from another case. He held the ink bottle in one hand and pen in another as he made annotations to his reports. He was right-handed and looked like a prissy puss. A big man holding a little bottle.

"They give you an air of distinction," she continued.

Mr. Lynsted frowned as if something on the ledger page puzzled him.

Grace wondered what he'd do if she tipped his hand holding the ink bottle toward his lap. It would be a shame to ruin such a handsome pair of breeches, but if he continued behaving this way, she might not have a choice.

With a loud sigh, she slipped her feet out of her kid leather slippers and tucked them under the hem of her dress on the seat, pushing his thigh with her knees . . . the closest she dared come to acting on her ink tipping impulse. Of course, one bump in the road and she would not be responsible for the damage . . .

But there were no bumps. The coach rode amazingly smoothly.

For a long moment she sat quietly and then started to hum a tune from her childhood. She hummed it louder and louder.

Mr. Lynsted studiously disregarded her.

"Are you angry with me?" Enough of the games. Where was the gentleman of the night before?

He didn't answer.

So she leaned her knees against his thigh.

That gained his attention.

"What?" he said, scowling at her offending knees.

"You aren't being companionable," she complained.

"We aren't companions. This is a business trip." He tried to turn his attention back to his scribbles and numbers.

Grace swung her feet to the floor. "Scotland is a long ride," she explained.

"Ummm-hmmm."

"If we ride in silence, the whole trip will seem ten times longer."

"It's unfortunate you are too frugal to hire a maid, Miss MacEachin," he said, not even deigning to look at her. "Then you would have someone to whom you may talk. However, I'm making this trip to set serious allegations to rest. I don't have to entertain you."

To whom you may talk. No one spoke with such

stilted formality anymore. At least, no one reasonable. And if he thought that set-down would shut her up, he was wrong.

"We must talk," she insisted, putting a lot more whine in her voice. "It isn't nice to not talk. Nor have I ever been disregarded before."

He looked at her then and smiled, the expression not nice. "More's the pity." He drawled the words out, making them last, before returning his attention to his ledger.

Grace's fingers ached to grab him by the ear and give it a savage twist. That would wipe the smug smile off his face. "What is the matter with you?" she asked.

"The matter? Nothing." He capped his ink, leaned over and put the bottle and his pen away in their proper little carrying case, and retrieved his satchel.

"You were much friendlier last night," Grace continued. "In fact, I almost enjoyed your company."

He pulled out a paper from his satchel and opened it, putting up a very effective barrier between them.

"I find you very rude, Mr. Lynsted," she declared. "What? Do you believe I have not been so ill treated before? I have. Back when I was first being presented. My family background was such that I should have been invited to all the events. Because of my father being convicted of a crime, *a crime he didn't commit"*—she had to be certain he remembered that—"the only invitations I received were for parties hosted by my relatives, who begrudged everything they did for me."

He stayed behind his paper.

The disdain hurt. It always did.

Over the years she'd reacted to it by running, or proving herself to be exactly what supposedly respectable people thought of her. Defiance was also a good reaction.

But if she was ever going to reclaim her life, to be the person she'd once believed herself to be, she could not let him cow her.

She tapped her foot on the floorboard, beating out the passage of time. They traveled in silence with only the sound of the horses, the rattling of the traces, and the squeaking of hinges.

He pretended not to be aware of her. She knew he was. Last night, this man had come across as honest. Today, he was a pretender.

"Usually people turn the pages," she observed, "when they read the paper."

There was a beat of silence, and then he flipped the page over.

"What is it?" she wondered. "Have your father

and uncle warned you away from me? Have they made you afraid of the 'Jezebel'?" She sneered at herself, all too aware of what those paragons of virtue and vice might have told him. "I liked you better when you thought for yourself."

The paper came down. His eyes were angry and she noted they weren't brown as she'd first thought, but a green. A dark, mossy green. "I do think for myself."

"And that is why you've had a change of attitude toward me between last night and today?" she challenged.

"It's not because I was warned off of you, Miss MacEachin," he assured her. "Quite the contrary, my uncle urged me to give you a *poke*."

The word offended her. She leaned back into her corner. "How godly of him."

He noticed her move away. "Don't worry. Your *virtue* is safe with me. And what my uncle is really saying is that you aren't the sort of woman a man asks to wear his marriage ring." He raised his paper again.

Grace knew that. It had been made painfully clear several times in her life. She'd lived beyond the pale of respectability. At times rebelliously so.

What caught her off guard was that Mr. Lynsted's saying it rankled.

He was her enemy. She should celebrate that he found her not to his exacting standards of a wife. After all, what did she care?

"*I* wouldn't consider marrying *you*," she informed him as if they'd been discussing the matter.

He concentrated on his paper.

"Not only is your family guilty of destroying mine," she continued, "but I wouldn't want someone with your *priggish* manner."

She glanced over to him. Was it her imagination, or did his fingers tighten on the paper?

Grace waited a good long moment before repeating herself. "Did you hear what I said?" she asked the newspaper. She laced her fingers together, happily preparing to annoy the devil out of him. "I said you were priggish. *Priggish, priggish, priggish*."

The newspaper came down.

"It is not priggish to have *standards*," he informed her, the outrage light in his eyes definitely bringing out the green. "In fact, it is a necessity— but then, you wouldn't understand because you don't have any."

"I do have a standard—truth," she insisted haughtily. "It's the only one that matters."

That remark hit home. "I wouldn't be making this blasted trip if I didn't seek truth." He started to bring his paper back up but Grace had enough.

She grabbed the top of the paper with her hand, bringing it down, crumpling it. She'd bored a hole into his arrogance and she wasn't about to relent.

"So what are your standards for a wife?" Her action had moved her from her corner of the coach, bringing her closer to him.

"What do you care?"

"I don't. I'm merely making conversation."

Annoyance flashed in his eyes. She tamped down a smile of triumph.

"She won't be an actress," he muttered. "Or a *Highlander.*"

"Am I being insulted?" Grace wondered. "I ask a simple question and you slur me?"

"There is nothing simple about your questions, Miss MacEachin. You are baiting me, plain and simple. You enjoy mocking me. Now here is the truth, the woman who wears my marriage ring will be all a gentlewoman should be. She'll be reserved, conservative, genteel, well-bred—"

"And *boring,*" Grace assured him.

"She *won't* be boring."

"She will," Grace pronounced with the voice of experience. "Because you can't make a list and order a wife to fit your personal specifications before you meet her. Wives don't come that way. They are people and people are always complex

and challenging. Or is that something your uncle and father didn't warn you about?"

The lines of his mouth flattened. "You go too far."

For a moment, she feared she had. This was no blustering male or one who could easily be controlled. There was steel in this man. Courage. Resolve.

Qualities she admired.

And he was ignoring her for his own reasons . . . reasons she sensed he did not want her to know.

"Marriage is a partnership of lovers," she said, holding his gaze. "And if there is one thing I've learned in my"—she paused, searching for the right word—"*adventurous* life, a mysterious element known as romance can never be valued too highly."

"I'm romantic enough, Miss MacEachin," he replied tightly.

And she had to let him know he was wrong.

"Truly?" she asked softly. "How romantic is it to order a woman as you would a steak pie? I want her genteel, I want her conservative, I want her plump but not too plump. Maybe plump here and slender there. And her hair must be yellow unless I'm in the mood for something red, or purple, or green—"

"Women don't have green hair, or purple hair. And I didn't talk about personal features but qualities of character. There is a difference."

"So you would marry a woman with green hair if she was boring?" She had to say it. She couldn't help herself and was delighted when his jaw muscle tightened.

"Boring was not on my list," he informed her. "*You* added it."

"Very well," Grace said. "I will amend my statement. It's not a concern if your wife has ten fingers and ten toes provided she goes to church every Sunday and prays at six on Tuesdays and never expresses an opinion other than the one you decide for her since intelligence wasn't on your list—"

"Why are you doing this?" He threw his paper to the floor. "Why are you spouting such nonsense?"

"Nonsense? I'm not the one ordering up a wife, Mr. Lynsted," she said.

"No, there is something else at work here. You are attacking me, but it isn't just me, is it, Miss MacEachin? This is something that has been on that female mind of yours a long time. You don't like men very much, do you? You think we are fools."

She did, but had never had a man astute enough to notice or bold enough to call her on it.

Edging back to her side of the coach, she said, "I don't like being categorized, Mr. Lynsted. I'm calling you on a hypocrisy. You aren't alone in your lists. Every man has them. The image of what his dream wife will be. They all want virgins while they chase me relentlessly. And once they do marry, they take on mistresses whom they treat better than those perfect wives."

"And you hate that, don't you?" he said, leaning toward her, intimidating her with Truth. "You don't like being left out, knowing you will never be the wife?"

"I prefer my own company."

"Liar," he accused softly.

In that moment, the coach rolled over a rock or deep rut in the road. The wheels bounced, throwing his weight toward her but he went farther than that. Abruptly, he threw himself on top of her, his arm reaching across as if to hold her down.

She'd not expected the move.

Her first response was panic, just as it had been years ago, only this time she was wiser. She reached under the seat, felt the knife sheath and whipped out her dirk. She pressed the razor-sharp edge against his throat.

Surprise crossed his face. He went still.

Her heart pounded in her throat.

His gaze held hers.

Neither moved, their bodies swaying together with the motion of the coach.

She swallowed. His weight was heavy on her body. "I'm not a plaything. I know men expect it, but I'm my own person now. I'm not that woman any longer. No matter what your uncle or anyone says. No one touches me."

Understanding crossed his face, and something else—compassion?

It embarrassed her.

He pushed his arm forward. She braced herself. She'd cut him if he tried to hurt her. He had to know she would—

A blast of damp, frigid air enveloped them before he pulled his arm back and there followed the click of a door being shut into place.

"The door came open," he said, the muscles of his throat moving against her knife. "I don't know why. It's a new coach. However, I didn't want you to fall out." Raising his hand to show he meant no tricks, he sat back up.

Grace didn't move immediately. It took several moments for her heartbeat to return to normal, and she was all too conscious of the fact that she'd tipped her hand. She'd overreacted and exposed to him, her enemy, her innermost fear.

He was such a strong man. A big one. An intimidating one. Now he knew how to frighten her.

Instead of gloating, Mr. Lynsted picked up his crumpled paper. He sat back against the seat, raised the paper, and once again began to read.

She reached down to the floor. She found her sheath and slipped the knife back into it before sitting up. She ran a hand through her hair, pushing the pins that had loosened back in place.

They rode in silence for a moment and then Mr. Lynsted murmured, "One other item to my list—the woman I marry *won't* pull a knife on me."

"More's the pity," she replied, trying to ape his earlier disinterest, and failing.

She'd been exposed. Made vulnerable . . . and he knew it.

Chapter Seven

They stayed in their separate corners of the coach as best they could after that.

When Mr. Lynsted finished reading his paper, Grace worked up the courage to ask if she could read it. He handed it to her without a word before returning to his ledger sheets.

The weather took a turn for the worst. Gray storm clouds covered the sun, threatening rain at any moment.

They had driven long and hard with only one quick stop along the side of the road for a stretch of the legs. Grace was very relieved when at last the coach turned off the main road.

"We must have reached the inn Dawson knows,"

Mr. Lynsted informed her, breaking their hours of silence. "He said it was suitable for the night."

Grace nodded, still not ready to talk to him. He'd kept his distance but she'd discovered she was too aware of him for her comfort.

After several turns down one road and another, the coach finally came to a halt. Grace stifled a yawn and put on her hat before she pulled on her gloves.

Mr. Lynsted did not wait for the driver to open his door but opened it himself and climbed out. Grace slid across the seat, ready to exit but his body blocked her way. He leaned back in to say to her, "It's crowded out. The yard is full of horses and vehicles. Wait in the coach while I send Herbert in to see if there are rooms available for us."

Grace didn't want to wait. She yearned for fresh air and yet with him blocking the door, what choice did she have?

She pulled back the curtain covering the window on her side of the coach that she'd closed to keep cold air out and was surprised to see exactly how busy the inn yard was. There were horses, sporty phaetons, and coaches everywhere, along with servants and gentlemen.

Leaning across the seat toward Mr. Lynsted, she asked, "What is going on here?"

He didn't answer her directly but stopped a passing gentleman. Grace couldn't hear what they were saying and had to wait until Mr. Lynsted informed her, "There was a boxing match about ten miles down the road. The winner is to fight Cribb. I suppose because this inn is near the post road, many thought they'd chance coming here for an early start home on the morrow." He pulled his head out and she heard him ask a passing gentleman who had won the match.

The name Cribb didn't mean a thing to her, but she was suddenly very weary and the walls of this coach were closing in around her. She wanted her supper and her bed and found it very easy to target her irritation at Mr. Lynsted.

She slid across the seat to the door. Mr. Lynsted was still blocking it with his body. For a second she debated giving him a goose in the hip to see if he would move, and decided against it. She'd wandered a long way from her mother's teachings on the manners and decorum of a young lady, but there were still some things she would not do.

So, she did what her mother would have advised her to do, she cleared her throat. *Several* times.

Mr. Lynsted either didn't hear her or refused to take the hint. He stood right where he was, discussing the fight with strangers and asking for more details. Apparently, a Scot named McGowan had defeated the favorite. The men had much to say about this unexpected win and proceeded to give it the same detailed consideration and discussion that Wellington probably offered over Napoleon.

Grace was going to scream if she didn't escape this coach in two more seconds. Convention be damned. She opened the door on her side of the coach and climbed out. Mr. Lynsted would be annoyed she'd disobeyed his order to stay where he wanted her, and the thought made her smile.

Since the door had opened on the road, she'd stayed well away from it. She was surprised how loose the catch was for a new vehicle and when she went to close it, she noticed it didn't close well. Curious, she poked her finger around the catch mechanism and discovered the tiniest bit of wood prying it open. She didn't know how it managed to lodge there but she flicked it out with her nail, and the door shut tightly.

She shook out her skirts and was reaching up to readjust her velvet cap when a high-perched phaeton almost skimmed too close to her. The ham-handed driver had been ogling her. He paid attention to his driving in the nick of time to move his wheels, overcompensated, and almost ran into an oncoming vehicle right in front of Mr. Lynsted's coach.

A shouting match between the two drivers resulted.

Grace ducked around the back of her coach and hurried around to where Mr. Lynsted and Dawson had been listening to the details of the McGowan fight from two other men.

Of course, the shouting match in front of them commanded their attention. Mr. Lynsted and the others became so caught up in the angry drivers they didn't even notice Grace's presence until the beleaguered driver who had almost hit her stopped mid-sentence.

He stood in his phaeton and pointed at Grace. "*Her*. There. She's the reason I almost ran into you. I had to swerve to avoid running her over. Stepped out in front of me."

All eyes turned to Grace, who became conspicuously aware she was the only woman present in the yard.

"I told you to stay in the coach," Mr. Lynsted barked without preamble. That angry muscle in his jaw had tightened and he was giving her the "glare," an expression he appeared to be perfecting around her.

Grace squared her shoulders. "While you discuss boxing? Well, I'm in search of a fighter by the name of Roast Chicken," she said. "Have you heard of him? I'd like him for my supper."

Mr. Lynsted's scowl deepened although his companions, including Dawson, saw humor in her small jest. However, they dared not laugh. They suddenly became interested in scratching their noses and looking to the ground . . . the cowards!

Fortunately, Herbert approached. He spoke in the ear of Mr. Lynsted, who shook his head.

"Dawson, is there another inn nearby?"

Before Dawson could answer, one of the other gentleman spoke up, "There's not an inn for an hour in any direction that will be less crowded than this one."

Mr. Lynsted looked to the inn and then to Grace. He obviously was not satisfied with the arrangements but gave a short nod of his head. Dawson and Herbert moved around her to unpack their luggage from the boot.

"Thank you, gentlemen," Mr. Lynsted said to the two standing with him. He offered Grace his arm. "We have little choice but to stay here for the night," he said and then frowned past her.

Grace turned to see a party of men who had been eyeing her. Mr. Lynsted's size and proprietarial air warned them away.

"Earlier, when I told you to stay in the coach, it was for your own protection," he murmured as he led her to the inn's door. "We have no choice but to stay here for the night, but considering the overwhelmingly *male* presence, you'd be wise to obey my orders."

"Perhaps you'd best add 'willful' to my list of sins then," she informed him, stung at being talked down to.

"I already have." He opened the door.

The inn was a lovely Tudor structure with beamed ceilings and a cozy rabbit warren of rooms.

Unfortunately it was crowded with not just men, but *sports*men. They came in all shapes, sizes, and from all walks of life. The taproom was filled to overflowing. Gentlemen crowded the narrow hallway or sat on every available surface in the side rooms. And however much attention she drew outside, she doubled it in here.

Mr. Lynsted was not pleased. That angry muscle in his jaw had appeared and didn't seem ready to go away.

He needn't have put himself in a pet. One sight of his big, hulking self behind her and the men quickly shifted their focus back to their drinks and conversations.

He took her elbow and directed her into a sitting room off to the left with a cheery fire in the grate. A comfortable-looking chintz-covered chair set empty beside the fire, the way to it blocked by a group of men talking.

"Excuse me," Mr. Lynsted said, his voice deeper than usual. They were going to ignore him until, like the others, they noticed his size and Grace standing beside him. They stepped out of the way.

Mr. Lynsted offered her the chair. "I'm going to find the innkeeper. I'll be right back." He said this last loud enough for the gentlemen to hear. And then, in a very quiet under voice, he had to add, "This is one of those circumstances when a lady's maid would have been a great help."

She bristled at the suggestion. "I can take care of myself."

"Yes, you have your knife," he agreed with a hint of disgust and left.

The truth was, she didn't have her dirk. She'd left it on the floor of the coach, a blunder that was uncharacteristic of her. The omission was certainly Mr. Lynsted's fault. If she hadn't been so frustrated and annoyed with him, she would have remembered something important like her dirk.

She studied the fire, watching the flames dance every time the front door opened and closed. More men entering the inn. She and Mr. Lynsted had obviously arrived just in time.

The air was full of masculine shouts of greetings, talk of the fight . . . and the mention of her name.

She'd been recognized.

Grace dared not look around her and invite unwelcome attention. She kept her head low, listening.

Then, she heard several men mention Mr. Lynsted's name. Their voices sounded patronizing as well as mildly surprised at his presence.

She had to look to see who was speaking and was shocked to recognize Lord Stone standing in the doorway surrounded by a group of his cronies.

It took all of Grace's courage to not jump behind the chair and hide. Stone was the man who'd attempted to bribe the stagehands, porters, and watchmen for access to her, the one others had warned her to stay far away from. She'd been blessed the stagehands and others had protected her. In the way of underlings, they'd managed to talk their way out of doing his bidding.

Stone was the son of a duke and impervious to the law. One of the girls in the opera company had been his mistress until a broken jaw, reputedly by Stone's hands, had left her unable to perform, and then he'd tossed her out.

There were other stories, whispers of behaviors so degrading and mean-spirited, Grace had not wanted to believe them. She hadn't wanted to grow closer to him either.

And now, here he was, looking down the hall and mentioning Mr. Lynsted by name.

Grace turned her back to the door, even as she strained to catch a word or two of what Stone was saying without drawing attention to herself—but it was too late.

A stool was plunked down beside her chair. Stone himself sat upon it. He was a tall, gimlet-eyed man with a lacy neck cloth and dark hair he combed forward in the style *á Brutus*. Many women thought him attractive.

Grace thought him reptilian.

"Miss MacEachin, who would have thought I'd meet you in the wilds of Biggleswade."

Her first instinct was to ignore him . . . but she knew that would only antagonize the situation.

"Who would have thought I'd meet you here as well, my lord?" She kept her voice cool, her back straight.

His gaze warmed in appreciation. "You are more lovely up close than you are on a stage."

She didn't answer. She held herself still.

He smiled as if sensing her apprehension. "Perhaps it is fortuitous that we are here together. I now have the opportunity to know you better. You have proven to be a difficult woman to know. I've tried my best to gain your attention."

"My career has kept me busy."

"But you are not busy now." His smile widened, turned wolfish—until Mr. Lynsted's voice cut in.

"She's also not alone."

Grace could have collapsed in relief.

The smile disappeared from Stone's face. He stood. "Lynsted."

"Stone."

Grace was stunned by Mr. Lynsted's curtness. It was as if he, of all the people of his class, was not intimidated by the rake.

"I have our rooms, Grace," Mr. Lynsted said, using her given name, and she understood. He was offering her the only protection Lord Stone would respect.

"You've won her? *You?*" Stone's accusation and disbelief rang off the ceiling beams.

Mr. Lynsted didn't answer him but took Grace's hand and led her from the room, Stone's mates stepping back to let them pass.

She could feel their gazes follow her and Mr. Lynsted as he led her down the hall to the staircase, where a girl waited to escort them up to their rooms.

"How do you know Stone?" he asked her in a low voice as they reached the top of the stairs.

"How do you know him?" she countered.

"I went to school with him. He's the devil incarnate."

"For once, Mr. Lynsted, we agree. He's been after me. Wanted to win that wager."

The girl opened a door on the right side of the hall.

"This is your room," Mr. Lynsted murmured. "Mine is across the hall. We're fortunate to have secured them. I'm not certain there are any others left."

"Yes, sir, we are full," the girl confirmed.

Grace walked inside. The room was a little larger than a good-sized horse stall but the sheets and the floor appeared clean, and a small fire gave the room warmth. Herbert had seen that her valise was waiting for her on her bed.

"Is the water warm in the pitcher?" Grace asked, nodding to the wash stand.

"Yes, miss," the girl answered. "And the soap is new, too."

Grace nodded her appreciation and the girl withdrew.

"I'll give you a moment to freshen up," Mr. Lynsted said, "and then I'll escort you to dinner.

Let's say in fifteen minutes. There is a rather nice dining room overlooking the garden."

"That sounds like heaven," she said, her dark thoughts of Lord Stone vanishing.

"Good. Now, don't open this door until you hear my knock."

"I won't," she agreed.

He paused by the door. "By the way, I took the liberty of ordering supper."

"What did you order?" she asked.

"Roast chicken." Something suspiciously like a smile crossed his face as he closed the door.

"If you aren't careful, you may develop a sense of humor," Grace warned, but there was no response. She heard the door across the hall open and close.

Fifteen minutes passed very quickly. Grace was barely ready when he knocked on her door, ready to escort her downstairs.

The crowd of men in the taproom and hallways seemed to have doubled in size, if that could be possible. Other than the serving girls in the dining room, Grace was the only woman there—and she was glad for Mr. Lynsted's presence.

By now, word had spread as to her identity and she could feel the men strip her naked with their eyes, but they kept their distance.

Their dinner was delicious. Of course, Grace was so hungry she have been eaten crow's meat and thought it tasty.

Conversation between her and Mr. Lynsted was sparse. He appeared as aware as she that, in spite of being seated at a table in the far corner, they were the center of attention. The situation seemed to make him as uncomfortable as it did her, which she found interesting. Any other man of her acquaintance would have preened over the impression he'd claimed her and won the wagers.

Mr. Lynsted acted awkward and almost embarrassed. Grace wasn't certain she ought not be a little offended.

Lord Stone sat with a group of comrades at a large table in the center of the room. Grace tried not to pay attention to them but they were loud and drinking heavily. New wagers were being made over whether the Scotsman McGowan could beat the current champion, Tom Cribb, when they met next month around London.

And then she heard Stone say to a man, "Ask her to sing. Tell her we want a song."

The man he'd given the order to was young, foppish, and had pretensions of being a Corinthian. He was also very deep into his cups. He leaned back in his chair, turning in Grace's direction, and shouted, "Sing us a song."

Stone kicked a chair leg out from beneath him and the man crashed to the floor. "I could have done that," he chastised the man and then sent an insolent grin in Grace's direction. "My apologies, Gracie love. Young men today lack manners." The others around him snickered.

Grace chose to ignore them and was pleased Mr. Lynsted did, too.

And then Stone called out, "So how are things with you, Dickie? Has life grown better or are you still the same shivering worm? Remember when we used to make you lie on the floor and pretend to shiver? Worm, worm, worm?"

Heads from other tables turned in their direction. Mr. Lynsted carefully buttered a slice of bread and took a bite.

Stone sighed heavily as if annoyed. Grace had finished with her meal and wished they'd leave. Mr. Lynsted seemed at ease.

A few moments later, Stone said to one of his comrades, "Natty, fetch that kitten over there. Bring it to me."

Grace had to look and sure enough, there was a curious kitten peeking out from behind the hallway door. It was a yellow cat with two white front paws.

"A cat?" Natty protested, even as he rose to catch it.

"A cat," Stone insisted. "I have a new wager."

Grace folded and unfolded her napkin. Mr. Lynsted appeared oblivious to Stone's presence.

"What sort of wager?" one of the gentlemen at his lordship's table asked.

"I'll wager five hundred guineas I can make that cat run a straight course from one side of this room to the other."

"You can't make a cat do anything," the gentleman said and his companions agreed.

"A straight line," Stone promised, taking the purring kitten from Natty. "Are you in?"

Before anyone could answer, Mr. Lynsted pushed back his chair and stood. "Let the cat go."

"This isn't your concern, Dickie," Stone answered.

"Yes, it is."

Stone laughed. "You tried to stop me one other time, remember?"

"I *did* stop you," Mr. Lynsted said.

"Not for long. I did what I wanted anyway."

Mr. Lynsted's jaw hardened, not with anger but resolve. "Leave the cat alone."

Grace had never heard of anyone standing up to Lord Stone. People usually dodged him, talking around him, mollified him. No one defied him.

The room had gone quiet.

Stone grinned, obviously enjoying being the

center of attention. "We used to lock you in your trunk, Dickie. Do you remember that?"

"I do."

"We'd hear you crying."

Mr. Lynsted did not say a word.

"And there was the time we pushed the trunk down the stairs," Stone continued. "What did you break?"

"You know."

"But the others don't," Stone reminded him.

"I don't believe the other gentlemen in this room are interested. Or they have too many of their own stories of being tortured at the hands of bullies to care about my own."

"*Tortured*, Dickie? Such a strong word."

"I've grown up, Stone. I don't cry any longer."

"We shall see," Stone answered, and before Grace knew what he was about, he held the cat down with one hand as he took the candle off the table and set her on fire.

Mr. Lynsted was across the room in the blink almost before the cat's howl hit the air. He doused the flame with Stone's own mug of ale, throwing the contents right into his lordship's face as he did so.

The cat took off running as Stone jumped to his feet, wiping his eyes as he did so. "*You bastard.* I ought to call you out."

"Please do," Mr. Lynsted answered.

Stone wiped his hands on his napkin. "There would be no sport in it."

"There never was sport in it, Stone. And we're not boys in school any longer. These men can think for themselves."

"*No one likes you.*" Stone spat the words out as he threw his napkin down, and then realized he sounded exactly like a small-minded schoolboy.

The snorts and titters from his companions and the surrounding tables were now at his expense.

Mr. Lynsted leaned forward. "You'd best leave the cat alone. This isn't like last time." He turned to Grace. "Are you ready?"

She was more than ready. She'd listened to the whole exchange with wide eyes. She'd jumped to her feet when Stone had burned the cat and now hurried over to Mr. Lynsted's side. He didn't linger but took her arm and directed her from the room.

"Be certain that whore doesn't give you a case of the spots," Stone called out after them. "I didn't like her when I had her. She's too hairy."

His insults shocked her. Grace started to turn around, ready to tie his tongue in knots. She was still shaking at what he'd been about to do to the kitten and really wanted a go at him.

Mr. Lynsted held her in place. "Don't take his

bait," he warned. "He's been exposed for the ass he is. But he can be dangerous."

"Someone should set fire to him," she answered.

"Agreed, but no one will. They've all been drinking steadily all day and are the worst for wear."

They started up the stairs. "What did you mean about what happened last time to a cat? What did he do?"

He shook his head. "Don't ask."

A dozen possibilities filled her mind, all of them horrifying. "And the things he said to you. Was he truly that mean?"

"Worse," Mr. Lynsted said, "but there were some who were more evil. Lower schools are beastly places."

He opened the door to her room. Grace went inside. He followed, shutting the door.

"And his comments about he and I—" She was shaking, she was so angry. "He's never touched me. He's wanted to but I've warded him off. The closest he's been to me is a few flowers."

Mr. Lynsted leaned back against the door, his expression somber.

"You believe me, don't you?" she demanded.

"Yes, I do."

"*Good.*" Grace paced from one side of the room

to the other. The only light in the room came from the hearth. She stopped when she was in front of it. Turned to him.

"Saving that cat has raised my opinion of you," she declared.

There was a beat of silence. "Thank you," he replied and then added, "I think."

Grace ignored the gentle jab. This was a serious matter. "I confess my opinion of you was not high. Your father and uncle destroyed my family. I realize that is not your fault," she said, raising a hand to stave off any protest he might offer. "I also understand you are traveling with me because of your sense of integrity and you have no obligation to entertain me although I was bored senseless riding with you . . . however—"

She broke off, not certain how to phrase herself and then decided honesty was best, especially between them. Mr. Lynsted had been bluntly honest with her. She could be the same in return. "I don't trust men."

He pulled back, as if he hadn't expected her comment. "Do you trust me?"

"No." She crossed her arms. "Or at least, I'm trying not to."

Her confession was a revelation to herself.

He was slipping past her guard, something

she'd never have imagined possible—especially since he hadn't put himself out very much for her.

"Do you still think I'm a prig?" he wondered, that same hint of dry humor in his voice.

"Oh, yes." She was serious. "Does that offend you?" she asked, hesitant. She didn't really want to insult him. He'd shown more courage downstairs facing Stone than she'd seen from any dozen men of his class in London.

He considered the matter and then shook his head. "Of course not. The truth is, I *am* a prig. I'm not popular for it. Probably less so now that I've openly made an enemy of Stone. But I am stuffy, and also reliable and honorable."

Important qualities. She agreed.

"Well, I'm not a—" She stopped. Some words were too ugly to say. "Whore" was one of them. She made herself say it. "*Whore*. I'm not a whore."

The word seemed to linger in the air. She hated it.

"I'm a singer and I have been a dancer. I have lived on the edge of society," she could admit. "But I've never sold myself. Ever. It's a point of honor of sorts." She knew how pitiful she must sound to him. "We all have our standards. Even actresses. That doesn't mean . . ." She let her voice trail off.

"Mean what?" he asked, hestitated, then said, "About you being the sort of woman a man marries?"

Well. He knew how to go right to the point. "I suppose your talent for plain speaking doesn't make you popular either?"

He bowed his head in concession to her observation.

Grace took a step back. If he could speak matter-of-factly, so could she. And she wanted to lay all her cards, so to speak, out for him. However she couldn't do it looking at him. She shifted her gaze to the floor, studying the tips of her coveted kid slippers as she said briskly, "I've had lovers in the past, but not recently. I've changed. I want to change. I want to be a person *I* respect."

She lifted her gaze to see if he understood what she was telling him.

His brows had come together as he digested her meaning. "Why are you telling me this?"

Grace reached for her courage. "Because I want you to respect me."

Mr. Lynsted studied her a moment as if sensing an ulterior motive. "All because I saved a cat?"

"Yes. And because you stood up for yourself to a man everyone cowers in front of."

"Some would say it is easy when you are as big as a house."

"It's *never* easy. I know that. Besides, you aren't that big. You are no Samson."

His brows rose as if she'd said something alarming . . . and then slowly he nodded, and she relaxed. He understood.

"Good night," she whispered, both relieved and pleased.

"Good night," he returned.

She waited, expecting him to leave.

He didn't.

Instead, he said, "Will you please hand me one of your blankets?"

"Why?"

"Because I'm staying right here."

Grace didn't believe she'd heard him correctly. "Here?"

"Yes, I'm sleeping in your room tonight."

"Oh no, you are *not*," she informed him. "Not with the male population in London walking the halls of this inn. Rumors will be flying."

"On the contrary, because half the male population in London is here, including Stone, I most definitely need to stay here."

All good will she'd built toward him vanished, replaced by all the years of wariness. "Is it the wagers? Do you want to claim the money? Or just appear to be my lover, because you will *not* be in my bed."

"So much for trust," he said under his breath and walked over to the bed and pulled the coverlet off it.

Grace's response was to grab hold of an edge of the blanket and attempt to pull it away from him.

Chapter Eight

$\mathcal{F}$or a few seconds, Richard found himself in a tug of war with Miss MacEachin. The woman was surprisingly strong for her petite size and hung on with the ferocity of a puppy who doesn't want anyone else to have its bone.

"Miss MacEachin, you are being ridiculous."

Her response was to pull harder. "Leave my room."

He let go. The sudden lack of resistance sent her falling back onto the bed. She bounced right back up, pulling her coverlet into her arms as if it were a shield against him.

"I'm not leaving." He ran a frustrated hand through his hair, and realized he was tired and

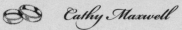

going about this all the wrong way—especially after her confession.

Actually, he found her confession unsettling. He didn't want to think well of Grace MacEachin or identify with her. As long as she was a "tart" or "whore" or "actress" or any of the words people used to describe her, he could keep her at a distance. His attraction to her was nothing more than male instinct . . . and not something as personal as admiring her or finding her likable.

He was also aware, she didn't see him as a threat. Maybe not even as a man. Women didn't confide in men.

"I'm not interested in winning wagers at your expense," he told her. "I have plenty enough money. And your virtue is safe," he placed a slight emphasis on "virtue," knowing she would assume the worst of his motives, but he needed the distance back. He needed his masculinity back. "After all you have your little knife to keep me at bay."

Her eyes widened at the insult to her favorite weapon.

He waved any protest she could have made away. "Keep the blanket. But I *am* staying here. Stone is not going to quit drinking and there is the real possibility he will try something very stupid. For that reason, I'm sleeping in front of your door," he said, taking off his jacket and throwing it on the floor in front of the door. He sat down. "If he opens even an inch, I'll push my hand down his throat."

"Do you really believe he would try such a thing in a crowded inn?"

"Do you think I'd be willing to sleep on the floor if I didn't?" he countered. "Stone doesn't believe rules—those of the law and those of civility—apply to him. He'd walk in here and rape you. I don't wish to sound harsh, but there is that sort of man out there, and he's one of them."

Her face had gone pale at his bluntness. Richard wished he'd not been so direct. He wasn't one for coating words, another fault she could lay at his door.

He stretched out. The floor felt good. He was tense, keyed up by her presence, the trip, and the possibility of at last having a reckoning with Stone. He hadn't acquitted himself very well when last they'd met . . . but that had been fifteen years ago. They were men now —

The blanket fell on the floor beside him.

He looked up. Miss MacEachin stood over him.

"Here. Take it," she ordered.

For a second he was tempted to tell her to stuff it, but then that would start matters all over again. "Thank you."

"You can have the pillow, too," she offered.

"I'm fine."

Miss MacEachin walked over to the washstand in the corner of the room by the fire. Her shadow made movements along the wall as she took the pins out of her hair. Her curls tumbled down around her shoulders, hitting the space between her shoulder blades, right where he thought it would. She quickly braided it into one long plait and washed her face.

Richard dragged his gaze away, focusing on the ceiling. His uncle's warning about not being attracted to Miss MacEachin echoed in his ears. He tried to think of Miss Abigail Montross and couldn't conjure one feature of her face . . . and yet the very light smattering of freckles over Miss MacEachin's nose was burned into his memory.

He heard the ropes of her bed creak. She'd lain down. God help him, he had to look.

She rested on her side on top of the bedclothes. She was still fully dressed, her hands folded beneath her head, and she watched him. She, too, still wore her shoes.

For a long moment their gazes held.

He didn't know what she was thinking, but his mind was recalling how soft and yielding her body had felt beneath him in the coach—even as she held a knife to his throat.

Richard rolled over to face the door. He had to keep control of himself.

"Thank you for saving that cat tonight," she said.

He gave a shrug. "You don't need to stay up," he said. "And you might want to become more comfortable than wearing your dress to bed. I won't look. You can trust me."

"I already do trust you," she murmured. "I wouldn't have said what I did earlier if I didn't."

Richard stared at the door. He was right. She didn't see him as a man.

"Besides," she continued, "you might need me and my dirk to help you." There was a pause. "Did you hear me? I was trying to make a wee jest."

He didn't answer.

Again, there was silence . . . and then, "So what did you break when Stone threw you down the steps in a trunk?"

"A collar bone. Had to leave school."

"Did they send him home?"

Richard gave a bitter laugh. "No one sends home a duke's son."

"How old were you?"

"Fourteen."

"I can't imagine he had the upper hand on you. Usually, people back off from big men."

"I wasn't big back then. I didn't start growing

until I was seventeen and finished with school."

"Ah," she said as if he'd said something very important. "What was it like when you returned to school?"

"I kept out of his way." *He'd won.*

"Did you truly take him to task over hurting an animal?"

"And people. Stone bullied everyone. I managed to escape his notice because he liked my cousin Holburn and let me by. He and his cronies beat a boy in my level so badly, he never quite recovered. His father was stationed in India and they sent him to him. I should have faced Stone then." Richard shifted his weight. "I felt like a coward until I saw him hurting a cat. They'd tied it by the tail from a tree and were trying to bat it with a stick. I went a little crazed and attacked him."

"What happened then?"

"All of his friends jumped on top of me. But I was angry and I fought back. They weren't used to anyone fighting back."

"And then?" she prodded. Her voice sounded interested.

Richard shrugged. "And then the tutors came running out to stop the fight. I was having the worst of it, but I had bloodied Stone's nose." He had to smile at the memory. "He was sniveling and crying."

"What about you?"

"I knew better than to cry. I'd heard what they said about the boys who cried."

"I know what you mean. People will offer pity to you when you cry but they won't respect you."

She was right. He wondered how she knew. He was tempted to ask . . . but that would bring him too close to her again. He lay silent.

"Tell me about the trunk."

He should ignore the request, end all chatter between them.

"Stone and his friends surrounded my cot one night and attacked me. I was little and skinny and this time no competition for them since they were ready for me. They folded me up in a trunk and tossed it down the stairs."

"Does Stone always travel in a pack?"

"Always."

"The coward."

Richard had to smile. His sentiments exactly.

"You are good with your fists," she said. "I noticed that last night."

In spite of wanting to keep his defenses up where she was concerned, Richard couldn't help but be flattered. "I train with Bill Richmond at his academy." He heard the eagerness in his voice. Embarrassed, he fell silent.

"Richmond is one of the best," she agreed. "I

thought most gentlemen preferred Gentleman Jackson's boxing saloon."

"I'm not playing at this," he answered. "I want to know the sport."

"Why?" she asked. A simple word that no one had put to him before.

Richard rolled over.

She lay on her side, cradling her head with her arms, watching him. She smiled. "Why boxing? Why not fencing?"

"I'm too clumsy for fencing. In boxing my height is an advantage. As is my strength. And there is grace to it. A formality."

"Not the boxing I've seen," she said. "Men double their fists and start hitting."

"Then you haven't seen it done right. I've studied it. I'm learning from a master. There is no one better than Richmond. Even Jackson will say it is so."

"The boxing lawyer," she murmured, and then yawned. "That's why you believe there are rules. Stay out of the rings at the country fairs, Mr. Lynsted. For your own safety."

"I have never planned on fighting for sport," he assured her.

"No, you've been planning on taking on Stone."

He opened his mouth to deny her statement . . . and then realized she was right. He could have said that every gentleman needed a sport and that Richard, being the big, clumsy ox he'd become, didn't have the grace or talent for many—but he would have been lying. That beating at Stone's hands had weighed heavily on his mind all these years. He'd failed to defend himself.

And now, he might have a chance to make that right—

Booted steps sounded in the hall, followed by drunken, schoolboy giggles.

Miss MacEachin sat up. She'd heard them, too.

Richard motioned to her to be quiet and earned a face from her at his impertinence for thinking she would give away they were awake. He had to smile.

Quietly, he came to his feet and placed his ear to the door.

"Which room is it?" one of the men in the hallway asked in a whispered slur.

"On the left," was the answer.

"No, right," another corrected.

"Keep your bloody voice down," another warned. "Lynsted is across the hall."

"That bloody bastard." It was Stone speaking now. "I'll crack his head open. How did he end up with a woman like that?"

Richard placed a light hand on the handle so he would feel it the moment it turned.

One of the men started to make a bawdy statement about Miss MacEachin but Stone shut him up with a furious, "Keep your voice down. If he finds out what we are up to, he'll be mad as a bear."

"He is a bear," someone muttered. "He's huge. Remember when he was so skinny we called him Straws?"

"Lynsted may be big, but he can't take on the lot of us," another man reasoned.

"I'd rather take on Grace MacEachin," was Stone's sly reply and he was seconded by a round of more male giggles.

The only light setting the scene was an oil wall sconce in the hallway and the hearth light in the room. Shadows appeared at the crack beneath the door.

The handle started to turn.

Richard stepped aside and raised one clenched fist.

In the hall, there was shushing all around. The door cracked open. A man peeked in.

Stone.

Grabbing the door and throwing it open, Richard let the man have it. Flesh hit flesh and bone. Stone grunted and fell to the floor.

Who knew the man had a jaw of glass? He was out cold.

Richard didn't waste a beat. He stepped over Stone's body and went out in the hallway, his fists ready.

There were three men out there, all so drunk they wove back and forth. They took one look at him, hiccupped, and then went flying down the stairs.

"You forgot your friend," Richard yelled. He picked Stone up by the jacket, and carried him over to the staircase.

Stone's companions were nowhere to be seen.

Richard sighed and turned back to Miss MacEachin's room. That's when he realized he had an audience. Besides Miss MacEachin, several other guests had stuck their heads out in the hall to see what the fuss was.

And here Richard was with a comatose Lord Stone over his shoulder.

All but Miss MacEachin pulled their heads in and shut their doors.

"What happened?" Miss MacEachin asked from her doorway.

"They ran."

"Well, what shall you do with him?" she said.

Richard grinned. "I'm taking him to the stables."

"Ah, where they keep the asses," she observed, and he had to laugh.

The door across the hall to his room opened. A

very sleepy Herbert peered out. "Hello, sir. I was wondering when you would be coming in."

"Not yet, Herbert. Go back to sleep."

"Yes, sir. Very well, sir. By the way, well done, sir. One blow. Good job." He shut the door.

"I was starting to believe he hadn't noticed the man unconscious on your shoulder," Miss MacEachin mused.

Richard found himself grinning. Miss MacEachin tilted her head as if she'd found something curious. "What is it?" he asked.

"You. I haven't seen you smile."

"I smile."

"Not like that. Usually it is tight as if it hurts your muscles to move." She considered him a moment. "You should smile more often, Mr. Lynsted. You are a handsome man when you smile. Good night. I'll see you in the morning." She shut the door.

Richard stood still, staring at where she'd just stood, uncertain he'd heard her correctly. She'd called him handsome. *Him*.

He was tempted to shake Stone to consciousness to see if he'd heard her say as much, too.

And this is what his uncle had feared. Miss MacEachin knew her way around men. With one word she made him light-headed, giddy even.

Richard turned on his heel and started downstairs. All was quiet. There was a large number of sportsmen without rooms who'd chosen to spend the night sleeping, or passed out, in chairs or curled up on benches. Again, Stone's cronies were not in sight. So much for camaraderie, although it pleased Richard to think he had them quaking in their very expensive boots.

Richard was serious about taking Stone to the barn and putting him as far away from them as he could. Sooner or later, the man would come to his senses and want revenge—but Richard no longer feared him.

A man who went down with one punch would be easy enough to handle. However, Richard didn't want any more gossip than had already started.

He carried Stone out to the stable. Drivers and servants were gathered around a fire on the other side of the yard. They didn't seem to notice him.

Years ago, Stone had played a terrible prank on one of Richard's schoolmates. He'd pretended to befriend him, gave him too much to drink, robbed him of his clothes, and tied him up to the school's signpost just for the sport of it.

Richard was tempted to do the same to Stone, but wanted a more subtle touch.

That's when he spied the loaded hay wagon under some trees.

In the stable, he found some rope and fairly clean cloth for a gag. He carried Stone over to the wagon, lifted the tarp covering the hay and dumped him into it. He quickly tied his hands and feet, then tied the cloth around his mouth. He tossed hay over the unconscious Stone and re-secured the tarp.

"Can I help you, sir?" a man's voice asked behind him.

Richard turned. A man in yeoman's garb walked toward him.

"Is that your hay?" Richard asked.

"Aye. Was there something you were wanting?"

"No," Richard hurried to assure him. "I'd noticed the good quality of your hay earlier, when I saw your wagon, and decided to have a closer look at it. Couldn't sleep," he added as an excuse for why he was prowling around in the dark. "Are you delivering it here?"

"I'm taking it on to London," the driver said with no little amount of pride. "It's quality stuff and that's where I'll receive the best price—especially this time of the year, when most hay barns are empty. Were you looking for hay?"

"As a matter of fact, I am. What time will you be leaving in the morning?" he had to ask.

"Before first light," the driver assured him.

" 'Tis unfortunate I'm going in the opposite direction."

"I haul to London on a regular basis, sir. Perhaps I can deliver to you on another of my trips."

"Yes, please do search me out. The name is Stone, Lord Stone. I'm in Mayfair."

"Yes, sir—I mean, my lord. I shall do so, my lord," the man said.

"Have a safe trip then," Richard said, thinking he rather liked being toadied to. No wonder Stone was so insufferable.

As he walked, the moon popped from behind the clouds and for a second, it was as if the universe smiled down upon him. Roddy Bankston and a host of other boys who had been brutalized by the likes of Stone had won one.

For the first time in his life, Richard felt like a man.

And he was handsome, too.

Chapter Nine

$\mathcal{G}$race didn't have any trouble rising the next morning after enjoying hours of deep, trouble-free sleep. In fact, she was looking forward to the day . . . and to seeing Mr. Lynsted.

She opened her door to go downstairs just as he opened his across the hall.

For a second, they stood facing each other, not speaking. When they had first met, his tall, brawny frame had attracted her. However, now that she knew him to be so honest, so forthright, she wondered how could she not have noticed how handsome he truly was?

"Good morning," he said.

He'd shaved. The clean, spicy scent of his shaving soap swirled in the air around her. "Good morning," she echoed, suddenly shy.

"I trust you slept well," he said.

"I did. And yourself?"

He laughed then, the sound startling her with the sense of newness about it. This was a man who rarely let down his guard, but he had . . . for her.

"I slept with the peace of angels," he answered, "and I trust Lord Stone did also. Don't worry about your bag. Herbert will see to it."

That's when she noticed the valet listening with great interest as he lingered in the room behind his master.

Grace took hold of herself. She wasn't one to go buffle-headed over men. They went buffle-headed over *her*. She'd learned the distinction the hard way and would be wise to follow the rule. *Especially* with Mr. Lynsted.

"Thank you," she murmured and came out in the hall. She carried her cape, cap, and gloves.

Mr. Lynsted fell into step beside her as they journeyed down to the dining room. "So, have you seen Lord Stone this morning?" she had to ask.

"I understand he is already on his way to London," he answered.

"He left? In the middle of the night? I'd always understood that Stone's consequence was so puffed up no one could ever convince him to do anything that wasn't his idea. How did you manage?"

"I can be very convincing when I wish to be," he answered, stepping back to let her enter the dining room first.

"I have no doubt of that," she murmured.

The innkeeper, his wife, and two of his serving girls were busy cleaning up after what had obviously been a very profitable night. Many of the guests were stretched out on benches where they'd passed out the night before. One man was curled into a ball under a table.

"Good morning to you, sir," the innkeeper greeted them. "It's a pleasure to see you are both bright and cheerful on a morning like this. Please excuse our mess. There's a clean table in the corner."

In spite of the sleeping bodies around them, Grace and Mr. Lynsted proceeded to have a very nice breakfast . . . especially when she realized he truly listened to what she said. An unusual quality in men, lacking in the circles she usually traveled.

And she liked his green eyes. They were intelligent, compassionate. She thought of the story he'd told her about his schools days the night before and wondered, if he had been as tall and muscular then as he was now, would he have become the same man? A man she found she could respect.

He also had the longest lashes. Any woman would have given her right hand for such lashes—

"Is something wrong?" he asked. "Are your eggs not to your liking?"

Grace looked down at her plate. She'd become so lost in listening to him and her own thoughts, she hadn't even touched her food. The irony was that here she was mooning over the only man in the whole inn who didn't bow and scrape to her.

"The eggs are fine," she murmured. "I was just thinking about the perverse nature of women." Herself in particular.

His brows came together in puzzlement.

She laughed. "Don't try to make sense out of my rambling," she warned him. "I can't and I'm the one with the thought." She dove into her food, aware that he was still watching her.

After the third bite under his scrutiny, she set her fork aside. "Is there a problem, Mr. Lynsted? Have you not witnessed a woman enjoying her meal before?"

"I don't understand women." He said this as a confession, almost apologetically.

She stirred her tea. "I often fail to understand men."

"This shouldn't be so difficult," he said. "Are

we not both human beings? Do we not want the same things?"

"In some areas," Grace said, "but the poets tell us differently."

"Poets? Do you pay attention to poetry? It's all flowery nonsense from people who think too hard."

Grace burst out laughing, finding she agreed with him.

He smiled, the expression almost self-deprecating as he confessed, "I'm a plain man and I like plain words and emotions. Do you see the innkeeper's wife over there?" The woman had just come into the room to pick up a tray of dirty dishes. "Do you believe her thoughts are so much different from her husband's? She wants to have good custom in this place. She wants food on her table for her children. Her husband wants the same thing. That's life. Men and women are more alike than they imagine."

"Yes," Grace agreed, "but that is everyday living. The hardship, the toil. Perhaps we are different in how we perceive each other beyond the practical."

Mr. Lynsted frowned as he if couldn't comprehend what she was saying.

"The courtship," she explained. "Life has many

layers. Certainly the innkeeper's wife wants him to recognize her for something more than working hard around the inn. Men think if they are working hard, it is a sign they care."

"Is it not?"

Grace set her fork down, finished with her meal and said thoughtfully, "'Tis . . . but perhaps she wants something more. Perhaps she would like some romance."

His gaze narrowed as if she'd said something shocking. "They've been married for years. Do they not have children?"

"But there must still be some romance," she insisted.

"Romance after years of marriage," he protested. "Look at them. They are like two old shoes that have walked the same path."

"All the more reason for romance," she answered.

"What is this—romance?" He sounded it out as if it were a foreign word. "What are you saying that is different from what I am saying?"

"I'm saying that just because two people have been married for years, they should want—" She paused. What *was* she saying? She was the last person in the world to be giving advice on marriage. "You are right. I was being fanciful."

"No, explain to me," he said. "What do you think it is like when two people have been married for years?"

There was an intensity to his question, an earnestness. He really did want to know.

"Just because someone has been married for years, they should still like each other. And be attracted to each other. In fact, from my friends who have been happily married, and I know only two—Fiona, Duchess of Holburn, and Constance Lachlan, who married the leader of my clan—it seems to me that when you truly love someone, then every day is better than the one before. Or so they told me."

"Does that make sense?"

Grace pushed the end of her fork on her plate, considering the question. "Yes. But I don't believe everyone feels that way."

He mulled over her words. "That may be true. I'm not around Holburn and his duchess. They still are newly married."

She nodded her agreement, fascinated that his lawyer mind had taken hold of this idea and was analyzing it.

"Most married couples I know," he said, "are like my parents. They live very separate lives. Mother has her interests; Father has his. They rarely spend time together. That's marriage."

"It's not like that for Fiona and Constance. They and their husbands seemed intertwined in each other's lives." She hesitated a moment and then, because a part of her needed to speak such, she confessed, "I thought like you at one time. Marriage just seemed too cold. I don't remember the time before my father was sent away. I sense it was happy . . . but I'm not certain. I was too young."

"And after he returned?"

"My mother left."

"She left?"

"She grew tired of being the pariah's wife. When he returned, she left." Left *her*. Grace focused on the food on her plate, a tightness forming in her chest.

"Do you know where she is?" he asked, sounding amazed a woman would walk out.

"I believe she has remarried and is living in Brussels."

"Your father is alive, isn't he?"

Grace nodded. "Of course he is. That's why we are going to Inverness." She placed her napkin on the table, crossed her arms, holding herself tightly. She'd not back away from this conversation. He needed to know just how much devastation his uncle and father had brought on her life. And yet now, she wasn't certain she wanted to discuss it.

"Did your parents divorce?" he asked. Divorce

was easier in Scotland than England but just as ugly an idea.

"Always the legal question first," she murmured. "No, they never divorced. Father was a man of the church. He would not do such a thing and he still honors his wedding vows. He truly loved her . . . and there is the tragedy."

"Then that makes your mother . . ." His voice trailed off. He looked away as if embarrassed for her.

"A bigamist," Grace finished for him. "Yes, she is. But she is in another country and what does it matter? Nothing to her." But it mattered a great deal to Grace. It had been a betrayal. Her mother, who had judged her so harshly after Harry Ellis's attack, had apparently one standard for Grace and another for herself.

Nor had she wanted anything to do with either Grace or her father. Once she'd found love, they'd become encumbrances.

At that moment, the innkeeper came out and took his wife's second dish-laden tray from her. For the briefest of seconds, their fingers touched and a smile passed between them. A longing the likes of which Grace had never known rose inside her.

Mr. Lynsted noticed them, too. "Is that romance?" he wondered.

"Being happy in your work when you are together? Yes," she said decisively. "The little things are the romance. The wanting to be together."

"And your mother didn't want to be with your father," he concluded. "Did you go with her?"

She drew her gaze away from the innkeeper and his wife and faced him. He leaned one arm on the table, his gaze intent. Why, of all the people who had crossed her path over the last five years, was he the first to ask questions?

"No, I didn't," she said. "I stayed with my father but I was very angry."

"About what?"

Grace shrugged. *About his having been sent away, about the way her life should have been, about the night Sir Nicholas Ellis's son had raped her and the number of men, so much like Lord Stone, who considered her fair game after Harry bragged about taking her.*

"It doesn't matter now," she said, rising to her feet. "I'm returning home. My father will have what he deserves, a fair hearing of his story."

"From me?"

"Yes."

"I assumed he'd want a magistrate if he wished vindication."

"It's too late for that, Mr. Lynsted. He's served the time. It's gone. But acknowledging his innocence is very important. When he sees you with me, when he realizes what I would do for him, then he'll be happy."

"I doubt if I will believe his story, Miss MacEachin. Will you be happy when all is said and done?"

Grace pulled on her gloves. The innkeeper and his wife had their heads together in the hallway now, arguing about something—and yet they stood so close to each other.

Before her mother left, her parents had stood far away from each other.

"Yes, Mr. Lynsted, as odd as that may sound, I'll be happy. You see, my father was right. Happiness isn't something others give to you. You must have peace in yourself. My taking you to listen to his story will say to him louder than words that I have faith in him. That's all he's ever asked of me. I just couldn't see it years ago. But now, all will be well."

He stood. "I pray it is, for your sake, Miss MacEachin."

"But you have your doubts," she added for him, smiling so he knew she meant no malice.

"I have my doubts," he agreed. "Shall we go?" He helped her put on her cape and they walked outside together.

The day was overcast with a bit of a wind but fine driving weather. The coach was packed and waiting for them.

When Herbert saw them coming, he opened the coach door. Dawson was already in the box, holding the horses.

"Good morning, sir," the valet said.

Mr. Lynsted nodded. "Good morning." He offered for Grace to climb into the coach ahead of him. She did, feeling the valet's eyes on her the whole time she did and knowing he was speculating over what she and his master had been up to for a portion of the night.

She should snap her fingers at what a servant thought . . . but she didn't. She couldn't. And therein might be the way she'd find herself again.

The old Grace, the girl who had been so eager to please, would have been mortified by what people thought. The woman she'd become had hardened herself against opinions other than her own. The woman she hoped to be was a melding of these two.

"There was a hay wagon under that tree last night, wasn't there?" she heard Mr. Lynsted ask.

"Yes, sir. I believe the driver pulled out before first light. Is there a reason you asked?"

"None in particular. Let's be on the road, Dawson."

"Right, sir."

Mr. Lynsted climbed into the coach, hanging his hat on the hook before pulling the door shut.

Once again, his huge body took up most of the space between them, but this time, Grace didn't mind. His presence was no longer unsettling.

Ever so slowly, her guard came down, and for the first time for what seemed like ages, she allowed herself to trust a member of the opposite sex. It was a good feeling.

Within minutes they were on their way again.

Richard had work he could do in his ledgers, but for the first time in his life, he chose not to put his nose to the grindstone—especially after Miss MacEachin asked him if he had a deck of cards in his satchel.

He did.

For the next nine hours of travel, including occasional stops for food or to stretch their legs, he didn't think about what he *should* be doing. Instead, he indulged himself in the frivolity of playing cards with a very beautiful woman.

But it was more than her beauty that attracted him to Grace MacEachin.

She was fun.

He *enjoyed* talking to her. She didn't make him feel like an awkward lug of a man.

Conversation was easy between them and not once did he experience a need to justify himself by mentioning his family's status or his position in his father and uncle's companies—points that wouldn't impress her anyway. Yes, he was related to the Duke of Holburn, but the *ton* seemed to consider him from the unsavory side of the family.

It didn't matter. She didn't care. Just as they had the night before and over breakfast, their conversation covered many topics. She listened to his opinions as considerately as he listened to hers.

If a week ago someone had told him that he'd be spending days in a coach with an actress and enjoying her company, he would have scoffed at the notion. Now, he basked in her presence.

Grace. The name fit her. He loved the sound of it.

He was also aware of why other men wanted her.

He wanted her.

All she had to do was give him a sly look from beneath her lashes as she contemplated which card to play next, and every muscle, every nerve, every fiber of his being went taut with desire.

He kept at a distance. His lust embarrassed him, especially when she was offering him her trust.

But what really kept him at bay was the realization that this woman had far more experience in bed than he had . . . because he'd had none. Most of the single men of his class and station had mistresses.

Richard had never pursued that course. He worked. That was what he did. His betrothal to Abigail Montross had been arranged by his father and hers. One day they would marry, but he did not feel a hurry.

There were times when he'd wondered if he wasn't a bit like his uncle, a complacent bachelor. Richard hadn't felt the need to pursue Abigail or any desire to bring about the nuptials.

He was feeling desire now. In Miss MacEachin's company, he was anything but complacent—

"Why haven't you married?"

Her question startled him.

"Why do you ask?" he parried. He didn't want to mention Abigail Montross to her. He didn't know why . . . but he had a suspicion, and it made him feel like any other man.

She considered her cards a moment before saying in the most casual tone, "Gentlemen of your class are usually married by now. Or on their way to being married."

"Not all of us."

"Don't you want to marry?"

Richard decided to be very interested in his cards. "Of course." Did she wonder about his attraction to women? She wouldn't if she knew how tight his breeches were right now. "But I have been busy with the family businesses and travel and all."

"So there is no time for a wife?"

"No time."

The lie flowed smoothly off his tongue—but any guilt he felt evaporated as Miss MacEachin gifted him with a smile so bright and sunny it robbed him of coherent thought.

For a second, he could only stare, stunned by the sheer, precious beauty of her.

"Gin," she announced, triumphant, bringing him back to the moment. "Show me the cards left in your hand so I can tally the points."

"I can't believe you beat me again."

"You aren't paying attention," she chastised him, spreading the cards he'd laid down on the seat so she wouldn't miss a point.

Perhaps she did know her impact on him.

The thought made him cautious. "I think you've beaten me enough for one afternoon," he said. Perhaps it would be best to put some distance between them. "I have some work to do." He reached for his satchel. Work would cure him of focusing on her.

She made a pretty pout. "One more game?"

He should say no.

"One more," he heard himself answer.

* * *

They spent the evening in an inn that was far more quiet than the one they'd been to the night before.

Dinner was excellent and Richard couldn't remember a meal he'd enjoyed more. Miss MacEachin surprised him by how well-read she was. Her experiences in life had given her a unique perspective on politics of the day and he found her comments not only interesting but also enlightening.

Of course they disagreed on the Irish question and she favored an independent Scotland, something he thought was idiocy. But she listened to his side of the argument, which few people ever did. Well, which his father and uncle rarely did.

However, what she was really doing was making him realize exactly how lonely he'd been in his life. How much he'd yearned for someone he could openly express his opinions and even his doubts to.

They talked late into the night. It was only after the innkeeper almost fell out of his chair, having fallen asleep waiting for them to finish, that Richard became conscious of the hour.

"Here," he said standing. "We should let that man go to his bed."

"His wife will wonder where he is," she agreed, rising.

They left the dining room. Richard wanted to offer her his arm, but held back, uncertain.

A woman like Grace MacEachin could do so much better than his luggish self.

They came to her room door first. He expected her to run inside. Instead, she lingered.

"I enjoyed this evening," she said.

"I did, too."

"It's not often people listen to me about my views of the world."

"I found them interesting," he said.

She smiled and Richard had an urge to pick her up in his arms and kiss her.

But he didn't. He wasn't that big of a fool—yet.

"Well, good night," he murmured, forcing his feet to move toward his door down the hall.

"Yes, good night," she echoed softly.

He tried not to look back at her. He didn't want to be that much of a puppy, but in the end, he couldn't resist. He had to toss a quick glance her way as he reached his door.

She was watching him. "Good night," she said again and then opened her door and went in.

Herbert was not waiting up for Richard. It was not lost on Richard that the valet had assumed he had spent the night before in Miss MacEachin's bed and had assumed he would do it again this evening. There had been too many winks and smug looks from Herbert and Dawson for Richard to miss the assumption.

His uncle would be pleased.

Richard didn't mind that the valet had gone on to bed. In fact, he enjoyed the solitude, so that he could replay in his mind everything she'd said over dinner.

The part of him that was still rational knew that all too soon this trip would come to an end. He needed to let go of his fascination with her— and yet, when he did fall asleep, his dreams were of Grace MacEachin.

They were both up early for the next day's travels.

Richard had spent a good deal of thought, while he was dressing, on a topic to share over breakfast, and was gratified when Miss MacEachin seemed pleased with the discussion.

Dawson informed him they would be rolling into Scotland by late morning. At the pace they were traveling, they would reach Inverness in two more days' time.

The day was a good one for travel, with a breezy sky and dry roads.

Richard and Miss MacEachin once again whiled away travel time over cards. He didn't even think about his satchel. He could always peruse accounts sheets . . . but he wouldn't have her much longer. Two days would pass as if a blink.

He knew he was being foolish. Miss MacEachin could destroy his family with her accusations.

But he liked her. A lot.

And for once, he was going to put common sense on hold and enjoy the moment.

They stopped at a roadside inn for a luncheon and ate outside. The air was still chilly but it didn't diminish their enjoyment of the food . . . or of each other.

Richard could remind himself that Miss MacEachin was an actress, but he didn't think she was acting when she laughed at his small jokes or listened intently to his opinions. And there were times when he caught her gaze drifting toward him as if reassuring herself he was there. He didn't believe that was acting either.

He thought she just might like him, even admire him a little.

Certainly he found her wonderful.

After several more hours on the road, Dawson pulled the coach over beside a swiftly moving river. "I thought we'd take a break here, sir," he told Richard as he opened the door.

"Good," Richard answered. "I'm in the mood for a stretch of the legs."

"I am, too," Miss MacEachin agreed as he helped her climb out of the coach. She looked around. "What a lovely spot."

"It is," Richard said, noting the lush greenery. The air was filled with the sound of rushing water from the river that could be seen through the trees. The road was not wide here. He turned to Dawson. "We aren't on the main road, are we?"

The driver smiled. "No, this route is more direct. Thought I'd save us some time."

"Excellent," Richard replied with little enthusiasm. He wanted all the time he could have with Miss MacEachin. He smiled at her.

She smiled back, pulling her cape closer around her. "March is always such a fickle month. The sun can be shining but the wind is cold."

"I know this area well," Dawson said. "If you need a moment of privacy, miss, there is a nice thicket down that path leading to the water that will protect you from the air."

"Thank you," she said and started walking in that direction, picking her way around the trees.

"Herbert, you go with her and keep watch," Dawson ordered. He smiled at Richard. "In case some fishermen are wandering around here. They like fishing off the rocks."

"The rocks?" Richard took a step through the trees so he could have a better look at the river.

Huge rocks formed rapids. "That water is too fast and too high for decent fishing," he observed. "If someone fell in, he'd be hard-pressed to survive that current."

Dawson craned his neck as if taking his own measure of the water and said, "You are right, sir. It would be a danger to fall in. This is the River Tweed. Mountain streams feed into it all the way to the ocean. Right now the water is cold as snow. I have to watch the horses to be certain they don't drink it too fast."

"Yes," Richard murmured, but his attention wasn't on Dawson. Miss MacEachin was no longer in sight. Nor was Herbert . . . and he didn't feel comfortable about this place.

Something was wrong, but he couldn't quite define what it was—except he sensed Miss MacEachin was in danger.

It was an odd notion. He wasn't a fanciful man, but the force of his suspicion was overwhelming.

Richard started moving down the path she'd taken toward the river, throwing over his shoulder to Dawson, "I believe I'll go check on Miss MacEachin."

Of course, if he found her, what would he say? That he had a strange feeling she might need his help?

Sounded silly.

"She's all right, sir," Dawson said, leaving the horses and coming down the path after him. "You know how ladies are. They take their time."

"I'm still going to check on her—"

Dawson grabbed his arm and swung him, catching Richard off guard. "I can't let you interfere, sir. It's for your own good. My lord's orders."

He pulled back his arm and threw his fist at Richard's face.

Chapter Ten

The path beside the raging water was steeper and rockier than Grace could have imagined. Her kid slippers offered very little traction as she picked her way carefully, conscious that Herbert dogged her footsteps. He had served as a watch during different stops they'd made, but his presence had not been this invasive.

The swirling rapids of the water seemed anything but peaceful and the air was cold and damp. Her hair curled tightly around her face. She wore her wool cape and the hem dragged the ground.

She tripped over one of the rocks and grabbed the trunk of a small tree to regain her balance.

"Are you all right, miss?" Herbert said, moving to stand even closer.

"I'm fine. Just clumsy."

Herbert didn't step back.

"You can go back up the hill," she said. "I'll only need a moment."

"Yes, miss," he replied dutifully, but when she took a step toward the sheltering thicket growing on the riverbank, he followed.

An inner sense warned her that something wasn't right. She stood no more than two feet away from the edge of the bank and could all too easily picture herself tumbling into the swollen river.

The image was so graphic in her mind she took a step back and so was somewhat prepared when the valet gave her a sudden, violent push toward the angry water.

Grace cried out in alarm and turned to run, but the valet caught her by arm and attempted to drag her toward the edge of the bank. However, she was no meek-and-mild miss. The blood of High-landers pulsed through her veins. She'd spent the last five years of her life living by her wits and she wasn't about to lose them now. Grace raised her knee and nailed him right between the legs.

The valet doubled over, releasing her.

She didn't hesitate but pulled out the dirk

strapped to her wrist. She'd bury it in the man's heart.

However, Herbert was prepared for the knife. As quickly as she had it in her fingers, he knocked it out of her hand. With a cry, she went scrambling for it but he grabbed her cape and started reeling her back toward him.

Grace slid out of the cape and made a mad dash up the bank. Unfortunately, she was hampered by her long skirts and the smooth soles of her precious kid slippers. Herbert tackled her before she'd gone far, knocking the wind out of her. The rough grass, sticks, and rocks scratched her skin while the earth's dampness seeped into her clothing.

"Thought you'd escape, huh?" Herbert whispered in her ear. "Not from me. Not after that kick you gave me—"

His voice broke off with a grunt of alarm as Mr. Lynsted grabbed him by the collar and pulled him off her.

"Leave her be," he ordered, shoving Herbert to the side. He then turned to her. "Are you all right?"

But Herbert wasn't giving up that easily. Before she could answer, he rushed Mr. Lynsted and threw all his weight on him. Both men fell to the ground and came up swinging.

Mr. Lynsted had height and size but the valet

was a scrappy fighter who didn't play by a gentleman's rules. He slammed his fist into Mr. Lynsted's abdomen with enough force to knock the air out of him and followed it up with a blow to the chin.

Two things went through Grace's mind—the first was relief that Mr. Lynsted had come to her rescue. She did not want to think him a party to her murder.

The second was that she'd best do something to help him.

Spying a good, stout branch not far from her hand, Grace picked it up, rose to her feet, and held it high, looking for an opportune time to crack it over Herbert's head.

She thought she'd found a good moment and swung the branch hard at the valet. However, Mr. Lynsted had been quicker and moved in for a jab so that the branch whacked him in the shoulder instead.

He grunted in pain and shot her a look that spoke volumes for what he thought of her help. It was at this time the valet slammed his fist in Mr. Lynsted's his face.

Grace didn't stop to think; she reacted. As Mr. Lynsted's head turned from the force of the blow, Herbert stepped aside, ready to deliver another punch. She threw the branch at Herbert, hitting him squarely in the chest.

The branch threw Herbert off balance. He lost his footing, staggered back toward the river, and then, for one awful moment, looked right at her in surprise before tumbling headfirst into the water.

Grace stared after him, shocked he'd fallen in. She heard Herbert thrashing in the madly rushing water, screaming for help, and then he was gone, carried away by the murderous rapids.

Mr. Lynsted threw off his greatcoat and his jacket. He began tugging off his boots.

"What are you doing?" Grace demanded.

"Going after him. He'll drown if I don't."

"*You'll* drown if you do."

"I have to try and save him" were Mr. Lynsted's last words before he jumped into the water.

Grace ran to the bank's edge. She looked to where she'd last seen the coachman's head. There was no sign of him—but now Mr. Lynsted was riding the racing current and Grace knew she had to do what she could to help him. She started running along the bank, crashing through bushes and stumbling over rocks to keep up with him.

Her cloak caught on tree limbs and small shrubs. She untied it and left it on the ground. She swore at her silly kid slippers and promised never to travel in anything but sensible shoes again.

Herbert's body popped up again in the water, fortunately on her side of the bank. She shouted to

Mr. Lynsted, catching his attention and pointing in the direction of where she saw the valet.

Mr. Lynsted began swimming with the current. Grace found herself rooted in place, watching the drama unfolding before her. Herbert had come up against an outcropping of rocks that held him fast. Mr. Lynsted caught up with him. He grabbed the neck of the man's coat and pulled him forward, only to have the current tear the body out of his arms.

This time, Mr. Lynsted let him go and Grace knew the man was dead.

For a moment it appeared the raging water would claim Mr. Lynsted, too, but he held fast to the rocks and Grace overcame her shock to run over and help him.

She balanced herself on a huge rock and bent down, grabbing a handful of his shirt at the nape. "Come on, Mr. Lynsted. Help me. You are too brawny of a man for me to do it myself."

He started to climb up but fell back, almost pulling Grace in with him. This next time, she lay flat on her stomach and used both hands to help support him as he tried again to crawl out of the water.

Her rescue was successful. He hefted himself upon the rock where she lay and fell beside her, breathing heavily.

It took Grace a moment to have the strength to sit up. When she did, she was shocked to see how badly his face was battered.

"Did Herbert do all that?"

"No," he said, the word little more than a groan. "Dawson and I had a round—*Dawson*." He climbed to his feet and began running back in the direction they'd come. Grace took off after him the best she could in her frivolous kid slippers.

Of course he was way ahead of her, charging through the brush and the trees, seemingly heedless of his wet clothes and his bare feet. He led her to the road and the coach—or where the coach should have been.

Seeing the empty space, he threw his hands up, his fists clenched in frustration. "He *ran*."

"Who? Dawson?" Grace managed to say as she tried to catch her breath.

Mr. Lynsted whirled on her, his face a mask of fury. "We had it out here. He tried to keep me from going to you. I *knew* something was wrong and he wanted to stop me. I knocked him out and left him on the ground while I went to check on you. He must have regained consciousness and took off with the coach. He has everything. Our clothes. My money. *God! I'm so stupid*."

Only then did everything that had just happened to her sink in. "They were going to kill me."

He gave a bitter laugh of agreement, folding his arms against his chest as if just starting to realize how cold he was. His breath came out in gulps. "And they almost succeeded."

"Your father and uncle tried to kill me," Grace repeated. "Just like they tried to have me killed in London."

"You don't know they were behind the attack in London," he argued, emphasizing his point by jabbing a finger in the air at her.

"I do. They *were*."

"My father is *not* a part of this. But my uncle—"

He broke off and started pacing as if the energy of his thoughts would not let him be still.

"Herbert was your *father's* valet," she pointed out coldly. He had to see the truth. He *must*.

"My father would *not* plot a murder," he ground out, clenching his teeth as if trying not to let them chatter.

Grace lost her temper. How could he be so blind? "Everyone knows the twins are close, that they finish each other's sentences, are rarely physically more than ten minutes apart from each other. If one has an itch the other scratches it."

"How do you know?" He was shaking hard now, his lips blue and his complexion pale.

"Because it's what *everyone* knows—except *you*," Grace repeated, determined to make him see the truth. "They almost married the same woman and some say they share her."

The last wasn't the wisest thing to say. It was a description someone had once given her to describe the twins, and Mr. Lynsted seized it.

"Now *that* is ridiculous. You are listening to rumor and innuendo from people who are jealous of my father and uncle's success. My mother is a good, honorable woman. And my father is an honorable man." There was an edge to his voice. She'd hit a raw nerve. Not all was as he wanted to believe.

She understood. She'd spent a lifetime of pretending. "Then what of your uncle?" she asked.

"*Leave it,*" he ordered. "Shut up about him."

"I wish I could, but the man has attempted to kill me *twice.*"

"Only once," Mr. Lynsted argued. His teeth were rattling in his head now with the force of his shaking. He turned away from her as if to shut her out.

Grace stared at his back and decided she'd never met a more stubborn man. His refusal to see what was clear to her made her angry. However, instead of arguing, she went stomping back through the woods to where his coat and boots were. She didn't find socks and remembered he'd jumped into the river with them on.

Her cape was still where Herbert had tossed it aside. She had no idea where her cap was but did find her dirk. She slipped the knife back into the sheath still strapped to her wrist, the leather wet from its soaking in the river.

Both her cape and his coats were damp from being on the ground. They'd just have to do. They were the only protection they had. The sun would set in another hour or so. The temperature would drop further.

She heard a twig snap behind her. She jumped, fumbling for her dirk.

"Me," Mr. Lynsted said. He spoke slowly, enunciating each word as if struggling for control of his frozen body. "Dawson . . . could . . . come . . . back. No . . . wait."

He was right. She threw his greatcoat around his shoulders. He huddled underneath it.

"Can you put on your boots?" she asked.

He shook his head. She bent down and helped him put them on. His flesh was blue and his joints stiff. "Come, let's find some help," she told him.

Cold air and wet clothes could kill. Every Highlander knew that. She watched him carefully as they walked a quarter mile or so along the river. Mr. Lynsted was a strong man but his strength couldn't protect him against bone-chilling cold.

Nor did she see sign of another human. No

smoke from a chimney or light from a lamp. They needed to make other plans. Even the walking hadn't helped to warm Mr. Lynsted.

She looked around and spied a level place in the woods up from the bank with a good wall of thick bushes, their branches winter bare, surrounding it on three sides. "We'll build a camp here."

He didn't say anything. He couldn't. He was shaking too hard.

Grace led him up the incline. "Stay here. I'll gather wood." She directed him to the haven provided by the bushes.

Mr. Lynsted nodded and then sank into a shivering ball on the ground. Her years living from hand to mouth had taught her how to use wet wood and make a fire. Grace found enough kindling and a few good-sized branches. She gathered as much as she could. It would be a long night.

She returned to their campsite. Mr. Lynsted didn't look any better but he wanted to talk.

"He wanted us alone," he said.

"Dawson?"

Mr. Lynsted nodded. "A m-more d-direct route." His tired voice was laced with bitterness.

"It's easy to catch someone off guard when they trust you," Grace answered, laying out her fire. "Don't think this is your fault."

"My u-uncle d-did this."

She chose not to argue. He'd learn the truth soon enough and she needed him to use his energy to save his life.

"Known him all my l-life," Mr. Lynsted chattered.

"Herbert? The valet? Yes, well you know some rotten people," she conceded, giving in to her own bad humor. She threw her cape over the top of the shrubs to create a three sided tent of sorts. She put on his jacket to keep herself warm.

Starting the fire was frustrating. Her fingers were cold and didn't want to cooperate. She used a piece of sharp rock, the blade of her dirk, and a piece of her petticoat. It was almost dark by the time she managed a spark. The flame grew and she felt hope.

She threw wood on the fire and sat back.

Mr. Lynsted crawled up beside her, holding his hands out.

"Dawson all. M-money, c-clothes, everything."

"I've been without money before," she said. "We'll survive."

His jaw tightened with anger. "G-go to Inverness. *We will*. Beforeuncleknowsdead."

She didn't like the way he slurred his words together and his chin rested on his chest as if his head was too heavy to hold up. Both were not good signs. She needed to keep him talking while she frantically tried to think what to do. "How long do you think we have?"

"Two . . . four." He swallowed. He hadn't the strength to say the word "days," and Grace knew she couldn't let him continue this way. He gave his head a sharp shake as if trying to clear his mind. "Dawson hasn't c-come b-back with the coach?"

"No. I haven't heard a sound."

"H-he's gone to my uncle. M-my uncle's m-man." He made a disgusted sound.

At least he hadn't grown disoriented—yet.

Grace reached over and put her arms around him. He was shivering again. Her fire wouldn't be enough to warm him up, and she was growing cold herself.

"B-bloody f-fool," he said.

"No, you aren't," Grace said. "You are the strongest, most couragest, noblest man I know. I wouldn't be alive if it weren't for you." She hugged him for encouragement before saying, "Now, take off your clothes, and don't argue with me."

Richard was absolutely certain the cold had gone to his ears and he wasn't hearing clearly.

Miss MacEachin knelt in front of him. "Do you

understand me?" she said in her wonderful, lilt-
ing accent. "It's growing colder. Wet clothes kill.
You must take them off."

"No."

"Please."

There was urgency in her voice, and he knew
she was right. Or perhaps he was just too tired to
care. His limbs had turned to lead. The simplest
move called for great concentration.

She was already undressing him.

He let her. He couldn't help. He felt a babe,
unable to perform the simplest task for himself—
and deep in the recesses of his mind, he knew she
was right. He was in trouble.

"Lie back," she whispered.

Richard collapsed onto his back. He was conscious of her unbuttoning his breeches but he felt
no reaction, and that was more of a concern than
his ceaseless shivering or how dull his mind had
become.

Miss MacEachin threw his greatcoat over him.
He huddled naked beneath it, turned toward the
fire and anxious for any warmth it might offer.
She threw a log on the flames.

"I need to go for more wood," she whispered,
or at least, he thought she was whispering. Her
voice sounded as if it came from a great distance.

He nodded.

"Try and stay awake."

Richard heard the plea in her voice. He'd try, but he was very tired.

He closed his eyes. He hoped she understood. He had no choice. His lids wouldn't stay open.

If only he could shake off this terrible cold. Then he'd stay awake. He'd do anything for her—

Another body snuggled up to his, pulling the coat so it covered both of them. *Miss MacEachin.* She was stretched out beside him, her legs along his. Her hips nestled his buttocks while her arms wrapped themselves around him.

It took several minutes before he realized, she was as naked as himself. Her bare flesh was against his.

Richard couldn't breathe. He couldn't think.

"This will help," she murmured. "We'll beat this. Together."

Slowly, Richard released his breath. The violent shivering ebbed but he felt colder than ever. She held him tighter. He wanted to tell her everything would be fine, but his lips couldn't form words.

For long moments she spoke to him, repeated, "It will be fine. All will be well."

And then he felt her hand on the most private part of his anatomy.

She cupped him, held him. "This will help," she whispered. She kissed his shoulder, his back, his arm.

Richard stared at the fire as her skilled hand brought him amazingly to life. He rolled over to face her, stunned, his confused mind not comprehending.

She looked down at him, so lovely in the firelight it almost hurt his eyes to look at her.

"It's all right," she whispered.

Her hair curled around her bare shoulders. His gaze fixed on her naked breasts. They were as he'd imagined, full and round, but the nipples were rosebud pink and tight from the cold.

He grew harder. Her hand tightened on the length and shape. The movement felt good . . . alive.

She rose above him, his black greatcoat around her shoulders. The firelight highlighted the curve of her waist. He caught a glimpse of dark hair at the juncture of her thighs. He raised his gaze to her breasts. Her beautiful breasts—

Miss MacEachin lowered herself upon his arousal, the intensity of her body heat overwhelming him.

He felt his release. It seemed to flow from every vein, every pore of his body, and filled hers. It shocked him with its intensity, its power.

So this was what drove men to madness.

At last he *understood*.

His heart pounded in his chest, pushing the blood through his veins and bringing him back to life.

Miss MacEachin leaned forward, bracing her hands on his chest. He closed his eyes, still assessing what had just happened. He could feel her watching him, knew her concern.

And then he felt himself harden again.

He was still inside her. He stretched, grew powerful, filled her.

Richard's hands went to her waist, holding her as he began thrusting himself up inside her. She leaned back. She knew what he needed far better than he knew himself.

This time, his release wasn't immediate. The heat between them grew more intense. Richard was driven to push himself further. He could hear his labored breathing. He opened his eyes, saw her above him, riding him. Her eyes were closed now and he didn't think there was a more beautiful sight than she, naked and moving to his rhythm.

He said her name. *Grace.* What a beautiful name! He repeated it, over and over until words were lost to him. The release began building in him. Hot, furious, demanding.

And now, poor wretched man that he was, he

had no choice but to hold her fast and complete what his Maker had designed him to do.

Her muscles tightened, holding him—and he was lost. Blissfully, completely, utterly lost.

He held her waist as he emptied himself into her. The force of life flowed between them—and Richard felt alive.

She'd done it. She'd saved him. He collapsed to earth.

Grace's body fell onto him. He brought his arms around her, cradling her close. Her head rested on his shoulder.

He didn't speak. He couldn't. Part of him was too humbled for speech; another part overwhelmed.

She'd changed him. Made him a man. God help them both.

Richard drew her with him as he rolled on his side toward the fire. He shut his eyes and within minutes his battered body fell into an exhausted sleep.

Grace lay very still, her heart pounding against her chest.

Dear God, what had she done?

She had no doubt she'd saved his life. His shaking had stopped and the color had returned to his skin.

But at what cost?

And she realized she was afraid of what he would think on the morrow. Men were funny creatures. She'd started to like Mr. Lynsted. *Richard.* Even his given name felt good to her.

She'd wanted to believe he admired her, too.

They'd started off enemies, but he'd earned her respect. Now, she didn't know what would happen.

He cradled her body with his own. His right hand rested between her breasts.

Mr. Lynsted was a well-formed man. Grace could count on one hand the men she'd been with . . . but she'd reached a point where there was no mystery, no power to the act of joining. It had become perfunctory, a matter of survival. She didn't desire men, they desired her.

However, tonight, the tables had been turned. She'd felt the quickening in her loins, experienced the sharp, fine edge of desire and been lost to the sensual satisfaction of release.

He'd taken her there, this giant, courageous man . . . whom she sensed had been celibate before this night. A moral man who'd unwittingly revealed the purpose to God's design to a jaded woman as herself, and she felt shame.

Certainly he would think the worst of her.

That's the way men were. Once they lost respect

for a woman, they became demanding, uncaring, or a host of tiny insults that cut at the heart.

And what did all this say about her? Was there something between her and Richard . . . something her actions this evening may have just destroyed?

Or had she, at last, gone completely wanton?

He stirred. Without waking, he grew hard again. His arousal pressed against her back.

Grace lay still, uncertain. He shifted. She felt him searching. She turned to him. He entered her swiftly, filled her, began moving inside her, and God help her, she was lost to the current of sweet, pure sensation.

Tomorrow she'd worry. Tomorrow, she'd protect herself from hurt . . . and from being destroyed the way only a man who'd slipped past her defenses could.

Chapter Eleven

$\mathcal{R}$ichard woke to the smell of cooking meat. He opened his eyes to see Grace holding a spit of meat over the fire. She was completely dressed, even wearing her wool cape, her hair curly, loose, and wild around her shoulders, the way he liked it best.

Vivid memories came rushing back to him. They weren't dreams. He was naked beneath his greatcoat. His body felt well used, content, *alive*. She'd saved his life. Her method had been unusual but very effective.

Grace noticed he was awake. Her gaze didn't quite meet his as she said, "Good morning."

"Good morning," he answered, his voice rough with sleep.

"I assume you are hungry?" she said. She looked clean and fresh, while parts of him smelled of sex.

"Starving."

"Then, you'd best dress. Breakfast will be ready any moment. I folded your clothes and put them beside you."

A vision of her sitting astride him rose in his mind. "Thank you," he said, sitting up and pulling his greatcoat around him. He was no longer self-conscious about his nakedness. In fact, he wished *she* was still naked. His body immediately eagerly approved the idea.

On second thought, he *was* self-conscious. He wasn't about to parade himself around aroused, especially since she had yet to make eye contact.

He rose to his feet, turning his back to slip his hands through the arms of his great coat. He gathered his folded clothes and picked up his boots. "I'll be back."

Grace didn't respond.

Richard made his way down to the river. With each step, he reminded himself he was a dunderhead.

He'd had sex. *He, Richard Lynsted.* And not just any sex. He'd had sex with the most beautiful woman of his acquaintance, and instead of being at ease, intelligent, *sophisticated* about it, he spoke in simple sentences. He didn't even know what a man should say to a woman after she'd turned his life inside out.

Thank you?

Please, may I have more? More, more, *more*.

A splash of cold water in the face brought him to his senses.

Richard scrubbed himself clean while frantically working up the courage to climb back up the bank and face her. He imagined it would be easier with clothes on but once he'd dressed, he still felt awkward and shy. His confusion was compounded by the understanding that Grace let him have a "poke," as his uncle would say, not out of attraction but out of mercy.

He'd had a mercy poke.

God, the thought was humbling . . . and yet, they'd had sex several times. He hadn't been able to keep his hands off her.

Heat rose to his face. No wonder she wasn't communicative with him. He'd been a randy fool.

Richard hated pulling his boots on without socks. Would hate more walking in them. It was a fit punishment for what he'd done.

He decided the best action would be to take his signal from Grace. If she wanted to discuss what happened between them, he would—although he hadn't a clue what to say. After all, he'd been alone all his life. He didn't express himself freely to others. It wasn't his nature.

His biggest fear was that *he* should say something first.

Grace was putting out the fire when he returned, kicking wet dirt and leaves over the smoldering flame. "Your breakfast is on that stick." She nodded to a stick staked into the ground.

"Thank you." He picked up the stick. "You look well this morning."

"I am."

His appetite left. There was an undercurrent in her curt "I am."

And he didn't know where to go next with it.

"Are you ready to go?" she asked. She had yet to look at him. "I don't know how far we'll have to walk to reach a cottage or perhaps even a village."

She was so capable. She made him feel like a damn eunuch.

"Grace, about last night—"

"Last night was nothing, Mr. Lynsted. We do what we must to survive. Are you going to eat your rabbit or shall we start walking?"

She didn't wait for a response but started up the hill toward the road.

Richard watched her a moment, annoyed by

her brisk authority. His memory might be a bit hazy because he was almost frozen to the core last night, but he recalled her being a willing participant. Had she not kissed his shoulder? His neck?

She'd disappeared from view, not once looking back. She behaved as she had when first they'd met. High-handed, distant, cold.

Richard tossed the rabbit aside and started up the hill after her.

He caught up with her on the road. His earlier discomfort and shyness had evaporated. He was boiling angry and surprisingly hurt. "Out with it," he ordered as he fell into step beside her.

"Out with what?" she asked, her eyes on the road ahead of them.

Richard used his longer stride to block her path. "I want to talk to you about last night."

She smiled, the expression cynical. "That's unnecessary. There's nothing to say."

"There damn well is."

"Oh, yes," she said, sounding bored. "Congratulations, you've won the wager on bedding me."

Grace would have walked around him, but he wasn't letting her go on that note. He took hold of her. "Why are you being this way?"

She frowned at his hand on her person. Last night he'd had his hands on her hips, her waists, her breasts . . .

He'd not remove his hand now.

Her lips compressed in resentment. She stared at some point on his wool greatcoat. If she thought he'd back down at her silence, she was wrong.

The doubts he'd nursed evaporated. "I don't like you this way. You act hurt."

Her eyes widened in surprise. For the first time that morning, she looked at him. "I'm not."

"I'd rather you let me freeze to death, than shut me out. That's what you are doing, isn't it?"

"Don't we have other concerns to worry over— such as Dawson hunting us down or having to walk our way to Inverness? This isn't important."

She didn't think *she* was important.

Richard had never thought himself astute, but he heard what she didn't say. He *felt* it. It would be far more simple to let her go, to keep the distance between them.

But that wasn't what he wanted.

Words he never thought he'd express came to his lips. "I know what it means to always protect yourself. To think no one cares. Or that you don't matter. But you do matter, Grace. Perhaps, a week ago I would have been a 'prig.'" He deliberately used the word she'd hurled at him. "I might have judged you, judged myself. I don't. Do you understand?"

She considered him, her blue eyes solemn—

and he knew he hadn't said the right thing. It wasn't enough. He knew that as clearly as if she'd spoken.

"I understand," she answered. "I—" She stopped, as if thinking better of what she might have said, drew a deep breath, and then released it, her gaze drifting toward the rushing river beyond the trees lining the road.

"Grace?"

She smiled, the expression forced. "I'm not angry."

"Then what is it?"

Another deep breath. A shrug. Then a confession, but not on the subject he wanted. "I worry about my father. And us. I don't want matters to change between us. No awkwardness. I did what I must."

"Yes," he agreed. She was evading his concerns. She didn't want to talk about the night before, and who was he to force her?

He released his hold. She nodded, her gaze slipping away from his and the wall once again rising between them.

She started walking and he followed. He could have told her that what had happened last night had meant something to him . . . but that would have called for trust, and he wasn't ready for that. Apparently no more than she was.

Besides, the only woman he'd been with was her. For all he knew, everyone felt this used after a night like the one they'd had.

She didn't owe him anything, so there it was.

"Do you believe Dawson will come looking for us?" she asked.

Richard appreciated a new direction for his thoughts. "I believe he'll go to my uncle. My one hope is my father will learn of this and ask questions."

Her silence reminded him that she thought his father was guilty.

"My father is not involved," he said.

"You don't want him to be."

"I don't . . . any more than you want to believe your father capable of a crime." Tired of defending his father, he took the conversation toward a new tack. "Tell me, what will you do once you clear your father's name?"

The smile that came to her lips was genuine. The tightness left her shoulders. "I don't know. I used to dream of going to my cousin's house and announcing to everyone they'd been wrong about Father. My uncle is an earl. Lord Cairn."

Richard had not heard of him.

"When I was girl, they would invite my mother and me to their manor but you could hear them whispering about us. We were the charity cases.

My uncle's money kept food on our table and a roof over our heads." She walked a few paces more and then added, "Mother was very envious."

"And you were not? I would be," Richard stated.

"I was too grateful to be envious," Grace said. "My cousin Jenny and her brothers had the best books. There were pictures in every one of them. Their governess would read to me. She said the others wouldn't listen to her but I always listened. My uncle always made certain I was included in whatever ball or rout or festivity they held."

"That was generous of him."

"It was. And he'd see that I had Jenny's cast-offs. Mother hated that I wore them, but I wasn't so proud." Her smiled faded. "When I've proven my father's innocence, I'm going to see my uncle. I'm going to thank him for what he did for me. I know he doesn't believe I appreciated it. I fear he's become sorely disappointed in me."

"If your father was falsely accused, and my uncle's actions make it appear that is true, then your family will understand."

"Do you think?" The cynicism returned to her face, this time in her eyes. "Will all the loose ends be tied up neatly? You are the last person I would have thought a romantic."

Her criticism stung. "If tying up the loose ends isn't what you want, then why go through this?"

"Because I want to go home." Her voice ached with longing. She glanced at him, suddenly shy. "Do I surprise you? I don't belong in London. I miss my Highlands and Inverness where I know every street and the name of every family who live there. It's taken me time, but I now know I should not have left. It's the only place I've felt safe."

"But you could always have gone home."

"I wasn't strong enough," she said cryptically. "I am now." Her words were more than a statement. They were a resolution. "You are starting to hobble," she observed, changing the direction of the conversation.

Even though he was curious to learn more about her past, Richard knew she was done. "By the end of today, I may be willing to kill for a pair of wool socks."

She laughed, the earlier tension between them slowly evaporating. "I imagine you might. We'll see what we can find."

"Find?" he repeated.

"One never knows what will crop up on the road. I've lived this life before. We'll barter or do whatever to find you socks."

"Do you think we might also find a razor?" he wondered, running a hand over his jaw. "Or am I pressing my luck?"

"We can try. You are already starting to look very roguish."

"Roguish?" he questioned, secretly hoping for a compliment, anything that would indicate she was as attracted to him as he was her.

"Yes," she said. "Another day's growth and we can pass you off as a highwayman."

The comparison pleased Richard. "From prig to highwayman. I sense I'm making progress."

"Aye, you are. But we'll have to find a dark steed for you. One that will make all the women swoon at the sight of you riding down the road upon it— what is it? What do you see?"

"I think there is a bridge up ahead. There, to the right. Can you see it?" He didn't wait for her answer but took her hand. "Come along."

She had to skip to keep up with him.

He'd been right. There was a bridge across the river and on the other side a good-sized village that included a mill on one side of the road and a small Norman church on the other.

"Come," he ordered, not letting go of the hand he had taken.

Three dogs barked an angry warning as they crossed the bridge. They were hounds of dubious parentage and they stood on the other side of the river, warning at a distance.

As Richard approached them, he held out his hand. The barking stopped but they didn't take a sniff. Instead, they kept their distance, escorting Richard and Grace as they entered the village.

There wasn't any activity on the street. Save for the turning mill wheel, all seemed very quiet.

"What do you think?" Grace wondered.

"I'm not certain yet," Richard answered.

"Perhaps we don't want to linger here."

"Perhaps . . . but first, let's find someone and ask where we are," he said.

There was no one in the mill house.

Richard started up the street toward the church, Grace trailing a step behind him. The cottages were freshly whitewashed with clean thatched roofs. One house had a lamb bleating in the walled front garden. Some chickens ran across the road in front of them. The dogs did not give chase.

At last, they saw inhabitants. A group of eight men and women huddled by the back of an oxen cart parked close to the church door. They looked up at the sound of Richard and Grace's approach.

Three more men stepped out of cottage doorways. They were dressed in homespun and had the air of good, solid yeomen.

Grace stopped. "Something is not right here," she whispered, pulling her hand from his. "The expressions on those people's faces are too solemn."

"The Scots are never over friendly," he said, sensing nothing of her concern now that they had finally seen inhabitants.

She reached for his arm. "Please, I don't feel good about this. There is something in the air here. Let's leave now."

Richard looked to the people standing by the cart. The dogs had trotted over to them. All seemed normal, albeit a bit quiet. Perhaps that was because of the March wind and the heavy clouds hanging in the sky.

"We can't walk to Inverness," he said. "We need help and this is the best we have for right now. Don't worry. I'll take care of you."

Grace shook her head, glancing around her. "We are strangers here and you are English. Sometimes it is best to keep moving."

"Why should you be worried I'm English?"

"Scotland is a long way from London, Mr. Lynsted. And there are many places where we Scots nurse grudges against the English. Let's move on."

"We will, once I discover where we are. Stand behind me if you have doubts."

She stepped into his shadow immediately.

The villagers were watching them now. Richard felt he had to speak. They would have looked like suspicious characters if he didn't. Besides, they were standing in front of a church.

"Hello," he said in greeting as he walked closer.

No one answered back, and that's when he noticed a man's legs hanging out of the back of the cart. He recognized his father and uncle's livery.

Richard moved toward those legs, almost certain of what he'd find. He hadn't gone more than a few steps when his hunch was proven correct in the form of Herbert's bloated, drowned body.

Sadness weighed down upon him. He'd known the valet the majority of his life. He wondered what inducement his uncle had dangled in front of the once loyal servant to make him willingly attempt to murder Grace—and what he could do to make his uncle pay for the crime.

"I know that man," he said to the group. He would claim Herbert's body and see that he was sent back to London and his family for a decent burial.

"You do now, do you?" a gray-haired, grim-faced man demanded with the air of a leader. A clergyman came out of the church. He was dressed in black from head to toe and had a long beard.

"I do," Richard answered.

"And I'm thinking we know you, too," the grim-faced man said. "We have a description of you."

"Of me?" Richard shook his head. "Why would you have a description of me?"

"Because a fellow you tried to kill, Dawson, the one that escaped, gave it to us," the yeoman said. "Told us you had already murdered one man by throwing him in the river. This here is his body, isn't it? We fished it out for you. And sure enough, you know him. Besides, there isn't many lads who have the size and looks of you. Or who appear as if they've been roughed up a bit."

"Dawson lied," Richard answered, conscious that the three yeomen blocked his escape in the opposite direction and the men around the oxen cart had fanned out. "I didn't kill Herbert. He fell into the river on his own."

"We'll let the magistrate decide that," the grim-faced man answered. "Take him, lads."

Before Richard could move, he was jumped on all sides.

Chapter Twelve

$\mathcal{R}$ichard's first concern was to protect Grace.

With a roar of fury, he shoved his attackers away. They came back with fists. He doubled his own and gave better than he received. First one man went down and then another.

The moment he could, he turned to Grace— except she was gone. Vanished.

He had assumed she was following him, that she stood behind him. She wasn't there, but a host of villagers had appeared from those silent, closed cottages and were coming to join the fight.

Richard knew his best option was to run. No one here was listening to reason. Grace had warned him. She had been right. Again.

However, before he could take flight, he was hit against the side of his head with something heavy and hard. There was a burst of light, and then his world went black.

Richard's eyes didn't want to open. When he finally did raise his lids, the world was still black, the air dry. He could not see even his hand in front of his face. He drifted off to sleep.

When he woke the second time, the morning sun blazed right in his face. He raised a hand to block the light, surprised to realize he was lying on the floor. A dirt floor.

Memories of seeing Herbert's body in the cart and being jumped by the villagers came back to him—and he knew wherever he was, it was not where he wanted to be.

Rolling over, he took stock of his surroundings. He was on the floor of an eight-by-eight-foot room with thick stone walls. The smell of onions, potatoes, and cured meats lingered in the air. The hooks in the ceiling rafter beneath a thatched roof confirmed his suspicion he was in a larder. The door was of heavy wood planks with a small arched window at eye level.

Of course, there was nothing in here now. Not even a stick.

His stomach grumbled with hunger. It had

obviously been hours since he'd tossed aside the rabbit Grace had caught and cooked.

Now he was happy she'd left him. His hope was that she'd managed to escape. In fact, she'd been wise to leave him. So far, he'd botched everything.

Carefully, Richard came to his feet. He still wore his boots. That was a good sign, but the bars over the small window in the door quickly sobered any optimism.

He walked over to them and peered out. The church wasn't far from his cell. He could see the mill wheel turning and villagers going about their morning business—

"So you are up, eh?" A man's grizzled face blocked his view. "Didn't think with that hard head of yours you'd be asleep so long. Must have hit you harder than I'd thought. Slept the night through."

Richard didn't answer. He worried about Grace, silently praying she was safe.

"Nothing to say, eh? Well, you'll be talking once you meet Douglas. He's gone for the magistrate. We decided not to wait for that man from London. We'll hang you on the morrow," he concluded gleefully.

"Hungry," Richard said, the word little more than a croak. He was going to need to eat if he wanted the strength to face his accusers. Actually, he wasn't that distressed they were fetching the magistrate. He had no doubt he could convince the man of his innocence.

After all, Richard was a lawyer.

The magistrate was a heavyset man with thick jowls and a tuft of yellow hair on top of his head and above each ear.

Court had been set up in the church's vestibule. The villagers had all crammed into the small space so they could see and hear everything. Richard surmised he had inadvertently supplied them with more excitement than they usually experienced in any decade of their quiet lives.

The smell of fried fish was in the air. Apparently, dinner was part of the magistrate's expected payment, because his court table was set with a plate and silver. Someone had already given him a stack of thickly sliced bread.

He buttered a slice as he gave Richard a look up and down. "You are from London, aren't you?" His lips curved into distaste right before he stuffed the whole slice of bread in his mouth. He had short, fat fingers that he moved with an effeminate air.

Richard bowed as best he could with his hands tied with three different knots behind his back. The villagers had wanted to ensure he wouldn't escape and hence their elaborate knot arrangement.

What he did wish is that he was clean shaven and didn't look as if he'd slept in his clothes. Then there wouldn't be any foolish accusations. The magistrate would see him as an equal.

As it was, he had to use his voice, manner, and credentials. "I am the Honorable Richard Lynsted. My father is Lord Brandt, my uncle Lord Maven, and my cousin is the Duke of Holburn. My family owns estates throughout England."

"I am Sir John Garson and we don't like the English much here," the magistrate informed him. "Especially English dukes. You know what the Duke of Cumberland did at Culloden. Whether you supported the uprising or not, his butchery tears at the heart of every good Scotsman. We are lowlanders here but the more we think upon it, the more we dislike the English."

A chorus of somber "ayes" met his pronouncement.

Anger flashed through Richard. He tamped it down. He prided himself on self-control and temperance.

"What are the charges against me?" he inquired, careful to keep his voice neutral.

Sir John stuffed more bread into his mouth before answering, "You are charged with the death of that man they fished out of the River Tweed."

Richard waited for him to ask how he pleaded.

The magistrate didn't say anything.

"I plead not guilty," Richard finally said, because he must have it on the record.

"We assumed that, sir," Sir John answered, his interest going past Richard to the doorway behind him.

Richard turned to see what he was looking at. A smiling village woman stood in the doorway holding a tray of fried fish.

"One moment, my dear," Sir John told her with a smile. "I must finish this trial."

"Yes," Richard agreed. "I wouldn't want your food to grow cold."

"*Silence,*" Sir John barked. "Your English humor is not appreciated here."

"I wasn't being humorous," Richard answered, his temper strained. He tried to keep control of himself and this trial. "I wish to tell my story."

"I suppose you will tell us you had nothing to do with that man's death?" the magistrate replied, folding his hands over his ample girth. "Come here, lass, and place that plate right here. Don't want you standing there feeling unappreciated."

The village woman did as he said, giggling as he lifted the covers and drew a deep whiff of her cooking. She sidled over to join the other witnesses to this "trial."

"Now," Sir John said, finally giving Richard his attention, "what say you?"

"I did not kill Herbert," Richard said. He'd given some thought to his defense, and after meeting the magistrate decided the clearer and shorter the story, the better. He would also leave Grace out of it. "He was traveling with me. He's been in a retainer in my family's employ for years. My coach and I were traveling to Inverness when we stopped for a short spell to stretch our legs. Herbert fell into the river. I tried to save him but was unsuccessful."

"Eh, now? And what happened to your coach and driver?"

"Dawson drove off," Richard said, choosing his words carefully. "Perhaps he jumped to a conclusion that was not correct."

Sir John leaned over a paper covered with hasty scribbles in front of him. "Dawson." He pointed to one of the scribbles and smiled up at Richard. "It says here your coachman accuses you of attempting to kill him, too. The man said he barely escaped with his life."

"He's lying," Richard answered.

"Yes, well, I don't believe you are being completely honest, Honorable Mr. Richard Lynsted.

And our dead man, this Herbert, appeared bashed and beaten." Sir John glanced over to the gray-haired yeoman Richard had spoken to the day before. "Douglas, is that not what you told me?"

"It is," Douglas answered.

"Nor do you look to have been enjoying a stroll in the country," the magistrate said to Richard. "In fact, you appear as if you were in a right proper row."

Richard said, "I received most of these bruises yesterday when this man"—he nodded to Douglas—"and a good number of others assaulted me for a crime I didn't commit. They hit me on the head and threw me into that larder over there on the church grounds."

"Ah, yes, the larder," Sir John repeated, nodding. "We've used it a time or two as a gaol, right, Douglas?"

"That's right, Sir John. But if I may say, Mr. Lynsted looked that rough yesterday when he came into Rachlan Mill. And the man who was driving the coach appeared as if his nose had been broken. He said he'd barely escaped with his life. Said his master had gone mad."

"Did he appear mad to you when you first met him?" Sir John asked.

"He appeared cautious," Douglas answered, "as if he had something to hide."

"And he knew the dead man?" Sir John asked.

"Recognized him immediately."

Now Richard understood why Dawson hadn't returned to finish the task he'd been charged with—murdering Grace. He'd set them up and left the job for these villagers.

Nor would his uncle be too sad to have Richard gone, too.

"You do realize," Richard said, "that none of the testimony presented in this court is valid. It's all hearsay."

"They take hearsay seriously in Rachlan Mill," Sir John corrected him. "A man's word is his bond."

"Well, my word, which is *my* bond, is that I didn't kill anyone. Herbert's death was an accident," Richard informed him. "And I have the right to confront my accuser, Dawson."

"We can't do that. He's not here," Sir John said, leaning over the plate of fish and giving it a whiff. He was obviously more worried about his food growing cold than Richard's trial. "Besides, you are being tried by a jury of your peers and they heard what this Dawson had to say—"

"What peers?" Richard blurted out, surprised at the statement.

"These villagers," Sir John answered. "They have been listening to the testimony."

"But they have been testifying against me," Richard protested. He'd be damned before he'd allow himself to be found guilty by this mockery of justice, especially when he could see by the villagers' expressions they thought him guilty. "I demand to be taken to London for my trial," he said. "I demand that Dawson confront me with these ridiculous charges."

"You aren't in England any longer, lad. In Scotland, we take care of our own justice," Sir John informed him. "I've had enough of you, the Honorable Mr. Richard Lynsted. A man's dead here and someone should pay for his death. How say you, jury?"

"Guilty." The word came out of them as one.

"Very well, he'll hang on the morrow." Sir John reached for his dinner plate.

"Hang?" Richard was stunned. "But I haven't done anything. It was self-defense."

Sir John looked up from tying a bib around his neck. "Self-defense?" He dropped the cloth and refolded his hands over his belly. "I thought it was an accident, Mr. Lynsted."

"It was," Richard said, cursing himself for a fool. "He attacked me and I defended myself. But I never meant for him to fall—and that is what he did, *he fell* into the river."

"And apparently the truth is something an

'honorable' gentleman like yourself stretches and changes for himself. Which is, in my esteemed opinion, very much like a lawyer."

The villagers murmured agreement.

"And does this new information change your opinions?" Sir John asked addressing them. "How say you, jury?"

This time their "guilty" was louder and more confident than the last.

"Take him away," Sir John ordered with a wave of his hand. "And," he added as an afterthought, "see that he has a good meal this evening. It will be his last."

Brawny young men flanked the trussed-up Richard and marched him back to his cell, unceremoniously shoving and pushing him the whole way across the church grounds.

They threw him inside the larder and locked the door, setting one of their number to stand guard. The one small blessing is that they cut free the ropes binding his hands.

Richard paced the perimeter of his cell. *They were going to hang him.* The idea was ridiculous, their charges unfounded, the verdict unprecedented— at least in his social circle.

If he was in London, he'd see that an inquiry was sent here to investigate this travesty of justice—

But he wasn't in London.

He'd never go there again.

They intended to hang him and would. This was their corner of the world. By the time anyone learned of his predicament and came to his aid, he'd be dead.

Such dark realizations would sober any man and they certainly did the trick for Richard.

Grace had warned him. And instead of listening to her, he'd been an arrogant fool.

He wondered where she was now. If she knew. He hoped she wasn't still in the area. He didn't want these bastards to catch her. Who knew what they would do to her? She'd been through enough humiliation and pain in her life.

The sound of hammering came from a distance.

Richard walked to the small barred window in the door and peered outside. His guard gave him an evil grin. "They are building the gallows now. Have to have it the right size for you." Richard turned back to his cell.

For the better part of two hours, he entertained a fantasy he could escape. He didn't test the bars since they were right in front of the guard, although he noticed they were made of wood and not of steel. Instead, he tried his brute strength on every inch of the cell's limestone walls to no avail. Initially, he was systematic and thorough, keeping his purpose quiet. Toward the end, his efforts turned frenzied and frustrating. There was no way out.

"Dinner's here," his guard shouted through the bars. "Stand to the back of the cell."

Richard immediately decided he would rush whoever came through. He'd put down his head and bowl right through the door.

However, when the door opened, a man entered with a blunderbuss pointed right at him.

Richard changed his plans. The gun was old but at these close quarters it could do damage. An older woman with a kerchief around her head placed a wooden tray on the ground. A cloth covered the food.

"I gave you hard cider," the woman said. "It's potent." There was compassion in her eyes. Richard was tempted to plead his case.

"Come along, Beth," the man with the gun said. "We'd best go home. We can retrieve our plates and fork on the morrow."

The woman ducked her head and left. The gunman followed and the guard locked the door.

"Well, so much for that escape attempt," Richard muttered. He knelt down and lifted the covers off the food, suspecting what it was by the smell of it. Sure enough, the plate was piled with the same fish the magistrate had been eating for his lunch.

Richard's stomach rebelled. It had been well over twenty-four hours since he'd tossed aside Grace's roasted rabbit. He needed his strength but he didn't think he could eat this.

And then he could imagine Grace arguing he must eat, he would need the nourishment, and so he forced the meal down.

A part of him refused to believe he would hang. There had to be an escape. Or perhaps that fool Sir John would come to his senses or have an attack of conscience.

And yet as the hours dragged on, he began to fear this might be the last night of his life. Not even the potent hard cider eased his tension.

Darkness fell. His guards changed. The new guard was a strapping lad with a shock of carrot red hair and a face full of freckles. He had to be all of nineteen and very proud to be serving his term as guard.

Richard sat on the floor of his cell. The only light came from the rush torch outside the door. It spread across the floor in rectangular lines though the barred window.

Even the moon and stars had disappeared, blanketed by clouds.

Going to the window, Richard asked the red-head for paper and pen.

"What for?" the lad asked.

"Last testament." What he really wanted to do was document what had happened. His father needed to know his twin's treachery.

"You don't have anything," the lad answered with a smirk.

Richard refused to give up. For a space of time, he used the spoon to carve his story in the serving tray. However, the letters appeared as nothing more than scratches.

Now Richard understood why condemned men made their marks in the stones of their prisons. It was their last attempt to let someone know they were there.

He turned his mind to what he would say on the morrow. He needed words that would convince them to spare him. He was not going to die. *He wouldn't.* Not on what had started off as a great adventure, as his way of proving to his father he was more than a clerk, and to prove to himself he was a man.

Perhaps everyone had been right about him. Perhaps he was nothing more than a great ox of a man who had intelligence but no wit, no daring, no bloody common sense.

Grace had tried to warn him. And he'd wanted

to prove her wrong because he wanted to be the protector. After all, what danger could lurk in such a small Scottish village?

He laughed bitterly. God, he was a fool.

And he prayed she was safe. He hoped she'd run as far from here as possible. There was the possibility she'd gone for help. He hoped not. He did not want her involved in this whole sordid business.

He also wished he'd taken a moment to tell her what he really thought about her. He'd tell her she was beautiful—but then she'd heard that from a hundred other men.

So Richard amended his thoughts. He decided, if he could speak to Grace one last time, he'd tell her how resourceful she was, and wise. And that he admired her intelligence and even her bluntness that could set his teeth on edge.

He'd tell her . . . he'd tell her he was in *love* with her.

The thought filled his mind.

Common sense told him he was being foolish. What was love? He wouldn't know.

And yet, the very air around him vibrated with the truth of that one thought. He'd fallen in love with Grace MacEachin—a woman who could have a prince or a duke.

She didn't need an oaf like himself.

And then there was the small problem of his uncle trying to kill her . . .

None of it mattered, he loved her all the same. Loved, loved, *loved*.

Love was different than he'd expected. It humbled him, filled him with conviction, made him want to jump up and down with joy, made him vulnerable and scared and secretive.

It seeped through his every vein, entering every muscle of his body, erasing pride, expectations.

He loved Grace MacEachin. He'd watched intelligent, powerful men throw over careers, friends, family, and honor in the name of love. At last he understood why. He didn't care if Grace was an actress or a whore or tart or duchess or Turkish princess.

He loved her.

And maybe that is what he would say on the gallows in the morning. Maybe instead of pleading his case, he'd profess his love, and then he'd die, but everyone who had heard him speak would be deeply touched and tell others, who would tell others, until all the world knew he loved Grace MacEachin.

Someday, somewhere, Grace would hear of his declaration and realize here was a man whose heart was true, a man who professed love with his last breath—

Richard picked up the cider jug and gave it a shake, realizing it was empty, and perhaps far more potent than he'd given it credit for.

Instead of mooning over Grace, he should be planning the words he'd use to dissuade the hangman—

"James Cannon?" *Grace.* He recognized her voice immediately.

Richard jumped to his feet and went to the window. All was dark beyond the torchlight.

His guard answered with a gruff, "Aye, I'm Cannon. Who goes there?"

"You don't know me," Grace said, stepping into the torchlight. "I'm Josie McGlynn from Dundee who is visiting her uncle Douglas." She wore her hair loose and curling around her shoulders. Instead of the blue traveling dress she had been wearing, she now wore a simple dark skirt and a white blouse with a neckline so low it exposed the round curve of her breasts. Her *petticoat.* She'd removed the bodice from her dress and was prancing around in the night in her petticoat. Her breasts rose like two high mounds above her neckline. Her nipples pressed against the thin cotton, beacons, as if there ever were ones, for any man.

"Douglas the miller?" James asked.

"Aye," Grace answered.

"I've not known he had kin visiting," James said, suspicious, as any guard should be.

"I arrived today," Grace said. "The village has been a bit busy."

"Aye, just a bit," James replied. "Come closer."

Grace stepped forward. She gave James a shy smile.

"What are you doing here?" he asked. "It's the middle of the night."

"I couldn't sleep," she said.

"And why not?"

A sly smile came to her lips. "I saw you today. I wanted to meet you."

What was she doing? Richard wanted to warn her back but feared tipping off James that they knew each other. He glared at Grace through the bars, ordering her away with his eyes.

She ignored him.

"Meet me?" James said.

"Aye. I like the look of you," Grace assured him. "I knew you would have the most important watch. My uncle says you are the only one he trusts."

James liked the sound of that. He straightened his shoulders, adding two inches to his height.

"May have a look at the prisoner?" Grace asked.

"Why would you want to do that?" James demanded.

Richard wanted to bang his head against the bars. What was she thinking? To use her dirk and slash both of their ways to freedom? Love and all charitable thoughts vanished from his mind in the face of Grace's foolishness.

"I've never seen a man who is about to die," Grace answered. "I'd like just a peek." She took a step toward the door, but James blocked her way and Richard's view.

"A peek?" James said. "I could give you a peek, but you can't have something for nothing, Josie lass. It's not the way of the world. Especially for lasses who like to wander around at night."

"What do you want?" Grace asked, a saucy note in her voice.

"There's a lot I want," James said, his meaning clear.

"I might be willing to trade you," Grace answered. "It would be good bargain with a handsome lad like you. They told me you are the one everyone wants in the village. I think I might like to have you, too."

"Oh, you could have me, lass," James assured her.

"A peek," Grace whispered.

"First something for me," James insisted.

"*Don't*," Richard barked harshly, curling his fingers around the bars and pulling them with all his strength as if he could break them free. He ached to use her name. To give a full command to his voice and tell her to run, but feared giving away her involvement with himself.

His outburst pleased James. "Here now," he said, taking the torchlight from its holder and waving at the window so that the flame burned Richard's fingers until he released the bars. Richard stepped back into the darkness.

"You stay back and keep your eyes to yourself," James ordered. He looked to Grace. "He's a tough one. As dangerous as they come. I have to watch him all the time. He didn't give the man he killed a chance."

"I can't believe you are so brave," she said. "I'd be frightened myself."

"Yes, well, perhaps it is best we don't dally this night. However, tomorrow after the hanging, I'd like to come calling."

Grace giggled in an uncharacteristic manner. "But I won't be able to have a peek at him if we wait. What say, I'll give you a peek of me and what you'll be seeing on the morrow if you let me have a peek at the murderer?"

The suggestion was arousing. Richard sensed James's interest.

He returned to the door, grabbed the wooden

bars. She couldn't do this. She must not prostitute herself for him.

James had no such noble ideals. "I'd like a peek," he answered, his voice husky with lust. "Better yet, give me a squeeze and I'll help you up a bit so you can see into his cell better."

Grace hedged.

"*No*," Richard ordered.

James laughed. "No? You should be saying yes. This is what you need for your last night on earth." He faced Grace, standing with his back to the cell door. "So how about it. Show what you have both to me and our condemned man. Let him die with a good memory on his mind."

"All right," Richard heard Grace say. "One peek, but you must keep your word."

"Oh, I will, I will," James promised.

She slid the thin strap of her bodice down over one shoulder, coyly cupping a hand over her breast so James wouldn't see as much as he wished.

There was a beat of respectful silence before James demanded in a thick voice, "More. Show me more."

"I want my peek at your prisoner first," Grace bartered.

"You'll have naught until I've a feel," James answered. "I've never seen such breasts before, lass, especially on someone so comely. Mayhap I have a mind for a taste."

"You promised I could look at him," she told him.

He gave a nasty laugh. "You want to see my prisoner very badly, don't you, lass? I don't believe you are with Douglas. He's not the sort of man to let his kinswomen walk around at night. I'd wager this gun that you have more interest in my prisoner than just wanting a peek. But you are in luck, Miss Josie lass, I've a mind to have more of what you are offering. Come here. Let me do what I want and then you can give a smooch farewell to your bonnie man."

Richard lost all sanity. *This man was not going to place his hands on Grace.*

With a growl in the back of his throat, he shook the bars with such force, one broke loose.

He reached through the window and before James was aware of anything, grabbed the lad by his red hair and jerked him up against the door. Richard had him now and could squeeze both of his arms through the opening to wrap his hands around James's neck.

Richard began crushing the life out of the guard.

$\mathcal{G}$race had known she was playing a dangerous game. Her original plan had been to either lift the keys from the guard or pass the knife to Mr. Lynsted. Then, if a chance presented itself, he'd have a weapon to free himself.

It was a wild scheme, but the only one she could think of in the short time since his trial.

And now all had gone terribly wrong.

"Mr. Lynsted, *please*, you are going to kill him."

He didn't release his hold on the guard.

She reached up, placing her hands on his wrists, trying to pull them away. "Mr. Lynsted. *Richard. Don't kill him.*"

Her words seemed to sink in. He released his

hands as if coming out of a trance. The guard's body fell to the ground.

With a soft cry, Grace knelt to feel for a pulse.

To her everlasting relief there was one. "He's not dead," she murmured. She rose to stand on her tiptoes and look through the window. "Did you hear me? He's not dead."

There was no answer. Richard had retreated to the cell's dark corners.

Grace returned her attention to the guard, looking through his pockets until she found the key to the huge padlock on the door. Her fingers trembled as she placed the key in the lock. The well-oiled lock sprung open with a click.

She had to move the guard's body in order to open the door. "Mr. Lynsted," she whispered. "*Come*."

When he still didn't respond, she went in after him. He stood quietly in the cell's shadows. She could make out his form. Reaching out, she grabbed the arm of his greatcoat. "We don't have time to waste. The guard could come to his senses at any moment."

His response was to rush past her. He dragged the guard into the cell. "Wait outside," he ordered.

Grace obeyed. A moment later, Mr. Lynsted came out, stuffing the guard's socks in the pocket of his greatcoat. "I need these," he said. He locked the door and picked the gun up off the ground.

"This way," Grace said. "I have a horse waiting through the woods."

"How did you come by a horse?"

"I stole it," she answered, already moving in the direction she wanted him to follow.

"*You what?* They hang people for horse thievery."

"They were already hanging you, so what does it matter?" Grace answered. "We'll ride it as far as we can and release it. Horses know how to find their way home."

But he didn't follow. He stood by the larder that had served as his cell. "Fine," she said. "Stay here. *I'm* leaving."

He started following her. When they reached the surrounding woods, he tossed the blunderbuss into the night. "You don't think we'll need that?" Grace asked.

"It's so old, we'd end up shooting ourselves with it," he answered.

The horse was waiting where Grace had tied it. "It's Sir John's," she explained.

Mr. Lynsted didn't respond. In fact, even though it was dark, she knew he hadn't even looked at her . . . and she knew why. But now was not the time to discuss the issue.

"My clothes are right here," she said, retrieving

the bodice she'd torn off her dress and wrapped in her cape. She shrugged on her bodice and laced up the back. Her petticoats showed between her bodice and her skirts but there was naught she could do about it without thread and needle. She threw the cape over her shoulders. "I don't have tack for the horse," she apologized.

His response was to mount up with little difficulty. He lifted her up to sit in front of him.

Grace's throat closed in fear. She'd been thrown from a horse as a child and was very leery of being on them, especially ones she didn't know. "I'm not good at this," she warned.

"I am. Hold the mane." He put heels to horse and off they went.

His body cradled hers and Grace could do nothing but trust him—and hold on to the horse's mane for dear life as they went galloping into the night. They charged down the road leading out of town for a good way before coming to the moors. Mr. Lynsted seemed to know exactly where he wanted to go. He pushed the horse off the road. They covered one large open field then zigzagged toward another.

After what seemed like several terror-filled hours for Grace, Richard brought the horse to a halt. He slid off and then helped her down. Without hesitation, he turned on the animal and waved his arms, scaring it off. The horse went running into the darkness, back the way they'd come.

Richard took a moment to put on the guard's socks, sighing with relief as he pulled his boots on over them.

She was jealous. Her kid slippers were not doing well. However, when he took her arm and began walking, she offered no complaint, even though she had to skip every third step to keep up with his longer legs.

The moon had finally come out, giving them some much-needed light.

Richard didn't speak. He didn't need to. Disapproval radiated from him—

Grace dug in her heels and pulled back with all her body weight. She knew it was nothing against his larger bulk, so she added the force of her indignation, her anger to the weight.

It worked. He was caught up short in mid-step. He turned with a scowl.

"I can't keep pace with you." Grace yanked her arm from his grasp. "Go on, if you want to walk like that. Take off by yourself."

"I'll do no such thing and you know it."

"Then you'll have to walk *with* me, won't you?" Grace demanded, practically trembling with rage.

His brows grew together. "This isn't about my walking."

"No, it *isn't*," she agreed.

"So what is it about?"

"It's about *you* and how *surly* you are."

"Surly?" He shook his head. "I'm surly?"

"And sanctimonious and judgmental and *mean*."

"Mean?" He shook his head. She noticed he didn't take on her other epithets. "I'm trying to save your life."

"I've been trying to save *your* life," she informed him.

And that is when it all came loose—all the tension, the anger. "I don't want you to save my life," he snapped. "Not if it means you must *whore* yourself."

The word was like a lash in the air between them.

Grace crossed her arms against her, holding her sides beneath her cape. She'd known what had him upset . . . just as her using her body had upset him by the river.

What she didn't understand is how much his charge upset her. He didn't say anything that hadn't been hurled at her before . . . except this time, he struck his mark.

Richard Lynsted had penetrated her air of bravado. He forced her to see herself as she really was.

As she didn't want to be.

"Would you rather have hanged?" she answered, her throat tightening.

He took a step back, his gaze shifting from hers. "You know I wouldn't. But the price . . . *damn it all*, Grace, the price was *too* high."

"It was *nothing*," she countered. "Nothing that I haven't offered before. And what do you care?" she demanded, lashing out at him. "You know I'm nothing. All I have is hair, breasts, and what's between my thighs. That's *all* I matter to anyone. That's all I've *ever* mattered."

"*That is so untrue.* Or is it what you want? You blame others, Grace, when you have the power to choose for yourself—"

"You don't know how it is—"

"Aye, so you tell me. I'm the sanctimonious one, the judgmental, surly one. Tell me, Miss MacEachin, which is the one of us calling names? Which one of us is truly judgmental?"

"I know what you think," she accused, wanting to defend herself because he was right. It was easier to hurl names at him than to once again face what she'd done, the woman she'd become.

She turned to walk off, needing to be away from him. He saw too clearly and it frightened her.

But Richard pulled her back. He took hold of each of her wrists, leaning so he could look her in the eye. "You know what I think, do you? Then you know I believe you are the most incredible woman I've met. You are honest, fearless, intelligent—"

Grace did not want to hear these words. They were not true.

She shook her head, shook her body, willing herself not to listen.

"What is the matter with you?" Richard asked. "Why do you deny what I say?"

"Because you're lying. You know it isn't true. You know what I am. I *am* a whore. I am *nothing*—"

He shut her up with a kiss.

Grace was stunned. She started to struggle, to push him away. This was how they all were. It's all they ever wanted . . . except his kiss was different.

It wasn't beastly or demanding or hard, uncompromising, overbearing.

He pressed his lips to hers as if to stop her from saying all the ugliness she found in herself. He kissed her as if begging her to be aware of what was good, what was right.

There was gentleness in this kiss but steel, too. Richard wasn't going to let her go—not until she let herself listen to him.

The furious shaking that had taken hold of her slowly ebbed. The hard pain in her chest eased and, ever so tentatively, she allowed herself to kiss him back.

She hadn't been aware that he'd taken hold of her wrists or of how tightly he held them until he released his hold.

He broke the kiss. They stood so close her breasts barely touched his chest. He leaned his chin upon the top of her head, his arms resting on her waist, a pose so endearing that it brought a reluctant, sad smile to her face.

"You don't know the real me," she whispered to him.

"I believe I do."

Those tears she'd struggled to keep in her throat came to her eyes. She shut them, trying to force the tears back and for once in her life, couldn't. They escaped with a will of their own. They would no longer be denied and she was powerless to stop them.

The story came out of her then, the words tripping over her tongue in their need to finally be spoken aloud.

She told him of Harry Ellis, Sir Nicholas's son, whom she'd wanted to marry with an unholy passion, of the rape and his cruel words afterward, of the meanness of others once they knew she'd been had and how it was all her fault for being so stupidly naive. She'd confessed all to her mother, who had been planning on Grace's beauty to free them from living like outcasts, especially after her father had returned home. Her mother had left once Grace told her she was ruined. Grace's foolishness had destroyed her mother's love and she hadn't the courage to tell her father, so she'd left. But the world was a dangerous place for a woman alone, especially one so young, and Grace had learned to survive on her looks and her sex.

And she wanted to go home. She now knew what Harry had done wasn't her fault but running away had been. She'd hurt people and she just wanted to make things right—with money, with the truth, with anything she could find.

To his credit, all Richard did was listen. He didn't try to offer advice. He was just there for her to hold on to. A solid rock of a man . . . a man she could trust.

At last her tears were spent. Everything bottled inside her, all the self-loathing, the humiliation was now there for him to see. Her head throbbed from the emotion. She leaned forward, resting her head on his chest, listening to his heartbeat. Her own raced madly as if she'd just run a great distance. Slowly, its beat changed, matching the steadiness of his own.

There it was, no more secrets.

And still he held her. His hold hadn't changed, not once in all her recitations of her wickedness. Nor did it change now.

Finally, she found the courage to break the silence. "Do you see how horrid I am?"

"I believe you are honest, fearless, intelligent," he said, repeating the words that had crumbled the shell she'd built around herself—and for once, she let herself believe it was true.

A change was wrought inside her. The tightness in her chest, the bitter anger in her stomach, the tension—all conditions she had assumed to be part of life—vanished. Evaporated. Disappeared . . . proving they'd been shackles of her own making.

And in their place grew a sense of peace.

"Don't do it again, Grace. Don't barter away a bit of your soul for me or for anyone else."

"There isn't much soul left."

"You're wrong. What's good inside us never dies. You have a magnificent soul."

A magnificent soul. He'd seen the worst in her, and still thought her good.

But he didn't offer her another kiss.

Instead, they faced each other as awkward strangers—and Grace didn't know what to do.

Men came to her . . . slavishly so if they were interested.

Richard wasn't anywhere close to being her slave.

She took a step away from him. Keeping her voice carefully neutral, she asked, "What do we do now?" She was uncertain of whether she spoke of Inverness or of the two of them.

His answer gave her pause. "We go to Inverness."

But this time, he didn't take her hand. He just started walking, albeit at a pace she could enjoy.

And Grace realized she hadn't given up all her secrets. She'd kept one.

She had not told him that his arms made her feel safe . . . and that night on the riverbank, the lust hadn't all been his.

Grace followed obediently. She focused on the shadow of his broad shoulders and back and realized that she'd fallen in love. That's really why she would have done anything to save him. *Anything*.

He'd come into her life and taken it over. Here, she'd thought she'd known her own mind, had become the woman she'd wanted to be, was complete and independent . . . and he'd shown her how empty she'd been.

Richard Lynsted was making her believe in love again.

The notion was frightening. She'd learned through Harry that she let down her guard when she was in love. That's the way he'd reached her. She'd dreamed of babies and a noble man and everything turning out for the best.

Life had taught her those happinesses didn't

exist . . . but then along came Richard, and Grace didn't know if she had the courage to believe again.

She should keep her distance. He'd already told her she wasn't the sort of woman a man married. He'd been brutally honest. He'd never give her a marriage ring.

Besides, what right did she have to covet one? She knew what the stakes were for the choices she had made. At that time, she hadn't cared. She'd relished being defiant. All that had changed. Richard had robbed her of that defiance.

Grace had to protect both her heart and her pride. They were all she had that was completely hers.

She just wished he hadn't already won her heart.

Richard had almost kissed her. He wished he had— and kissed her with the wild, untamed need roiling inside him.

Then she could be angrier with him than she was now, but at least Richard would know why she'd withdrawn.

He sensed the tension in Grace. She was as distant as when they'd first met.

God help with the mercurial moods of this woman. One moment she was as defenseless as a lamb and in the next she turned into some female warrior who wore her pride as her armor.

Of course he understood pride.

Any other man of his acquaintance, including his cousin Holburn, would have taken another kiss back there. But he hadn't.

He was more of a coward than he'd imagined.

And so they walked on.

Around dawn they reached a level stretch of road winding through woods. Richard noticed she was limping. He frowned at the kid leather slippers she wore. They were excellent for the dance floor or to set off a fashionable dress, but they weren't good sturdy shoes for trudging over the Scottish landscape.

What puzzled him was that she'd not said a thing. He'd carried on about socks and Grace was stoically walking her feet into nubs.

"Sit down," he ordered. "Let me see your feet."

"They are fine," she said, the flash of defiance in her blue eyes warning him to keep his distance. Dear God, he'd felt the heat of those eyes for the last three hours. They'd been boring holes in his back.

He sensed there was something she expected him to understand, and he didn't, but he'd had enough. He was bloody tired and hungry. She had to be feeling the same, but her Scottish stubbornness wouldn't let her admit it.

Without another word, he took advantage of his superior size and swung her up in his arms. He deposited her unceremoniously on her bum upon an outcrop of rock. Before she could kick and carry on, he slipped her shoe off and swore softly under his breath.

"The soles are almost worn through. You are practically walking barefoot. And your feet are bleeding." He couldn't believe what he was seeing. She'd rubbed her feet raw. He knew how he felt with a blister, and this was much worse.

She snatched the shoe out of his hand. "I'm not complaining."

"No, complaining would imply common sense. It is far more in your character to keep walking until your feet are nothing but stubs."

"No more talk about my character," she warned, pointing her shoe at him—and yet, he noticed she didn't put it on immediately.

He knelt in front of her. "You have great character. You have wonderful character. I thought we'd settled that. I need a strip of your petticoat."

"Why?"

Richard didn't bother to explain himself but lifted the hem of her skirt and started tearing the thin white cotton.

She leaned over to stop him but the material ripped easily and he had the amount he needed for one foot at least. Without asking for permission, which she would not grant anyway, he picked up her shoeless foot and began wrapping it.

He tried to be careful and not hurt her. Her stocking was torn and bloodied. He couldn't imagine the pain she'd suffered without a whimper, and all while he'd complained about his blisters.

And the whole time he was bandaging her, she looked daggers at him.

Finished with the one foot, he said, "I need another yard of petticoat."

"Are you asking this time?"

Prickly Grace. He smiled in spite of his tiredness. "I can take again, but this time it will be higher up. I thought it only polite to say something before I rooted under your skirts."

He'd thrown the words out without considering their import. The heat of a blush rose becomingly to her cheeks and made him realize what he'd said. However, instead of being the old Richard and hiding behind formality, he tilted back his head and roared in laughter.

Grace stared at him as if he'd taken leave of his senses, and that made him laugh all the harder.

Laughter. He'd rarely indulged in it. There had been no laughter in his home or school. No laughter in business and little pleasure either.

But here he was, penniless, out of the wilds of

Scotland after almost being hanged, having battled his way through old nemeses and traitorous servants, and he felt more alive than he ever had before in his life.

He was not only enjoying himself, he was also becoming the man he'd always thought he was.

And then Grace began laughing, too.

No music was sweeter than Grace MacEachin's laugh. Not even her singing could compare. It caught his attention, held him spellbound. He could listen to it forever and n'er grow tired of the sound.

She stopped laughing when she realized he watched her.

Her expression turned sober.

For a long moment they stared at each other. "What did I do, Grace, to make you angry? I had thought by now we would trust each other. Instead, I find you suffering in pain rather than turning to me for help. Why is it? And what can I do to make it right?"

"You've done nothing," she said. "It's me. It's what I want to do that has been giving me fits."

"What is it then?" he said. "Do you want to slap the mouth off my face for being the ungrateful scoundrel I was to you back there? You were right, Grace. I don't know you and I had my say. I am judgmental. But that doesn't mean I don't—"

He stopped. He was about to say *that doesn't mean I don't love you.*

Then she'd really laugh.

"Mean what?" she asked.

"Mean that I don't worry about your feet," he answered.

"My feet?" Grace repeated.

"Your feet," he agreed.

There was a beat of silence, and then Grace said, "We aren't talking about feet."

"No." He barely whispered the words.

Something was in the air around them. Something powerful, wondrous . . . and then she started to lean forward and he realized that, miracle of all miracles, she was going to kiss him.

But before their lips could connect, there was the jangle of harness tracings and the thud of hooves.

Chapter Fourteen

A dray stacked with cages of chickens and pulled by a chestnut horse spoiled the kiss. The driver of the wagon sat up, a sign he'd seen them, and Grace lost her nerve. She pulled back.

Richard released a frustrated breath. "We are not finished with this," he said.

"No, we aren't," she agreed.

He kissed her nose. "Stay here." He rolled up to his feet and stepped out into the road to meet the wagon.

Grace turned and hastily ripped another strip of her petticoat to wrap her other foot. She didn't make it neat as Richard had but it would serve. Carefully, she stood. This was so much better. She was surprised she hadn't thought of doing this before.

The driver had pulled to a halt a good distance away from them. Grace knew why. The sight of such a large man with a two days' growth of beard on a lonely stretch of road would give even a saint pause. The driver was an open-faced fellow with a wide-brimmed hat and a good amount of Scottish reserve.

Holding his hand out to show he meant no ill, Richard approached him. "Excuse me, good sir, we wonder if we could trouble you for a ride?"

The driver's distrust didn't ebb. "I'm not running a ferry," he said and picked up the reins. He would have gone on without a second look except Richard refused to step out of his way.

"Please, sir, it's my wife. We've been traveling to see her family in Inverness, but our horse fell and had to be put down. We've been walking for hours . . . and she is in the family way."

Wife. It was a loaded word. One that brought her closer to him. She folded her hands demurely in her lap, appreciative of her cape that hid her slim figure.

But his claim also brought about a change inside her, too. She squared her shoulders, lifted her chin, experienced a sense of pride.

She chose to ignore how easily the small fibs

slipped off his tongue. *He*, a man who had once refused to lie, and she knew then he'd do anything to keep her safe.

Safe. Her life had always been a struggle . . . because she'd been alone.

Richard knew exactly what words to say and they worked on the driver. He began walking to her, a huge smile on his face. "We have a ride," he informed her with pride. "Can you walk? Did wrapping your feet help?"

"Let's see," she answered, reaching for the hand he offered. Her feet were still sensitive but felt much better.

He tucked her hand in the crook of his arm and led her to the dray. The driver was rearranging his load to prepare a space for her. "Here you are, missus," he said. "It's not the most comfortable but it will save you a walk."

Placing his hands on her waist, Richard helped her up onto the dray. "If you lean this way, you won't be in danger of tumbling out," he said.

Grace looked over her shoulder as one of the hens reached out to peck at her cape. She wasn't fond of chickens, and yet her body appreciated this chance to rest. She rested her head on her folded arm. "I shall be fine. Where will you be?" she asked Richard.

"Walking alongside," he told her.

"Come up here and sit beside me," the driver ordered. Like most Scots, once he'd offered a helping hand, his reserve quickly thawed. "You are a brawny man, but Sweet Bonnie can pull us and four more men your size if she sets her mind to it."

"Yes, ride," Grace said. Richard must be exhausted, too. He'd endured far more trauma than she had over the last day.

He took their advice and climbed up beside the driver. In fact, the two of them made a comical pair—the tall, broad-shouldered Richard and the short, skinny Scot.

With a clucking noise to Sweet Bonnie that set all the chickens clucking in reply, they were on their way, and that was the last Grace remembered until Richard's hand on her shoulder gently shook her awake. She didn't want to open her eyes but he was insistent.

"Grace, we must unload the wagon."

She would have turned away except that a hen reached her beak through the cage slats and tried to peck her hair. Grace forced herself to rise. She looked around, disoriented. There were crowds of people passing them by, many of them carrying bundles.

"Where are we?"

"A town called Lanark. It's market day. Our

friend Malcolm is bringing his chickens to sale. Come along, Grace, we need to unload the dray, and that includes you."

She let him help her out of the wagon, smiling shyly at their driver as she rubbed the sleep from her eyes. "Did I sleep long?"

"Three hours at least," Malcolm said.

Richard directed her to sit on a stone mounting block while he helped Malcolm with his chickens. After a shaking of hands, Richard took Grace's arm and they started walking through the stalls and wagons set up for market.

Lanark itself was a bustling town. At one end of the street was a huge stone church that gave the shopping and haggling around it a stately air.

Grace's stomach rumbled.

"I'm hungry, too," Richard said as if she'd spoken. He stopped. "We need money."

"We could sell the buttons off your coat," she said, lifting them up for him to see. "Someone would pay a pretty penny for them." She yawned and apologized, "I can't help myself."

He frowned at the black horn buttons. "We need lots of money. Dawson must be in London by now. My uncle will be on his way."

"What makes you believe he'll come? Dawson may tell him he'd fixed you good."

"My uncle is a thorough man. He'll want to see

with his own eyes. I also believe my father would want to know the facts."

His father. Grace kept her opinion to herself. "Lanark isn't far from Glasgow. We are maybe two days' ride from Inverness."

"Good. My fear is that my uncle will try to reach your father. And he may learn you are alive. He'll want to shut the two of you up."

Grace raised a hand to her head. "Shut us up?"

"He's already tried it twice, Grace."

She nodded dumbly. She'd not considered that her quest for justice would endanger her father. "We must reach Father first."

"We *will*," Richard assured her. "But we won't do it walking . . ." His voice trailed off. "How much do you believe I can receive for these buttons?"

Grace took a moment to inspect the buttons and Richard was amazed to discover he hardly considered Grace's looks any longer. Oh, yes, he saw those clear blue eyes, creamy skin, and shining black curls but what he valued was her honesty. Her goodness. Her courage. He admired her as well as loved her.

"They might bring a guinea for all five," she decided.

"Then let's sell them," Richard said. "And the coat while we are at it."

Grace nodded agreement and went plowing

her way through the marketplace with an air of authority. Richard followed and marveled at her bargaining skills. She visited several stalls and two tinkers' wagons before she found her price.

The tinker also purchased his coat for another three pounds. Richard hated to part with it but they'd discovered such a fine coat was not in great demand at this fair. Grace tried her best but could not find a better price.

Next, they broke their fast with sweet ale, piping hot buns, and a wedge of hard, tart cheddar.

The food made Richard sleepy.

"I believe we need some sleep before we try to book passage to Inverness," Grace said.

Richard didn't argue. He was exhausted.

She took his hand and led him to the church, where they found a secluded corner and sat in a pew next to the wall. He stretched out his arm and Grace nestled up to his side. Within seconds he was asleep.

Richard woke to having his shoulders shaken. A bit groggy, he looked around and saw the vicar, a gray-haired, bushy-eyed gent, frowning down on them. "No sleeping in this church. Move on, move on." His breath carried the whiff of gin fumes.

Grace was still asleep. He woke her gently. "Come on, love, we need to leave."

She didn't want to wake and tried to snuggle deeper.

Richard gave an apologetic frown to the vicar before saying, "Gracie, wake."

This time, she drew a deep breath and opened her eyes. He didn't think there was anything more lovely than Grace opening her eyes and looking around the world. She smiled at him, the lazy expression setting all his senses on the alert.

Even the vicar appeared bemused.

Richard took her arm. "We've overstayed our welcome," he whispered.

Her lips formed a soft "oh" and she came to her feet with him. Together they walked out of the church's cool darkness and into the marketplace. The trade had picked up quite a bit over the last two hours or so that Richard estimated they'd been asleep. The walkways were crowded with shoppers and the number had easily doubled.

Grace stood at his side and yawned. "I want to go back to sleep."

"Come on, lass. We have to figure out a way to Inverness. We have what to our name? Almost four pounds? That should pay our fare on the Mail, hopefully sitting inside the coach." He took her hand.

Grace moved closer to him, leaning her head against his arm lest she be overheard as she suggested, "We could steal a horse."

He knew she was teasing. "We already have that crime chalked up to our name. Been there, " he said briskly, "and I'm not willing to try it again. One sentence over my head is enough."

"I could sing," she offered.

"Aye, and everyone would pay to hear you," he agreed, distracted by a bill some boys were going through the crowd and handing out. The name "McGowan" had caught his eye. McGowan was the Scottish fighter who had won the bout he'd heard about their first night out of London.

"Here there," he called to the boy. "Let me see that."

The lad ran over and handed him a sheet before moving on.

"What is it?" Grace asked.

"An advertisement for a fighting contest. Remember McGowan, the Scot who won his match that first night out of London?"

She shrugged her shoulders. Of course the name wouldn't mean anything to her. Women didn't follow boxing.

"He's taking on all comers this afternoon," Richard explained. "It says here, the person who could last three minutes in a prizefighting contest with him would win twenty-five pounds. If he is knocked out, the purse goes up to fifty pounds."

"A fifty?" Grace frowned. "He must not plan to lose."

"I'm certain he doesn't. He's very good, if what I overheard that night in the inn is correct."

"If he is so good, why is he here?"

Richard knew the answer. "To make money and to stay ready for his fight with Cribb. It will take a few weeks before things can be arranged. A fight like the one he'll have with Cribb for the title will need time to run the odds up. What's the man to do in the meantime? He charges each challenger two pounds for a round."

Grace made a disbelieving noise. "Why would any man pay to fight?"

"To say he did," Richard answered. "Or test his skill or his mettle. Who knows? There might be one of them who could win the big purse."

"I just don't understand why, if this McGowan is so important, he would be in a fight all the way up here."

"He's a Scot. These are his people. Besides, up here it will be harder for him to be observed by the London crowd and the wagers will be higher against him. He'll make a fortune if he beats Cribb." He looked again at the paper. "I'm going take this chap on."

"What? *No.*"

"Grace, I can do it. I'm handy with my fists. I have size. I've studied the sport. I can stay with him for three minutes."

She shook her head and started walking. "What you are is light-headed from hunger and lack of sleep. Come, we'll find something to eat and then you will thank me for being sensible."

"I'm going to fight, Grace."

The resolve in his voice made her halt. She turned. "I don't want you to."

"You believe I will fail."

"And have your face pounded in for your trouble," she admitted. She walked back to him. "It's not that I don't think you are brave or strong—"

"You believe I will bungle it, the way I have everything else that has happened to us on this trip."

Grace placed her hands on his arms. "That's not true. I think nothing of the sort."

"Then it is what *I* think. Look at the facts, Grace. If I'd listened to you in the first place, I wouldn't have been so foolish as to leave Dawson by the coach. I'd have been more suspicious and I wouldn't have gone walking up to the town elders in Rachlan Mill."

"You make me want to give you a shake the way you gave me one last night," she said, her eyes alive with fury. "Do *not* feel sorry for yourself for what has happened. I won't let you. You've been everything honorable and good."

"That's why I *must* fight, and I *will* win, Grace. I promise I will. Fighting isn't only about strength and experience. It's also about cunning."

She rolled her eyes heavenward. "Richard, this McGowan has been *winning* at his fights. He knows cunning."

"I've trained as a lawyer, Grace. We have a cunning that is all our own. *Three minutes.* If I stay on my feet against him, we'll have enough money to not only ride to Inverness in style but have a good night's sleep and a bath before we go."

And he would vindicate himself, he could have added . . . but there was more to his request. Richard *wanted* this fight. He'd trained for it. His boxing master, Richmond, had told him he had talent. Here was the chance to test himself.

"I can beat him. Grace. I *will*."

She wasn't convinced. Worry etched every line of her face.

"Believe in me, Grace. I believe in you. Now, I need *you* to believe in *me*." He knew he was throwing it all on the line.

"You are determined to fight, aren't you?" She didn't wait for his answer, but worried: "Why couldn't you have been attracted to a different sport?"

"Because with my big hulking size, I wouldn't have been so good at it," Richard said. "You don't think I didn't try fencing? I stumbled over my own feet and almost stabbed myself in the chest. I was a laughingstock. But my fists . . . Grace, I understand this. And I'm not afraid to take a blow."

"You make it sound so simple."

"It *is* simple. One man against another for three simple minutes."

"This isn't going to be the type of fighting you are accustomed to," she warned.

"How would you know?"

"Because wherever there are men, there are fights. This is bare-knuckle fighting, Richard, and they are fighting for money, not sport. There will be no rules. I've never had the stomach to watch one, but I've seen the shape of the men who have come back from them and I thought them a right silly group of fools."

"We could be in Inverness by tomorrow night. Think of your father."

"I think of *you*."

The implication of her words shot straight to his heart. He stared wanting to believe there were deeper feelings behind them.

He waited, expecting her to retract her statement.

She didn't.

Instead, she rose up and kissed him on the lips.

Richard dared not move. Dared not breathe. The words *I love you, Grace* roiled in his mind, but he lacked the courage to speak them aloud. If only she would give him one more sign, then he'd declare himself—

Her lips left his. She brushed his whiskered jaw with the back of her fingers. "Don't be noble."

Noble? Was that all she thought he was being? And what was the kiss? A way to bring him in line? To save him from harm?

Everything masculine inside him revolted.

"I'm no Galahad searching for some holy grail that he'll never find," he said, stepping away from her. "I can do this, Grace. I will."

He turned and began moving toward the nearest clump of men. They would know where McGowan was.

Grace was stunned by Richard's anger.

What had she said wrong?

Why were men, especially this one, so insistent upon proving themselves?

She knew the answer. He wanted her to believe in him. Richard Lynsted had pride, and Grace understood pride. Why else had she done so many foolish things in her life?

She wanted to save him from himself. But that wasn't what he was asking her to do. All he wanted was for her to believe in him.

Such a simple request, and yet it called for all her courage. If she put her faith in another, what if that person failed her? Or turned on her? She'd had that happen, too.

Life had taught her there was only one person she could trust, and that was herself.

And Richard.

Not once had he failed her. Events hadn't always unfolded as he'd thought they would, but he hadn't left her and he would never betray her.

Nor would he marry her, that devil inside of her whispered, searching as it always did for what was wrong with each man she'd met, belittling him until she packed her bags and left. Except this time was different. This time, Grace had the wisdom to respond with maturity.

The truth was, with her past, few men would offer her marriage no matter how many times she repented.

Furthermore, Richard wasn't asking for heart and soul. He just wanted her to place a little faith in him.

She could do that. She could do *more* than that.

This man had slipped past years of her distrust and disappointment, and she loved him enough to follow him into the fires of hell if need be. Soon they might have to part because she would never measure up to his ideal, but for right now, they were together and she realized that was enough for her.

Awe filled her at exactly how unselfish love was. She'd not imagined she could ever be so. She'd always expected tit for tat. Now, she would support him because what was important to her man was important to her—even in something so foolish and potentially dangerous.

He'd started walking away from the group of men, moving with a sense of purpose. He'd found his fight—and she'd not let him go alone.

Grace lifted her skirts and began running after him. When she caught up to him, she slipped her hand in his.

He looked down at her, his expression still grim. That was all right. Grace had a purpose. She'd stand beside him no matter what.

Chapter Fifteen

Richard led Grace to a field at the edge of Lanark where a crowd of men were gathering. Apparently Richard wasn't the only one interested in the purse.

Boxing was not outlawed in Scotland the way it was in England. Although even there, as long as the fights were held away from populated areas such as the one they'd stumbled upon their first night on the road, authorities did very little to interfere with the matches. Still, even though the sport was legal, Grace thought there was an unsavory air about it.

The fight was man against man until one of them went down and could not rise for thirty seconds. There were few rules. Grace thought of them more like codes of conduct. Hitting an opponent below the belt was considered unsporting and, if a fighter did need a break, he could drop to one knee to start a thirty-second count while he gathered his wits up again.

The men lining up to form a queue were of all shapes and sizes—burly men with arms the size of cannons, whipcord-thin lads who were as hard as leather, old men wanting to prove their strength and validate their youth, and young men wishing to prove their mettle. More than a few were almost as tall and strong-looking as Richard.

A good number of women waited with their men. Some were hard-looking or carefree. The majority appeared anxious.

Grace took a step closer to Richard, knowing what category she fit into.

He'd been quietly looking around, taking in his competition. He hadn't said a word to her since she'd joined him.

As she studied the other men present, she realized that Richard had become the best-looking man she'd ever seen. He was masculine and strong, but he also had character.

His hand still held hers. He might be angry but he had not forgotten her. She clasped her fingers around his, not wanting to let him go.

On one side of the field was a brightly painted covered wagon much like a gypsy caravan. It had a green bed and a yellow hood with a howling wolf painted on the side.

The calico-curtained door at the back was flipped aside and a bantam rooster of a man climbed down. He wore a dandy's yellow pantaloons, bright blue jacket, a cherry-striped vest and red shoes with pointed toes. Tight brown curls of hair stuck out this way and that from under the man's blue wide-brimmed hat. It sported a huge pheasant feather that sliced the air with the movement of his head as he boomed out, "Here now, I'm the McGowan's manager. Do what I say." Grace was surprised he was English. "Contestants line up. Right over there. McGowan wants a look at you."

The crowd of men moved to comply.

Grace didn't want to leave Richard even after he let go of her hand. She stepped back with the other women. The day was growing warm. Spring was in the air. Grace took off her cape and folded it over her arm.

McGowan's manager began marching back and forth in front of the line of men, holding his hat out for their two guineas. Two of the men didn't have the funds and had to move to join the onlookers. One tried to argue his way into a bout, but the manager nodded to a barrel-shaped man with a hard jaw to escort the man out of the queue.

The woman next to Grace, a young thing who was very heavy with child, made a soft cry of alarm. The man being ordered out of the line was hers. She hurried to join him with the onlookers. The young couple put their heads together and clasped hands. Grace couldn't help but pity them. They probably had more need of the prize purse than she and Richard.

She glanced over to him to see if he'd noticed the couple. He hadn't. He was listening to McGowan's manager go over the rules.

"We start the bouts at three. That's an hour from now and as you can see the crowd is already forming. If your knee hits the ground and you are there for a count of thirty, you're out."

"Who does the counting?" one of the contenders asked.

"I do," the manager said. "So if you are going to knock out the McGowan, you'd best do it good and right so I can't cheat on the count."

A nervous laugh met his comment. The manager puffed up his chest. "I'm not teasing you, lads. Fighting is a dirty, grim business. If you want out of your bout, you go to your knees for thirty—that is if McGowan hasn't knocked you out."

"What if I stay in for the three minutes?" Richard asked.

The manager smiled, the expression not particularly nice. "Then you receive twenty-five pounds. But you have to stand and take your blows like a man. I warn you, I run a clean fight. Even the vicar of St. Nicholas Church will be here and he'll vouch for me. I've seen some who think they can run around like a chicken without its head for three minutes and win the twenty-five. We'll have none of that. Oscar will see that you face your opponent, and I should warn you now, McGowan will not be pleased with you. He's not a friendly man when he isn't pleased."

Three more men stepped out of the queue. There were now twenty men, Richard being one of them, ready to face the McGowan.

One of the men in line asked, "Will there be time in the day for him to fight all of us?"

"We shall see, won't we?" the manager said as if that was the least of his concerns. "Any other questions?" There were none. "Very well, stand tall. McGowan will want a look at you. He's the one who decides the order of the fight." He went over to the caravan and gave the side a knock. "They are ready for you, Mr. McGowan."

Everyone's eyes turned to the calico curtain.

There was a dramatic pause, and then the curtain opened for a man to climb out. He had to bend over to fit through the door, and once his feet hit the ground, he unfolded, and unfolded, and unfolded his body.

The McGowan was as tall as Richard and he looked more like a crofter than a fighter. There was little humane intelligence to his face. His nose and eyes appeared scrunched together and his thick lips curved into an expression of disdain. He wore his shirt hem out over his homespun breeches and on his feet were heavy wool socks and worn, sturdy shoes. His hair flowed past his shoulders, a dirty yellow mess that made Grace itch to look at it.

Heedless of his audience, McGowan stretched his arms in a yawn. His big gaping hole of a mouth held very few teeth. He scratched his belly with a groan of satisfaction and then dropped his arms to his side—and his hands almost reached his knees.

Grace shifted her weight from one foot to the other. She'd never seen such long arms in her life.

Or a nose as flat. He'd taken a hit or two there and it wasn't a pretty sight. It was barely recognizable as a nose.

Another occupant of the tent climbed out. This person was a blowzy bawd with impossibly red hair. She scrambled out of the tent, her blouse gaping loose and exposing almost every inch of her impressively large, soft breasts.

She took a moment to hike her blouse up and tie it at the neck. Her feet were bare. She reached back into the wagon for her shoes and socks.

"Thank you, sir," she said, giving McGowan a cheeky bump with her hip as she passed him, clearly enjoying the attention her appearance was receiving.

McGowan grabbed her around the waist, drew her close to him so her feet were off the ground, and was about to bury his whiskered face in her neck to give her a gobble of a kiss—when his gaze fell on Grace. His piggy eyes homed right in on her.

He dropped the bawd. She wasn't ready for his release and didn't catch herself. Her bottom hit the ground and caused her to give a surprised wheeze.

McGowan began walking toward Grace. "I want this one." He had a voice as gruff as the rest of him.

Grace took a step back. McGowan's manager raced forward. He caught the fighter's shirt tail and tried to drag him back, receiving a shove in the face for his trouble.

But Richard was already there to protect her.

He stepped into McGowan's path. "She's mine," he said.

McGowan pulled back so that he could give Richard a good look up and down. "I want her."

Richard tapped the fighter's forehead with three fingers as if to wake him up. "You can't have her."

"I think I can," McGowan replied, looking past Richard's shoulder to where Grace stood, horrified at the turn of events and at being the center of attention.

"You are wrong," Richard answered, taking a step over to block the fighter's view of Grace.

McGowan took another look at Richard. He reached for the collar of his jacket and rubbed it between his fingers. "Good coat," he said.

Richard didn't answer.

"Good boots," McGowan continued. "No farmer. No Scotsman." He turned to his manager. "I fight him for the girl," he said, pointing at Grace with a jerk of his thumb.

"The girl?" the manager echoed.

"Aye, the girl. I want the girl. Fight him for the girl. Do it." McGowan retreated to the corner of the wagon, where he dipped a ladle into a rain bucket and drank deeply, his piggy gaze on Grace.

His manager puffed his cheeks and released his breath. "Very well." He looked to Richard. "He fights you for your woman."

"No," Richard said as if he thought the man simple-minded. "She's not a prize. She's not a part of this."

"You'll be the last fight of the day," the manager offered. "Everyone will be here."

"I'm not fighting. My woman is not a prize." He turned to Grace. "Come along, let's go."

The manager held his hand up to stave off Richard's departure. "You want a bigger purse," he said. "We can manage that. A fight between the two of you will be something to see. I'll double the prize if you win."

"I'll not risk my woman," Richard said. He held out a hand to Grace but before she could go forward, McGowan placed himself between them.

The swiftness of his approach alarmed Grace. He moved fast for a man of his size.

"I fight you for the woman," he said. "You win, you keep her and the purse. But you won't win— you are not a fighter."

The other contestants and onlookers had created a circle around them. Grace could see anger at the boast build inside Richard, especially in front of this crowd.

"I would win, but my lady is not a part of this," Richard said.

McGowan's thick lips curved into a cocksure smile. "His *ladee*," he mocked, looking around at those gathered around them. "Such a fancy man. Makes me want him to eat dust." He held his hands up as if shaking in terror and earned a good laugh for his silliness.

"Come, Grace," Richard said

"Come with *me*, Grace," McGowan said, echoing Richard's king's English. "Let me show you what a real man can do with a pretty thing like you."

"He's a good one," the bawd cheerfully endorsed. "Kept it up all night till I thought it wouldn't come down. I'm aching all the way through." She hunched over to demonstrate what she meant and the crowd couldn't help but laugh.

Richard started to step around McGowan but the fighter again blocked his path. He shoved Richard's shoulder, making him take a step back. The humor had left McGowan's face. "You've never fought before in your life, have you, mate?" he said. "You are running because you are afraid."

"The lady is not a prize," Richard repeated, his voice tight but controlled.

But Grace knew the cost of this confrontation. It was his rounds with Lord Stone all over again. It was what he'd fought against.

"Oh, she is a prize," McGowan corrected him. "I imagine she is a right, tight poke."

Richard's fingers curled into fists.

Grace was certain their audience couldn't overhear all of what was being said, but they knew Richard was being baited and they judged him less for not rising to defend her.

He would judge himself less as well.

"We'll accept your offer," she heard herself say. "My man will fight you for double the purse. And we'll share it with that couple over there." She nodded to the pregnant woman and her man, who couldn't afford to fight.

McGowan's tiny eyes gleamed with triumph. "You are my prize if he loses."

"I am."

"Grace, what are you doing?" Richard demanded.

She looked to the manager. "We are here at three?"

"Aye, missus, be waiting under that tree yonder." The manager nodded to a chestnut on the other side of the caravan.

"Tell the vicar at St. Nicholas to put his money on my man," Grace instructed him, raising her voice for all to hear.

"And what is the name of your man?" the manager asked.

Grace thought fast. Richard wasn't going to answer. He stared at her as if she'd gone mad. She was certain they didn't want to use his real name, especially since there was an order for his hanging under it.

Inspiration struck. "Why, John Bull," she said. "A bold, proud Englishman who is going to teach this Scottish pig some lessons."

Her declaration was met by a chorus of catcalls and derisive comments.

"Englishman versus Scot," the manager said, quick to capitalize on the rivalry. "We'll see you at three, John Bull."

McGowan lingered, insultingly letting his eyes rove over her person, until Richard grabbed him by the chin and turned his head away. The Scot laughed and meandered off one way.

Richard stomped off in the other.

Grace hurried after him.

"What did you do?" Richard demanded in a furious under voice once she'd caught up with him.

Conscious that eyes were upon them, Grace took his arm and led him down one of the roads leading to the market. "What we have to do. Richard, you can beat him."

"I want to murder him." Richard's stride grew longer, faster. She had to hurry to keep up with him. "But I would never, *never* put you up as the prize."

"I know," Grace said. "That's why I had to do it myself."

He stopped so abruptly she almost ran into him. They stood on a side street, not far from

St. Nicholas Church. He faced her. "I must not do this fight."

"Why?"

"Because what if I lose?" he asked as if the reason was clear.

"You told me you would *not* lose."

His brows came together. "Is that what this is? An opportunity to throw my words back at me? Didn't I say I wasn't willing to risk you?"

"I know, and that's why I risked *myself*—"

"There's *no* risk involved. You *threw* yourself away. You told a field full of people that you were worth nothing."

The accusation stung like a swarm of hornets. "I told a field full of people that I believe in *you*."

"You don't know that I'm going to win, Grace," he countered, the light in his eyes livid. "If I fail, do you think this is the price I want to pay? It's one thing to take a beating. Another to let you go off with that disgusting pig of a man."

"You aren't going to lose," she told him. "I know you won't."

"And I'm not so certain," he shot back. He turned and began walking away from her.

"Where are you going?"

"To think," he threw over his shoulder. He turned a corner and he was out of sight.

Grace waited a moment, willing him to return.

She took a few steps after him and then stopped.

He would come back. She knew he would. His pride would make him fight.

But the question was, would he come back *to her*?

She started walking after him.

Richard walked as far as he could without leaving the village. Grace didn't understand. She'd decided that he would be her rescuer in spite of his proving he couldn't rescue anyone.

He *had* looked forward to the challenge. He'd wanted the fight—until Grace had become involved. Now his confidence waivered. He couldn't bear to think of the consequences if he failed her . . .

With a shake of his head he tried to erase all the vivid images in his mind. Of course right now, he didn't just want to knock McGowan out, he wanted to rip out his throat.

And he didn't know what he wanted to do with Grace. Witnessing her put herself in danger on his account made him crazed.

She'd been raised well. He didn't understand why she continued to toss herself away—and twice she'd done it for him.

Twice.

Richard sank down on a rough-hewn mounting block, startled, humbled, and frightened by her sacrifice.

No one had paid attention to him. He'd worked for both father and uncle and had received little notice for what he'd done for their business. He'd been an outstanding student in school, excelled at all his studies, and yet people discounted his brain because of his size . . . or, at least, that is what he'd told himself.

But a part of him feared it was true.

"Before McGowan made his challenge, you believed you could beat him," he heard Grace's voice say from behind him. "You asked me to believe in you, Richard. I do."

"You know the times I've failed." He refused to look at her.

"I know only the number of times you've thrown your heart and soul into something you believe in. I know you aren't afraid to do what is right. I know I trust you with my life."

"You are trusting me with *more* than your life," he told her.

"I'm trusting you because I love you."

He couldn't have heard her correctly. He went still, hoping she'd repeat herself. Hoping it wasn't a trick.

"I know I'm not the sort of woman a man like you loves," she said, her voice tight as she held back tears. "I didn't want to love you. You were my enemy and yet, everything you did, I admired. You are like no other man I've ever met. And I couldn't stop myself from falling in love with you—"

Any other words she was going to say were cut off by his whirling around, coming to his feet, and sweeping her up in his arms.

Richard kissed her. He kissed her the way he'd dreamed of kissing her. Fully, completely, possessively. *She loved him.*

He didn't hold back. He couldn't. He loved her, too. Passionately.

And the wonder of the kiss was that Grace kissed him back.

They breathed the same air. He wrapped his arms around her. He'd never let her go. *Never.*

He tasted the salt of her tears. He kissed them. Kissed her eyes, her cheeks, her nose.

She held him as tightly as he held her. Her fingers curled into his hair. "Does this mean you care for me? Please, Richard, even a little?"

"I worship the ground you walk on. You are more important to me than my own life."

Her gaze met his. "Then you'd best last three minutes with McGowan."

He leaned his head near hers. "Ah, Grace, you know how to put pressure on a man."

She started laughing and he found himself laughing with her. He, the man who never laughed. He'd done more living, more laughing during his days with Grace MacEachin than in all his life before.

But what was truly amazing was that he was no longer alone. They stood side by side, two against the world.

The miracle of this moment sent shock waves through him. The March wind blew around them and yet nothing could touch them, not when they were in each other's arms.

"You won't let McGowan win," she said. "Your pride won't let you, not once you step in to fight him."

"You have such faith in me?"

She nodded, and then she said something that changed his life. "There isn't anything I believe you can't do."

"Is it almost three?" he asked.

"It may be."

"Then come along, lass. I have a fight to win." He took her hand and together they marched to the clearing.

The crowd had quadrupled in size while they'd been gone. The boys who'd been handing out the bills now collected twenty pence a person to watch the fights. The atmosphere was one of a

fair, with women carrying trays of pies and jugs of cider and ale for sale.

Everyone seemed to know who Richard was. They cleared a path for him and Grace to the caravan, where McGowan stalked his turf like a wildcat. When he saw Grace, he stopped, a toothless grin spreading across his face.

Richard would never let him touch her. He placed her cape around her shoulders, a silent warning to McGowan to take his eyes off her.

The betting was against Richard. He could hear the wagers being called from all around him. Even grandmotherly old ladies had come for the fight and had bet he'd lose.

The manager came to McGowan's side. Under the tree next to the caravan stood the other men who had signed up to win the purse.

"I want her up here," McGowan shouted, pointing his finger at Grace. "Bring her here."

Richard tucked Grace's hand in the crook of his arm and led her to the wagon, where a dais has been hastily constructed. A chair was placed beside it for her to sit so that all would see her.

"You go join the others," the manager instructed Richard.

"No, I'll stay right here," Richard answered.

The manager started to protest and then nodded to Oscar. "Keep an eye on him."

Oscar took a position next to Richard.

A group of men had been selected to join hands in a very large circle to keep the crowd a distance from the fighters. Richard removed his jacket, boots, and socks as the others had done. Some had even taken off their shirts. He removed his neck cloth but kept the shirt on. That's what McGowan did and that is what he would do.

The manager started the contest. Richard had anticipated the dozen other fighters would take up at least an hour or so before he and McGowan fought. He was hoping the first matches would wear down the fighter.

He was wrong.

McGowan dispatched the other contestants in less than eighteen minutes. After watching the first two challengers get knocked unconscious, the next three men walked off without fighting. The remainder dashed out of the ring within seconds of facing the champion. The manager attempted to prove true to his word and force the fellows back, to the hearty amusement of the crowd.

Richard knew the passage of time because the manager gleefully announced it.

Not one of the other contestants had any boxing form. Richard had watched them with a critical eye, just as he watched McGowan. Of course, he hardly had the opportunity to see the Scot in

action because most of his opponents vanquished themselves.

Grace sat with her hands clasped tightly in her lap. He placed his hand on her shoulder.

At last, all eyes turned to him. He was the last contestant and this was the match they'd all gathered for.

McGowan crooked a finger at him, ordering him to step into the ring of men.

Richard kissed Grace. "For luck," he whispered.

Her face was pale, her brow worried, but she smiled.

"I know what I'm doing," he promised her and walked into the ring. He put up his fists, taking his stance.

However, the manager handled this bout differently from the others. "Take it easy, man," he ordered. "There will be plenty of time to raise your fists. But first, let me give you a proper sendoff." He strutted past the boxers to address the crowd. With a flourish, he announced, "This fight is between Royce McGowan—"

The crowd cheered.

"And John Bull."

Catcalls and boos met Richard's name. He raised his fist in a salute anyway, proud to be representing his country against this hooligan McGowan, and noticing the betting was against him.

"It's bare knuckles," the manager announced, "no rules, and let the best man win the wager. Shake hands, lads."

He stepped out of their way as Richard turned to shake his opponent's hand—but McGowan wasn't in the mood for shake.

Instead, he took advantage of Richard's lack of protection and brought a big meaty fist the size of a small anvil barreling into the side of Richard's head so hard his neck snapped back.

Darkness blinded Richard and with a will of its own, his body went down.

His knees. He had to stay on his knees . . .

Chapter Sixteen

$\mathcal{S}$hocked silence met McGowan's unfair punch. Grace watched Richard go to his knees, his eyes losing their focus. She rose from her chair and came down from the dais, moving as close as she could to him. "Richard, please, *Richard*."

He didn't respond but stayed on his knees.

This was exactly what she had feared in the beginning. A fight in a Scottish field was a far cry from two gentlemen sparring in a fancy boxing saloon.

The crowd recovered their voice. The bidding had been against John Bull and many saw their wager was about to be won. They let out a cheer, shouting McGowan's name as the manager began the thirty-second count.

"This isn't fair," Grace protested to the manager. He laughed and kept counting.

The crowd started counting with him. "Eleven . . . twelve . . ."

Grace panicked, not for herself but for Richard. "Richard, *you must fight this unfairness.*" Such a task would have set him to work in the past. She prayed he heard her.

For his part, McGowan was pleased with his handiwork. He adored the crowd's cheering and then his attention turned to Grace.

"Come here, my pretty, pretty. Let me show you what a real man has—"

Any other suggestions he had were cut off in surprise as his feet came off the ground.

McGowan had been so interested in her, he'd not paid attention to the count and had failed to notice his opponent was back in action.

Richard lifted the Scot and tossed him as if he were a caber, a huge log thrown for sport. He made it look effortless. McGowan landed hard on the ground.

The crowd caught its collective breath and while some began shouting for McGowan to rise from the dirt and start fighting, another group started calling to place a wager on the Englishman.

Again, Richard put up his fists in proper style. Grace thought he should have jumped on McGowan while he was down and pummeled him silly . . . but then that wasn't her man. He would fight fairly, and he would win. Her faith would not waver again.

McGowan raised his fists and moved forward. He had the longer arms but in a matter of seconds and three short jabs, Richard proved he had speed and agility his opponent lacked. He was also better than the Scot at protecting his head.

Grace found herself clenching her own fists and had to fight the urge to punch the air like so many of the men around her in the crowd were doing.

Richard was nothing short of brilliant. He really could fight, even she could see that. And now that he knew McGowan used dirty tricks, he seemed to thwart every one of them before they started.

At one point the Scot threw all his weight into a punch and as Richard blocked it, McGowan rammed his other punch below the belt. But Richard was a canny one. He'd obviously been expecting such a trick because he turned at the last minute and McGowan's blow bounced off his hip.

Richard now had the hearts of the crowd. Scots had a passion for a good fight.

Three times McGowan went down on one knee, holding it just long enough during the thirty-second count to recover and come up fighting.

But it didn't do him any good.

Richard moved like a man possessed. He dictated the fight, hitting McGowan at will, keeping him off balance so his longer arms were not effective weapons.

McGowan grew desperate. The smile was no longer on his face.

Nor was the crowd behind him. He did not fight well and had started doing more running then punching. The times he tried to step out of the ring, the onlookers shoved him back in with admonishments to "own up," meaning they wanted him to be a man and take his punishment like a dozen other fighters had before this bout.

And then it came, the deciding blow. Richard's fist struck McGowan right below the chin.

The fighter reeled back. He balanced on one foot, and then went down with a crash.

Richard stared at him, his fists up as if expecting him to rise again. Grace shouted to the manager, "Start your count."

The man gave her a dazed stare as if he couldn't believe his man was out.

Grace counted for him. "One," she shouted. "Two."

The crowd took up the count. Richard still waited, ready for anything.

And when the crowd finally reached "Thirty!" Grace ran into the ring and threw her arms around her champion. "I knew you could do it."

His arms came down over her and he stumbled backward. Laughing with happiness, she almost fell with him but he caught them both.

"I did do it, didn't I?" he said, sounding amazed.

"You are the *best*," she assured him.

He laughed, the sound carefree and joyous.

After that, he was rushed on all sides by well-wishers. They'd enjoyed the fight and even though many had lost a wager against him, the sport was such that there could be no hard feelings. Before Grace knew what anyone was about, Richard was being dragged from her arms and carried away for a pint at the pub, but he shook them off.

He walked back to where McGowan's manager knelt on the ground, still trying to bring his fighter to his senses. He had McGowan sitting up but the man sat with his head resting on his knees and didn't appear ready to move any time soon.

"You owe me money," Richard said.

The manager made a low growling sound in the back of his throat. "You've ruined him."

"Nonsense. He can go on to fight Cribb. No one who is important will know about this."

"Word has a way of being spread."

"And you'll deny it." Richard held out his hand. "Double the purse for a knocking out, remember? A hundred pounds. I'll thank you kindly for it."

At that moment, McGowan came to his senses with a snort and a groan. The manager shrugged Richard off. "I must see to him first."

Richard took the manager's arm and brought him to his feet. "I have no desire to interfere with McGowan's fight with Cribb, but I might change my mind."

The manager reached into his pocket and pulled out the purse. He began counting money into Richard's hand.

McGowan lay back on the ground with a groan. Grace was concerned but one of the elderly ladies who had watched the fight told her, "Don't be worried. It's his pride that is keeping him down there."

"You are certain?" she asked, concerned.

The woman made a blowing noise through her lips, dismissing any doubts.

"A hundred pounds," the manager said, having counted out the money. "Now take off. I never want to see your likes again."

Richard looked to Grace, both of his hands full of money. He had done it. He'd told her that he would win the fight and he had. Her heart brimmed with pride in him.

And then his gaze slid to the young pregnant couple she had noticed earlier, the ones who the manager had tossed out of the competition because they lacked the fee to compete.

Before Grace knew what Richard was about, he walked over to the couple and, offering them a handful of his winnings, said, "Here, buy something special for your wife and the baby."

The husband was speechless. "Sir, you, you—"

"You are to be thanked," said his practical wife. She held out her apron and Richard poured the money into it.

Everyone watching was touched by the gesture. Grace most of all. She'd thought him so wrapped up in the fight he hadn't noticed earlier the plight of the couple.

Richard looked to the crowd, who now gave him unwavering support. "Is there a pub in this village?"

The answer was a hearty chorus of "ayes." Someone mentioned the Crown's Thistle.

"I think we should celebrate. I'm buying the first round." Richard said. That's all he needed to say. Such an announcement was met with an even louder shout of approval. Richard took Grace's arm before they were swept away from each other by the tide of people happy to show him to the pub.

The crowd carried them through the maze of

streets to the hewn oak door of the Crown's Thistle, a public house and inn down the row from St. Nicholas Church. They all squeezed through the door and drinks were quickly poured all around. Richard went up to the bar while Grace lingered by the door.

Two serving girls began filling tankards from a tapped keg as fast as they could. The tankards were picked up and handed around the room to man and woman alike. Even the vicar who had thrown them out of the church was amongst their number. If there were any hard feelings over losing a wager over Richard's fight, they didn't appear in evidence as the Scots raised their drinks to salute Richard's health.

"A good man you have there, missus," someone said to Grace's right.

The gent on her left quaffed his ale as he approvingly added, "Knows how to use his fists."

"Well, I had some worries in the beginning. McGowan leveled him with a powerful blow," another commented, and talk about the fight was on. It was almost more entertaining than the fight itself.

Richard listened, throwing in a word or two that everyone in the room held their breaths to catch—and from her vantage point, Grace realized he had come the distance. He'd not bothered to retie his natty neck cloth. His jacket was open and the shine had long ago left his boots. But he looked younger and more at ease with himself. No one would call him a prig now, not with two days of whisker shadow on his jaw. It gave him a rough, dashing air, and more than one woman in the room had her eye on him.

The men were all reliving the fight with him. The women closed in around him, caught up in the men's excitement and in being close to the hero of the hour.

Grace leaned against the door frame and watched Richard bask in being the center of attention, and realized this was what he'd once dreamed of—to be included. He was especially celebrated because apparently from what she could overhear McGowan had not endeared himself to the villagers. During the two days he'd set up camp here, he'd chased their daughters and bullied their merchants into providing him free food, drink, and whatever else had met his fancy.

"He's already packed and out of here," a man proclaimed who had just joined them. "His wagon and everything is gone. So here's to John Bull." Another round of toasts ensured.

For his part, Richard smiled with modest good humor. He didn't brag or boast like so many men would have. He let the villagers tell the story of the fight back to him, and they enjoyed every moment of it.

And Grace fell deeper in love.

She'd known many men in her life but this bear of a man with a lawyer's mind, an accountant's habits, and a knight's spirit outshone them all.

At that moment, Richard looked around the room, his brows coming together in concern. He caught sight of her at the doorway and the tension eased. He held out his hand, motioning her forward and bringing the attention of everyone in the room to her—especially that of several comely village girls standing as close to Richard as they could.

A man's voice called out, "To John Bull's lady and the bundle of joy that will soon grace their lives."

Both Richard and Grace were startled until they saw the toast came from the "Chicken Man," who had given them a ride that morning. He stood against the back wall with a few of his mates.

"Ah, a baby," one of the matrons interpreted with approval. "Are you bearing, lass?" she asked Grace.

Thankful she still had her cape on, Grace nodded.

Tankards and glasses were lifted higher as toasts had to be announced for the baby. Grace joined Richard, who brought his arm around her shoulder as he offered her a glass of golden ale.

He didn't move that arm as the toast was repeated but left it resting there with easy possessiveness.

The village girls backed away, losing interest now that they knew he was taken.

"See what happens when you tell a fib?" Grace whispered to Richard.

He laughed, the sound free of his usual tightness. "It's not such a bad thing, is it?" he offered. "In fact, I like the feeling of having you mine."

And she liked the idea of being his . . . but had never thought to hear it from his lips when first they'd started this trip. Words couldn't form in her mind, other than a desire to throw herself into his arms and tell him to never let her go.

He leaned close to her ear and gave it a kiss, a sign the ale was having its effect. "Don't tell me I have shocked Grace MacEachin?" He sighed and said with the candor of ale, "I can't help myself, Grace. Every time I look at you I turn buffle-headed."

"Buffle-headed?"

"You know what I mean."

She did.

"I turn buffle-headed around you, too," she confessed.

Time stopped.

The crowd, the noise, the drinking good humor around them faded.

There was just him.

He brought his other arm around her, hugged her close. He understood. He *knew* . . . because he felt the same?

His lips brushed her hair. Several women cooed an "ah," and someone murmured, "That's so sweet."

A man standing close said, "Here, mate, have another drink before you do something you'll regret." His wit was met with several guffaws over how he already had done something he'd regret. Married humor, the sort couples with long-standing affection understood.

She, Grace MacEachin, was part of that conversation.

Richard wasn't the only one to have his life changed this trip.

A yawn escaped her.

"It's been a long day," Richard murmured.

She nodded. "You are holding me up." But she wasn't thinking about sleep.

A glance up at the look in his eye told her he wasn't either.

"Come along," he said. "Ladies, gentleman, good night," he announced.

They didn't want him to leave, convinced him to have just one more ale. Some of the lads that had more than their fill started to follow them out the door, but Richard gently pushed them back.

In the hallway, they came upon a red-haired woman with two chins wearing a mob cap and a clean apron over her dress. A set of keys was at her waist. Earlier, she'd been in the taproom serving drinks.

"Excuse me," Richard asked. "I need to see the innkeeper about a room."

"You are looking at him, or her," the woman said with a smile. "I'm Mrs. Fraley. I prefer being called an inn mistress over innkeeper."

"Well, inn mistress," Richard said with the good humor of ale, "we need a room. Do you have one available with hot bath, soap and razor, a good comfortable bed?"

Mrs. Fraley laughed. "I believe I do."

"Is the bath big enough for two?" Grace wondered. At the other woman's raised eyebrows, she explained, "My husband"—how sweet those words were—"is a good-sized man."

The inn mistress nodded agreement. "Aye. As of fact, my late husband was a good-sized man. I happen to have such a tub. Come along."

"We'd like a good meal, too," Richard said.

"Roast duck?" the inn mistress suggested.

"Perfect," Richard answered.

"One moment please," Mrs. Fraley said and disappeared down the back hall. When she returned, she said, "We have the water heating for your bath and the girls will be up with the tub soon."

"I can carry it up," Richard offered.

"Absolutely not. You are our guest of honor," Mrs. Fraley said, indicating they should follow her up the stairs. "Business has not been so brisk," she confided. " 'Tis a good thing you came to town, sir. We've not come together for a good evening at the pub for a long time."

"Why is that?" Grace asked. The pub was the center of village life.

"The times," Mrs. Fraley answered. "The world is changing. The old ways no longer matter the way they once did. The landowners talk about raising sheep instead of taking care of their kinsman. But then, missus, you are Scottish and know what I mean. Ah, now, here we are," she said as she stopped at a door. She used one of the keys on the ring tied to her waist and opened the door on a charming room that made Grace gasp in delight.

A lovely four-poster bed covered in a blue counterpane and stacked with several large feather pillows took up a good amount of the floor space. In one corner were two upholstered chairs beside a small side table. Mrs. Fraley lit the lamp on the table and then went to work lighting the fire in the grate.

There was a knock at the door and a serving girl entered with a covered tray full of delicious-smelling food and a stoneware jug. Grace's knees went weak from hunger. It had been a while since they'd had a decent meal.

Behind the girl came a hired man carrying a huge ornate tub.

"Set it in front of the fire, Olin," Mrs. Fraley instructed. "And go fetch the water."

Within twenty minutes, Olin had carried enough buckets up and down the stairs to fill the tub full of steaming water. Mrs. Fraley provided milled soap scented with roses, a razor, and linen towels. She smiled as she closed the door on Grace and Richard.

Grace poured each of them a glass of cider from the stoneware jug. She now raised it in a salute to Richard. "To Sir Galahad."

He laughed at her reference and set down his glass. Placing his arms around her waist, he drew her to him. "I fear I'm no celibate." His arousal, strong and insistent between them, gave proof to his words.

She set down her own glass and looked up to him, so full of love she could have burst from it.

"Very well," she said softly. "So what shall it be first—the bath and shave, dinner or—"

She stepped back, reached behind and unlaced her dress, letting it fall to her ankles before she finished her question. "Or do you want me first?"

Grace knew the answer she wanted. Her body ached to join with his.

And to her everlasting gratitude, he came straight to her.

Chapter Seventeen

$\mathscr{R}$ichard was a God-fearing man, but he had not expected God to bless him. He prayed but hadn't believed in divine intervention or that God truly knew his deepest secrets, his doubts, his wants—until now.

Taking Grace in his arms, having her cling to him as tightly as he held her made him realize how deeply he'd lacked faith. Her love defied rational explanation. He was a lump of a man, full of human failings. She'd seen him at his worst and at his best—and loved him anyway.

And if that wasn't a gift from God, Richard didn't know what else could be.

He carried her to the bed. They didn't speak as they undressed each other. He was so nervous his fingers shook. She seemed just as anxious.

They worked together. While he unlaced the back of her bodice, the one she'd ripped from her skirt to save his life, she unbuttoned his breeches. Throwing their clothes to the floor, he leaned Grace back on the bed.

She was so very precious to him. He kissed her eyes, her nose, her chin, the curve of her breast. Her lips curved into a smile. Her hands ran down his arms, over his chest, along his side.

Richard took his time making love to her. They'd been through so much together. In the short span of their acquaintance, he'd come to know her almost better than he knew himself . . . and that's because he loved her.

Her legs parted, cradling him. Richard reached for her hand. He pressed a kiss in her palm, closing her fingers over it before slowly sliding himself inside her.

Grace's eyes widened and then her lashes lowered as she made a satisfied sound. "My man," she murmured.

He leaned over her, brushing a stray curl back from her cheek. She turned, kissed his hand, and he said what was in his heart. "I love you, Grace. I adore you."

Tears came to her eyes. Richard wasn't certain what he'd done. He'd upset her. He'd held very still, enjoying the sensation of being joined with her, but now, he started to pull out. She stopped him, her hand on the back of his neck.

"Don't you dare stop now," she warned. "We're only beginning." She began moving her hips, letting him know what she wanted, and he was only too happy to oblige.

Together they moved, his rhythm matching hers.

"What did you say to me?" she whispered in his ear. "Please tell me."

"I love you, Grace. I love you, I love you."

She purred at what he was saying as if she could not hear it enough. The intensity built between the two of them, and he realized this was what making love was. It wasn't just the coupling. It was this need to be closer, to share not only their bodies but also their lives.

There were no barriers between them. The act of sex was no longer about lust, but about giving. Not about desire, but about sharing. Not about that moment of release, but about that moment of life, of creation.

Richard felt the quickening inside her. Deep muscles tightened, held him, melded with him. Her eyes had closed, her lips parted as she drew a deep wavering breath, and he didn't think she could ever be more beautiful to him.

He found his own release. He buried himself deep, losing his mind, his soul, his very being, in the wonder of her.

This was his woman. The one he wanted by his side forever.

She'd branded him. Marked him. He'd never stray. In this moment, he was hers.

Grace held Richard tight.

She'd not known the act of mating could be like this.

It wasn't just that her body joined with his. There was more. They *fit* together. He, a giant of a man, and she, as petite as they come—they meshed like pieces of a puzzle. And it wasn't just their bodies that perfectly connected. Their minds and hearts were in harmony, too.

At last, she understood. Life, *her* life, suddenly made sense.

Grace had been looking for *him*. All her experiences, all the trials, the evils, the small successes had been bringing her closer to him—and to being the woman he needed, too.

She loved him.

And miracle of miracles, he loved her, too.

The world came back into focus in that persistent way. She melted into the comfortable softness of the mattress, playing with his hair, stroking it. His weight felt good on her.

He raised himself up to look down at her. Their noses were inches from each other. He smiled. She smiled back.

"I love you," he said.

Grace could have laughed with happiness and that wonderful sense of completion. "I have never loved anyone," she said. "But I love you, Richard Lynsted. I love you with all my being."

"You must," he agreed. "You've put up with my whiskers."

She ran the back of her fingers along this jaw. He turned his head and kissed them. "Let's have a bath now," Grace suggested. "And then I'll give you a shave."

The offer didn't need to be repeated. Richard rolled off her, scooped her up in his arms, carried her over to the fire, and lowered her into the tub of still hot water, but not before he'd threatened to drop her into it. She shrieked with laughter and gave him a kiss to behave.

He sat down beside the tub and picked up the soap.

"What are you doing?" she asked, knowing full well.

"I thought I'd give you a scrub."

"And then do I receive the opportunity to return the scrub?"

His smile widened. "I was hoping you'd offer." He reached for her foot, her most ticklish part, and scrubbed her up from there. It wasn't long before they were both in the tub together.

Later, Grace straddled his legs in the tub as she gave him a shave. She'd not done it before. Richard teased her by pretending to be nicked here and there, but overall, she believed she did a very good job. The task was a challenge with her subject intent on teasing her breasts and nibbling on her earlobes, her most sensitive spots.

But her favorite part of the evening came when they curled up in bed beside each other, their bodies spooned together, his arm resting protectively over her shoulder.

"So, what is the biggest difference?" she whispered, setting her wonderings to words.

"We are no longer alone," he answered, a yawn in his voice.

He was right. Her life had been busy and full of challenges so she had not realized how tired she was of always being alone. Even when there had been a man in her life, she'd been lonely because there had been no meaning in those relationships. None at all.

"I wish you'd been my first," she said.

He snuggled her closer, surrounding her with his masculine presence. "I am," he said confidently. "I'm the first you've loved."

That was so true. She was no longer alone. She was loved.

Grace rubbed her back against his chest and fell into a deep, untroubled sleep.

Richard was the first to wake.

The day was well under way when he opened his eyes. Grace still slept soundly and he didn't have the heart to wake her—although he was sorely tempted.

Instead, he watched her sleep, realizing her well-being meant more to him than his lust. *He loved her.* The words had a music all their own.

He wanted to marry her. He wanted her to be the woman to wear his ring. He couldn't imagine spending even one day more of his life without her as his wife.

Richard became a man with a mission. He would buy her a marriage ring. He knew a ring would surprise and please Grace. They could marry here in Lanark. He was certain the vicar at St. Nicholas would perform the ceremony. Banns were not needed in Scotland. For that reason, couples eloped here all the time.

But first, he had to have a ring.

He rose from the bed and hurriedly dressed. They were going to need some new clothes, too. Especially Grace. The dress she'd ripped wouldn't be decent much longer.

Shaving was a bit of a chore. Looking in the small mirror over the washstand he could see a number of places she missed and he had a good idea why. He'd done his best to distract her.

He rinsed off his razor, catching a glimpse of her in the mirror. She hugged the pillow like someone who enjoyed her sleep, whereas he never missed an early morning. But the difference, like all the others between them, made her more perfect to him. They were a team. When one was weak, the other strong. When one was afraid, the other bold.

The ring he'd buy would be a simple band. First, he'd arrange for their transportation to Inverness and with the rest settle his bill and buy the ring. Then, in London, where he would have easy access to his funds, he'd buy her the marriage ring of her dreams. And earrings and a necklace to match, he decided. He'd deck her with jewels from head to toe. He was a wealthy man and he wanted to spend it all on his wife.

As he left the room, closing the door quietly behind him, he wondered if she'd want sapphires the color of her eyes, or perhaps rubies. The bold red would look good against her skin and with her black hair.

Mrs. Fraley was sweeping out the taproom. "Good morning to you, Mr. Bull."

Richard laughed at the title, but didn't correct her. "Good morning. I need to settle the bill, Mrs. Fraley."

"You are going to break your fast, aren't you? Your wife needs her food for the bairn."

The baby. He'd forgotten their ruse.

In fact, by now it might not be a ruse. Grace might actually be carrying his child. The thought filled him with pride. *His* child. His family.

"Something must please you," Mrs. Fraley observed. "You have the largest smile across your face that I've seen on any a man."

"Yes, Mrs. Fraley, something has pleased me. It pleases me very much. We'll breakfast here but I want to do a bit of shopping. I'd like to buy a dress for my lady and a ring. I also need to hire a vehicle to take us to Inverness to meet her father. Where should I go to find all these things?"

The inn mistress directed him to the blacksmith on the other side of Lanark who could help with the horses and mentioned a dressmaker who often had items made up. The ring was more of a challenge. There had been a tinker in the market that carried gold.

"I'm assuming you want it of gold and not base metal?" she asked, her tone letting him know what his answer should be.

"I do."

"Then go to the field where you had your fight and see if the tinker is still there. His name is Liam. He's an Irishman and has the charm, although he'll talk your ear off, and you into a higher price if you let him."

"I won't let him."

"Good," she said, smiling her approval. "If your lady wakes, what should I tell her?"

"Don't tell her about the ring. That's a surprise. Just say I've gone to hire a vehicle to take us to her father's. That should be enough."

"Very well, sir."

Richard paid for their room and went off to see the blacksmith. There weren't any vehicles to be had around Lanark but he knew someone leaving for Glasgow after noon who could give him a ride there. "You can hire a fine post chaise in Glasgow," he told Richard and sent his son off to deliver a message to Angus Livingstone asking if he would like passengers. "He'll say yes. He saw your fight yesterday and will want to give you some tips." He said that last with a wink before turning back to his fire and anvil.

The dressmaker did have a frock that should fit Grace. The dress was the dark green of summer with a square neck trimmed in lace. The dressmaker had been refashioning it for a local woman who had decided she no longer liked the color. "Some women can never make up their minds," she confided to Richard.

"Would you wrap it up?"

"Certainly. And if it needs a stitch or two to make it right, bring her by," the dressmaker offered. "By the way, that was a good fight yesterday."

"Yes, thank you," Richard said.

The dressmaker didn't take more than a blink to wrap the dress in paper. Richard left the shop with a sense of pride over his purchase. He liked the color and thought it would suit Grace. He also liked having a woman in his life and buying gifts for her.

His next search was for the tinker. He caught Liam the Irish tinker in the field of yesterday's fight, just as Mrs. Fraley said he would. The man was readying to leave but was more than happy to open his cart when he heard what Richard wanted.

"A marriage ring," Liam said, searching through the boxes and bins in disarray inside his cart. "Keep them all here, well, I thought I did. I tell you a man would lose his nose, or something more important, if it wasn't attached to his body." He laughed at his own humor and went digging some more.

"Here it is," he said at last, pulling out of a tiny box a dirty wad of rag.

Richard wished now he'd not come. He'd been gone an hour. Grace might be up and wondering where he was. "That's all right. I don't really need the ring." He started to walk away but Liam grabbed his arm.

"Here it 'tis, right where I thought it would be," he said, pushing back the dirty cloth to reveal a ring of solid gold.

But it wasn't just any ring. Tiny, delicate leaves were carved into the design and after every third leaf was a Celtic symbol.

"It's a lover's knot," Liam said, pointing to the four symbols. "One to the north, one to the south, then the east and west. The symbol has no ending and no beginning. It means forever."

"I'll take it," Richard said, holding the ring to the light. The band was a delicate thing. It seemed tiny. He slipped the ring on his own hand, fitting it to the top of his little finger. "How much?"

"Ah, well, a ring like this . . . 'tis one of a kind."

"All I have is twenty pounds," Richard said.

"That hurts," Liam said, dramatically clutching his chest. "Look at the ring. I carried it straight from Ireland, I did. And you can only offer twenty pounds?"

"It's all I have," Richard answered, wise to the tinker's ways. He handed the ring back to the man. "Thank you."

He turned away, started to walk off when Liam called him back. "Very well, twenty pounds but only because I have a soft spot in my heart for a lover—and because you did so well in that fight yesterday."

Richard pulled out the coins before the tinker could change his mind. With a good day, he set off with his purchases, very pleased with himself.

Grace would adore the ring and the idea of marrying her before they left for Glasgow took greater hold in his mind, so his step was light as he hurried back to the Thistle.

As he approached the inn, he saw a movement in an upstairs window and recognized Grace. She caught sight of him and opened the window. Her hair was loose and free over one shoulder. She was wearing the blue dress with the ripped bodice.

"I have something for you," he said proudly, holding up his dress package.

Her eyes lit up. "Bring it to me."

He laughed and ducked into the inn, nodding

to two old men who had taken up residence on a bench outside the door. He took the steps up to their room two at a time.

Grace was holding the door open, waiting for him. He held out the dress package. She carried it into the room and ripped off the paper.

Her breath caught. She raised the dress, shaking it out. "This is lovely," she said. She held it up to her person.

"Will it fit?" Richard asked, a bit anxious. "The dressmaker said we could stop by and she'd take a stitch or two if it didn't."

Her answer was to give him a big loving kiss. "Let's see if it fits," she said and started to undress.

Of course, then she couldn't try on the dress because Richard couldn't help himself and went for another kiss . . . which led them back to the bed.

Holding her in his arms, he toyed with the idea of giving her the ring now. He decided against it. Offering the ring shouldn't be like a man giving presents to a mistress. It should be done with some formality, some style. He decided he'd do it over breakfast.

Rising from the bed, he gave her another kiss and began to dress. "You take your time," he told her. "I'll go down and tell Mrs. Farley we are almost ready for breakfast."

"Wait," Grace answered. "I won't take long to dress, plus I could use your help tying the sash on the dress."

She was true to her word. Grace wasn't a fussy woman, nor did she need to be. She threw the dress over her head. "It's a bit long and a tad snug here," she said, indicating her bodice. "But I don't think you will mind."

"Not one complaint," Richard agreed. The dress was spectacular on her. The high waist emphasized the fullness of her breasts. The sleeves were short with the same lace trim as the bodice and the material was such that the skirt seemed to move and sway with her every movement.

"It's so elegant," Grace said as he tied the sash into a low bow the way she instructed him to do since such a style was all the rage. She stepped back, holding her arms open. "What do you think?"

"I believe I have very good taste," he said.

She laughed. "I agree." She folded her old dress and picked up her cape. "Let's go for our breakfast. I'm starving."

"And when we reach the dining room, I have another surprise," Richard said.

"What is it?" Grace asked.

"Downstairs," he insisted.

She threw open the door. "Then let's go."

They went downstairs, laughing and arguing over which one was the more hungry and could eat the most.

However the laughter stopped as they entered the dining room. They had visitors.

His father and his uncle sat at a table drinking cider and coffee. They wore traveling clothes and their boots were muddy as if they had ridden very hard. His uncle noticed him first.

"Richard, at last we've caught up with each other."

His father rose from his chair. His face was pale and he looked very tired.

Not his uncle. He was the picture of good humor and health. "Please, sit down and join us," he invited. "We ran into a traveling fighter and their manager in Glasgow last night who had unkind words to say about John Bull. Your father and I sensed it was you. I say, I'm glad to see you took my advice, nephew, and have been enjoying your time with Miss MacEachin. Well done." He gave her a wink before adding, "There are some wagers on the betting books that will pay off handsomely—but you already knew that."

Chapter Eighteen

*G*race was absolutely certain Lord Maven was baiting her. She had more faith in her man than that. Richard was incapable of using a word like "love" lightly.

So she found it easy to keep her composure and walk into the room, holding out her hand to say, "Good morning, Lord Maven, did you bring your murderous coachman with you? And, Lord Brandt, have you hired a new valet yet?"

Her words wiped the smirk off Lord Maven's face. The brothers exchanged glances.

In truth, she found it eerie how similar the twins looked in appearance. Even the lines of their faces seemed marked in the same places. And the way they were looking at each other just now, as if they could communicate without words, was also unsettling.

Richard came up behind her, placing reassuring hands on her shoulders. "Father, I need to know, did you order Herbert to murder Miss MacEachin?"

His father turned from his twin. His gaze landed on Richard's hand on Grace's shoulders before he looked back up and said soberly, "Yes, Richard, I did."

For a second, Grace didn't believe her ears. She had been right, but she felt no elation. If anything his father's matter-of-fact admission sickened her.

Richard's hand squeezed her shoulder. "Well, then you will understand why we can't stay a second more under the same roof together. Come, Grace." He started out the door with her at his side.

"Don't be dramatic," his uncle said, stepping into their path.

"By your order, Herbert attempted to kill her and almost cost me my life," Richard continued. "And you are accusing me of being dramatic? Be honest, uncle, my death would not sadden you. You have considered me an intrusion since I was born. Perhaps you have hoped Miss MacEachin and I die together."

"*I* would not see you harmed, Richard," his father said. "And you are unfair to Stephen. You are our heir, for God's sake. It all became a bit carried away."

"Yes, why would we wish to lose the one man who knows *all* our business affairs," his uncle chimed in. Grace detested his flippancy. "After all, a man must do what he must to protect his interests."

"Apparently I didn't know all," Richard said. "I didn't know about your roles stealing Dame Mary Ewing's money. Perhaps you should have had me murdered . . . since you will be handling your financial matters alone in the future."

Grace was so proud of him she could have kissed him. He started to walk out again.

"*Wait*," his father called out. "Richard, you deserve to hear the full story. You *owe* us that much. If after hearing our tale you wish to leave, then go with our blessing."

"Yes, Richard. A hearing. That's all we ask," his uncle agreed.

Richard stood in indecision and Grace knew he had to hear the story. But she had one important question. "Did you send the men who attacked me after my final performance?"

"No," Richard's father said. "We were surprised to hear of the attack, and I'll be honest enough to admit we were not disappointed by it. But it did give us the idea to have you disappear on the road to Scotland."

"Why should we believe you?" Richard asked. "Thinking back, I didn't sense you were so terribly surprised when I told you of the attack."

"That's because we'd heard the rumors," his uncle said. "We were hoping someone else would take care of Miss MacEachin for us."

"And what were the rumors?" Richard demanded.

"That Lord Stone had had enough of Miss MacEachin's ignoring his gifts and flowers. His besetting sin is pride and he bragged to everyone he would bed her. They said he was thinking to do things the rough way by kidnapping her. He was to be out of town for several days but had invited a party of men to his hunting lodge for what he promised would be a grand treat. I believe, Miss MacEachin, *you* were to be the treat."

Her stomach turned at the thought of it.

"However, a curious thing happened with Stone," his father continued. "He disappeared for several days but showed up in someone's hay bin. He'd been bound and gagged, so no one knew he was there. I suppose pride kept him from making too much of a fuss. Anyway, he was dumped into the bin and no one was the wiser until a stable lad went to feed the horses and out popped Stone's head."

His uncle started laughing. "They said after they took the gag off, they wanted to put it back on because he was so foul."

"And did he say what happened?" Richard asked, his voice carefully neutral.

"He refuses to discuss the matter," his uncle replied. "You went to school with him, didn't you, nephew?"

"I did. We weren't friends."

"The man has very few," his uncle agreed. "By the way, a number of people saw the set down you gave him. Word is all over London, along with speculation over who threw him into the hay wagon."

Richard didn't answer . . . but Grace sensed the twins knew and respected him for it. *She* certainly did.

His father turned to her. "Miss MacEachin, my twin and I are wise enough to know when we've been bested. You know your story could ruin us. But please, you and Richard, sit and hear our side. It is the least you should do before passing judgment."

Grace knew if she made a move toward the door, Richard would go with her. He was that loyal.

However, a part of her wanted to know what the twins would say after denying even knowing her father. She moved toward the chair Lord Maven held out.

Mrs. Fraley entered the room, noticed she had new customers and came rushing over to the table with breakfast plates for Lord Maven and Lord Brandt. She smiled, her expression warm and sunny. "Are you ready for yours and the missus's?" she asked Richard.

"Yes, we are," he answered.

Lord Maven waited until Mrs. Fraley had left to say, "The missus?" He started laughing.

Grace ignored him. She looked to Richard's father. "Tell me the story. Richard says you never were in Scotland but that isn't true, is it?"

"No," the man admitted. "Stephen and I were both in Inverness at the time that Dame Mary's fortune went missing."

"And did you steal it, Father?"

Lord Brandt had trouble meeting his son's eye. His uncle had no such difficulty. "We did. But not in the way you believe it to be."

"What other way of stealing is there?" Richard demanded, but the question went unanswered as Mrs. Fraley returned to the table with more plates loaded with food.

She set the heaviest plate in front of Grace. "You are eating for two." She looked around the table. "Is there anything else I can be finding for you?"

"We are fine," Richard answered.

The inn mistress bobbed a quick curtsey and left.

"Eating for two?" Lord Maven said.

"It's quite a story," Richard answered, not even flinching under his uncle's curiosity. "Let's hear your tale first."

His uncle sighed, folded his napkin and placed it on the table. "Do you tell him, Gregory, or do I?"

"You may."

Leaning an arm on the table, Richard's uncle started in, "We went to Inverness on a fishing trip. The truth was we were dodging our creditors. We'd invested in a ship that had not returned. We'd gone flat out on it. Gambled all, and the ship disappeared. There hadn't been a word of it and it was three months late coming into port. While on our fishing expedition, we met Reverend Jonathon MacEachin. We became friends, and he confided he needed advice. One of his parishioners, Dame Mary Ewing, was advancing in years. Indeed, she was very frail and often confused. She was also very wealthy and she wished for him to help her handle her finances. Supposedly, one of her servants had stolen a large sum from her and she didn't want to have it happen again. She asked the good reverend to serve as her man of business."

"Why did he go to you?" Richard asked, the same question Grace was wondering.

"He had no experience in these matters and we did, even if our own finances were teetering precariously," his father answered. "We sat down with Reverend MacEachin and Dame Mary and advised them both on how such a relationship should work. That's all we did."

"*Nonsense*," Grace said, the word exploding out of her. She'd not touched her meal. She had no appetite for it.

"Here we go again," Lord Maven muttered, pushing back his chair. "At last you can see how difficult she is," he told Richard. "She refuses to believe us."

"What is wrong with their story, Grace?" Richard asked.

"Because there is more to it," she said. "Your names came up in the court documents and the money went missing after you met with my father." Their explanation did help her understand some of the missing pieces of information. "Besides, if it was all so innocent, you would have said so in the beginning and be done with me. There's more here you are not telling."

Richard's father drew a long drink from his tankard. He set it town, his hands cupping the pewter mug, as he looked over at his twin.

"Tell her all," Lord Maven said. "It doesn't matter."

"Obviously, it does," Grace answered, "or else you would be out with it by now."

"Dame Mary had a sizeable fortune," Richard's father said. "And she wasn't certain of all of her accounts. We helped Reverend MacEachin document them and gave him some advice. Dame Mary was a very generous woman. She trusted easily." He looked right at Grace as he said these statements as if he wanted to impress upon her their import. "We had some investments we wanted to make. Opportunities we couldn't take advantage of because of our funds being tied up with that deuced ship—"

"So you helped yourselves to her money and let Father carry the blame," Grace said, elated to at last have the truth.

"*No*," Richard's father answered. "Dame Mary considered the money a gift."

"A gift?" Grace repeated, letting her disbelief show.

"Yes, Miss MacEachin, a gift. Or you could say a payment for services performed. After all, she and the reverend asked us questions that we answered. The money came at a fortuitous time. It righted our fortunes and provided the stake that Richard has used to multiply our accounts tenfold."

Grace couldn't sit at the table any longer. She stood. "Who would give such a generous gift? My mother was right. You took the money and my father paid the price."

"Miss MacEachin, your father was found guilty in a court of law," Richard's father said.

"An *English* court," Grace said. "*English* law."

"Only because that is where Dame Mary's relatives filed their claim." Lord Maven pushed his chair back in anger.

"Then if you are so innocent, why are you here?" Grace challenged. "Why did you want to stop Richard from hearing the truth?"

"Because it doesn't sound good," his father answered, his own temper growing heated. "It sounds as if we were taking advantage of a senile woman—"

"You *were* taking advantage of her," Grace stated flatly.

"Not according to the law," his father flashed back. "And I like to think we've done good things with the money. Invested it wisely."

"But it wasn't yours to invest," she countered.

"On the contrary," his uncle said, "it was, and,

unlike your father, no court found us guilty of taking it without permission."

"If you are so innocent, why would you fear my telling the story to a magistrate?" she challenged.

"Because we have our share of enemies, Miss MacEachin," his father said. "Certainly you can appreciate our situation. My brother and I decided early on to reject the lavish lifestyle celebrated by most of our contemporaries. We prefer piety and a moral code. When a man makes that sort of decision, he is judged harshly by his fellows. They don't like being reminded that we are all sinners. If word of your accusations, true or not, reached the papers, our reputations would be ruined."

Richard stirred on that statement. "And perhaps there is a bit of guilt mixed in there as well, Father? For all of your fine posturing, you and my uncle are not above taking shortcuts where money is concerned, moral code or not. After all, you've already admitted to attempting murder."

Grace wanted to kiss him for that statement.

The color drained from his father's face. "We became carried away. A man's reputation, Richard . . . it's worth more than gold."

But his twin wasn't so contrite. He turned to Grace, his eyes alive with dislike. "Let's talk truth. On whose information do you base your accusations? Has your father made them?"

"Yes. He told me that he was unjustly accused. You ruined his life and mine. A *gift*?" She infused the word with disdain. "All that he should have had, should have been, you stole from him when you let him pay the price for your thievery."

His uncle came to his feet. "Miss MacEachin, you go too far."

"I don't go far enough, or you would be locked up by now, Lord Maven."

Richard had stood, too. He was at Grace's side.

His father leaned his elbows on the table, burying his head in his hands. "I knew it would come to this, Stephen. I warned you. I said it would be this way."

"Only because Miss MacEachin is the daughter of a lying clergyman," his twin answered.

Grace wanted to carve his tongue out for the insult. Richard caught her arm before she could attack. "You owe her an apology, uncle."

"Do I?" His uncle shook his head. "Years ago we helped MacEachin. Were we more than handsomely rewarded for our services, mayhap even excessively so? Of course. But we were anxious to put our mark on the world and no funds to do so. And then, here was this dotty old woman and her conniving clergyman anxious to give us money, and we took it. Were we a touch greedy? Perhaps."

"And we have paid dearly for involving our-selves with Dame Mary and your father," Richard's father said, rising from his chair. He held a beseeching hand out as if begging her to under-stand. "When the charges were made against your father, we feared we'd be roped into his misdeeds, too. We prepared ourselves. And then nothing. No one charged us."

"*My father charged you.*"

"No, he didn't. Not in any court." Richard's father took a step around the table toward her. "I don't know what he told you or your mother, but he never implicated us—"

"Because we are innocent," his twin finished for him.

Grace didn't believe them. "If you are so in-nocent, then why wouldn't you want Richard to know the truth?"

"For the reason you don't believe us," his father said. "A cynical mind would assume we had access to Dame Mary's fortune and applied pres-sure, *but we did not.*"

Richard stepped in front of her. "Enough," he said. "There is one way to discover the truth, and that is for all of us to go to Inverness as we are planning to do."

"The truth?" his uncle muttered. "The truth for her is whatever she wishes it to be."

"Miss MacEachin is a forthright and honest woman," Richard returned in her defense.

"Is that so?" his uncle challenged. "Then why is she pretending to be your wife, *Mr. Bull*? And what is this I hear about a babe on the way? Not that I don't think there couldn't be one from the activities I suspect you have both enjoyed—"

"Mind your tongue, Uncle," Richard said, his voice a growl.

His uncle turned away with an angry wave of his hand. He looked to his brother. "I can't wait until he and Abigail Montross are married. I thought he should enjoy himself, but I didn't expect him to be so foolish as to not understand the tart's place in his life."

"Who is Abigail Montross?" Grace asked, her mind catching on the name. Had his uncle said Richard was to be married?

Richard had taken a step toward his uncle, the green coming out in his eyes in his fury—but he pulled up short at her question.

Before he could answer, his father said in a matter-of-fact voice, "She's the young woman he's betrothed to. They are to marry this summer."

Marry.

The word echoed in her ears and Grace was stunned at how much she'd been counting on Richard's honesty.

But he wasn't honest. He was going to marry and he'd not said a word to her . . . because?

A list of reasons came to her mind—that she didn't matter, that he considered her a whore, a plaything, damaged goods.

Richard turned to her. "Grace, it's not what you are thinking."

She walked out of the dining room, and she kept walking. She walked right out the door and into the street. She didn't know where she was going, but she had to walk. Something was wrong with her mind. It couldn't seem to accept the idea that Richard was marrying. She should have known better. Of course he would marry. He was at the age when a wealthy young man like himself is expected to meet the altar—

But she had believed him when he'd said he loved her.

She believed.

"Grace," he called, running up behind her. She was tempted to lift her skirts and start running. She didn't do that. She had more dignity than to race through the streets. Instead, she kept walking, her head high.

"Stop, will you?" he demanded, falling into step beside her.

She ignored him and kept walking.

"I've been betrothed to Abigail Montross for years. She means nothing to me and I mean nothing to her. We barely speak. That's one of the reasons there hasn't been a wedding. Neither one of us cares."

Grace frowned, a torrent of words aching to unleash themselves on him while a cold numbness started creeping through her.

"You must talk to me about this," Richard said. When she still didn't stop, he grabbed her arm and turned her to face him.

That's when Grace lost all civility, all sense. She hit him with the flat of hand. Slapped his shoulder, his arm, his chest. He refused to let go.

"Yes, hit me, Grace. Hit me hard. You are angry, as you well should be—"

She stomped her heel on the toe of his boot with all the weight in her five-foot, three-inch frame.

That made him let go—only she didn't run away. At last her feelings found a voice.

"Why didn't you tell me? Why weren't you honest with me?"

"Because I didn't think about her. *You* are all I think about."

"If that isn't a greedy, conniving male answer, I've never heard one," Grace shot back. "I *loved* you. Of course, that's what you wanted, wasn't it?

For me to lose all good sense so that you could worm your way into my bed. Here I am, finally having a sense of self-respect, and I meet you."

His brows came together. "Grace, you know that wasn't the way it was." He reached out to her.

She shook off his arm. "I know no such thing." But instead of keeping her distance, she moved in closer. What she had to say was for him alone. "I *trusted* you."

He pulled back, as if the words struck him harder than her blows.

"You knew I wanted a different life," she told him. "What sort of woman I wanted to become. And you took advantage of that." She gave him a hard shove with both hands. "Don't come near me. I want nothing to do with you."

"But, Grace, I love you," he said. "Do you hear me? *I love you*." He practically shouted the words as if not caring who overheard him on the busy street.

"You don't know what love is," she told him and started to walk away.

However, Lord Maven and Lord Brandt had caught up with them. They blocked her path.

She gave them a brittle smile. "Excuse me, my lords." She would have gone around them but Lord Maven held out his arm.

"A moment of your time, Miss MacEachin. I

understand you are upset with my nephew. However, we still have the issue of you believing my brother and I are responsible for a crime. I suggest we solve this matter now by continuing up to Inverness and speaking to your father."

"I'll speak to him once I arrive there," she replied coolly, wanting to put distance between herself and Richard.

"On the contrary," his father said, "we've hired a vehicle, we have money. Why not travel with us in style rather than . . . what? Beg rides all the way to Inverness?"

Grace raised her hands to her head, her temples pounding. They were right. She didn't have a shilling to her name. "I don't want to ride with him. I want nothing to do with him."

"He will ride up in the box with Dawson," his uncle offered magnanimously. "You won't even have to look at him."

"Grace, you are being ridiculous," Richard said. "Just listen to what I have to say—"

She cut him off by holding a hand palm up against him. She looked at Lord Brandt and Lord Maven. "When will we leave?"

"As soon as you are ready," Lord Brandt said.

"I'm ready now. Where is the coach?" She didn't wait for an answer but spun on her heel and marched back toward the inn, where common sense said the coach would be. As she left them, she overheard his uncle say, "I told you to bed her, nephew, not fall in love with her."

Grace didn't hear Richard's reply.

They were a day and a half's travel to Inverness. True to their word, the twins kept Richard away from her. He didn't ride in the box but rode on a hired horse alongside the coach. His father and uncle rode with him.

Grace sat in the hired coach, alone.

She wouldn't let herself think or feel when it came to Richard Lynsted. For his part, he seemed to know she wanted nothing to do with him. He kept his distance and yet his presence was always with her.

For the first time in her life, she experienced a broken heart, and she never wanted to fall in love again if this was the result.

That night, she climbed into bed in the private room the twins had procured for her at an inn, and slept like the dead. She didn't want to open her eyes in the morning. Sweet oblivion was so much better than the pain that made it difficult for her heart to beat.

But Grace was no coward. She rose, dressed, and put her best face on. They had brought the bags that had been on the coach when Dawson had taken off so she had her clothing and personal items. She changed into a light blue walking dress and left the vivid green gown on the bed. She didn't want it.

Nor was she anxious to break her fast once she saw Richard waiting downstairs for her.

She started to turn and walk back to her room but he stopped her by saying, "Running, Grace?"

That straightened her back. She faced him. "From you? Yes. I am. You aren't good for me, Mr. Lynsted. You aren't the sort of person with whom I wish to involve myself."

"With whom?" He shook his head. "I remember being accused of being priggish when I used such stilted English. You didn't hesitate to mock me. So what is it now, Grace? Have we switched roles? Are you now the one hiding behind indifference?"

Her response was to march down the stairs and into the small dining room without a sideways glance at him.

Once they were on the road, Grace kept her mind busy by remembering her father the last time she'd seen him. He'd been thin and had acted defeated. Her mother had just left, he was having trouble finding work, and Grace herself had been young and very angry. Her mother's sudden defection had been a betrayal, one she'd felt somewhat responsible for, since she was no longer the virginal daughter who could have married well and improved their lot.

Before she'd left, Grace had done everything she could to make him pay for what she felt were her own shortcomings. And then she had run away, certain there was a better life for her elsewhere. She'd been very wrong.

Grace tried to imagine how life had treated him while she was gone. He must have been lonely without wife or daughter. She prayed he'd found work and had earned respect. She was certain he'd been eaten alive with anger over the unfairness of his sentence. Certainly she and her mother had been. But would it have broken him completely?

Guilt for running away and leaving him rested heavily on her, especially now that it was coupled with uncertainty. Lord Brandt and Lord Maven made a convincing argument of their innocence, but of course they would. They had everything to gain by convincing her they were blameless.

One thing Grace had learned over her years of wandering—no one is completely pure. The twins were fooling themselves if they thought she believed their story. After all, her father was blood. He was where her loyalty lay, and by the time they reached Inverness, she could easily picture her father on his deathbed, waiting for her so he could beg forgiveness before he breathed his last.

She heard Richard asking for directions to the home of Jonathon MacEachin. She didn't expect anyone to know immediately, so was a bit surprised when the man he asked said MacEachin's home was by St. Ann's Church.

Grace let down the window and leaned out. "Did you say St. Ann's?" she asked.

"Aye, missus, I did," the man said. He was a ruddy-cheeked man of good Scottish stock and didn't appear to be one for telling stories. St. Ann's was where her father had been the vicar before his trial.

"What does he do there?" she asked.

"Why, missus, he's the sexton."

Grace sat back in the coach, a bit stunned that the church had taken her father in. Her once proud father who had run the parish was now reduced to being its caretaker.

The coach went forward. The sights along the street were all familiar to Grace. She'd avoided returning to Inverness, avoided any of the memories.

They turned a corner and there was St. Ann's.

The coach came to a halt. Grace didn't wait for someone to open the door but opened it herself.

She hopped down from the coach and followed the stone path through the cemetery that led to the sexton's cottage in the back.

She knew it well. There had been a time when her mother had lamented not being able to move into the modest cottage.

Grace knocked on the door. She sensed Richard and the others followed but she wanted to be the first to see her father. Tears threatened. It had been a long time.

The door opened, but a young woman no older than Grace stood there. She was blond, rosy cheeked, well fed, and very obviously pregnant. Two dark-headed children, the oldest around the age of four, came running into the cottage's main room to see who was visiting. They came to a halt and hung back shyly at the sight of Grace.

She smiled at them and then turned to their mother. "Excuse me," she said. "I'm looking for Jonathon MacEachin. I thought this was his residence."

"It is," said the woman. "I'm his wife."

Chapter Nineteen

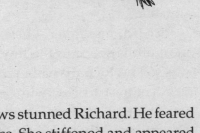

The woman's news stunned Richard. He feared their impact on Grace. She stiffened and appeared ready to collapse. He stepped to her side, reaching for her arm, but she shook her head and moved away from him.

Mrs. MacEachin noticed the current of tension between them, and then her gaze narrowed on Grace. *Did she know who she was?*

His uncle had a huge grin on his face. He obviously enjoyed the surprise. "Is Mr. MacEachin in?" he asked the wife.

"May I tell him who is calling?" she asked.

"Old friends," his uncle answered.

Mrs. MacEachin frowned. She was not a fool

nor easily pleased by his uncle's smile. Grace hadn't moved, so Richard said, "Please, we'd like a moment of his time."

His request, or his tone of voice, reassured her. "Thomas," she said to her oldest son, a wide-eyed lad of four. "Go fetch your father. He's working on that drain ditch."

"I know, Mother," the lad said, and took off out the door at a run, as if sensing the urgency of the situation.

Richard, his father, uncle, and Grace took up most of the space in the tiny cottage. The ceiling was so low, Richard had to stoop.

In contrast to his twin's gleeful enjoyment of the situation, Richard's father seemed subdued. He surveyed their surroundings and then said to Grace with a surprising empathy, "Here, we'll wait outside. Come, Stephen."

Stephen appeared reluctant to leave, but at his twin's silent insistence, sighed heavily and went out the door. Looking to Richard, his father asked, "Coming with us?"

Grace seemed oblivious to Richard. Instead, her gaze was on the child Mrs. MacEachin had picked up, a girl of about two who had Grace's same wild, black, curls.

Richard wasn't about to leave Grace alone. The

color had returned to her face and she seemed to be breathing easier again—but who knew what other surprises awaited her? "I'll stay here."

"Please sit," Mrs. MacEachin offered, indicating the rocking chair and an upholstered chair before the hearth. "May I fix you something to drink? A lovely cup of tea? I had the kettle boiling before you knocked."

Grace didn't answer so he spoke for her. "Thank you, that would be nice." Neither he nor Grace sat.

Mrs. MacEachin acted happy to have something to do. She sat her daughter down, handed her a rag doll that had seen much love, and set to work at brewing their tea. The child gathered her doll under one arm and placed her thumb in her mouth. She watched the visitors as she sucked, the small frown line between her eyes reminding Richard of Grace.

The cottage was neat as a pin and very obviously a happy home. The leaded-glass windows shone as a testimony to Mrs. MacEachin's housekeeping and the stone floor was covered with colorful hand-braided rugs. All of the furniture was sturdy and serviceable but marked with good use. Family meals had been served around the supper table, where the children had been free to be themselves and the scuffs on the bench showed it.

There were two rooms off to the side, bedrooms. Richard could see the corner of a crib through the door.

Mrs. MacEachin handed them their tea in pottery mugs. She didn't pour a mug for herself. Instead, she moved back beside her child.

Richard took a sip. "It's good. Thank you."

Grace stood studying her father's wife. She didn't lift the mug in her hand.

A few moments later Richard heard a man's voice outside the door. MacEachin. He'd recognized his father and uncle. There wasn't much said, and then he entered the cottage.

Grace's father was a thin man with deep lines in his face. His sparkling blue eyes were much like Grace's . . . except his held a sense of peace.

For a long moment he and Grace stared at each other, two strangers. Finally, he looked to his wife. "Eileen, would you take the children outside for a walk?"

"Yes, Jon, I will." She still did not know who Grace was, and her husband did not seem to feel a need to introduce her. That action alone said louder than words her father's attitude toward her.

And that is when Richard understood. Grace had longed for family. She'd returned to prove her love to her father. Richard knew all too well that need. Hadn't he undertaken this trip to demonstrate his love to *his* father? Hadn't he longed for the moment when, just once, his father placed Richard's opinion over that of his twin's?

It would never happen. The bonds between the twins were stronger than the ties of father and son—and a man's responsibility to a woman bearing his child would always take precedence over his care for his daughter.

Grace sank down on the bench at the table. A graceful movement of capitulation. She already knew she'd lost. She set the mug down. Her father's wife left the cottage with the children. Through the opening and closing of the door, Richard could see the twins, their heads together as they stood by the coach, waiting.

Jonathon MacEachin pulled the upholstered chair toward the table so he could sit facing his daughter. "You are looking well, Grace."

She didn't answer.

He continued, "Eileen has been a godsend to me. She helped me reclaim a part of my old life. I've also been blessed with more children. They've made my life good."

"But you *had* a wife," she said simply.

"A wife who went on with her own life as if I wasn't there," he answered.

"You were a man of God," Grace said.

"That was a long time ago," he replied. "A man

doesn't stop living because his wife leaves him."

"But you are *married* to my mother," she insisted.

He shrugged. "Not in my mind. A man doesn't need a court to tell him his marriage is over. After all, your mother took a husband, too. No harm, I say."

"I've been singing in London," she said, her voice faint. She dropped her gaze to her hands, lying useless in her lap.

"So I've heard," her father said.

Grace raised her eyes to meet his. "You've heard? And you have done nothing to contact me?"

There wasn't a moment's hesitation or remorse. "You are the one who left, Grace."

"I was confused."

Her father shrugged. "I know. Your mother taking off the way she did in a cloud of accusations and complaints was difficult. Georgina blamed me for so much. Funny how she waited until I returned to leave."

Richard thought of the rape, wondered if the man knew. Grace's hand as she reached up and pushed the handle of her mug shook slightly. He suspected she wondered the same thing. He sat on the bench beside her and covered her hand with his own. Her eyes followed up his arm, and then to his face as if just realizing he was in the room.

"He knew I was singing in London," Grace whispered to Richard as if she could not believe he'd not wanted to make contact.

Before Richard could answer, she looked back to her father, her composure returning. "I brought this gentleman to you, Father. His name is Richard Lynsted."

Mr. MacEachin appeared startled. "Brandt's son."

"Aye," Richard said. He didn't like MacEachin or the way the man was handling this reunion. Grace was better off without him.

"I want you to tell him your story, Father," Grace said. "I want him to hear the truth about what happened to Dame Mary's money."

A great sadness settled over MacEachin. "Grace, no good will come from going there."

"*The truth*, Father." She paused and Richard realized she was no longer certain of the story. "I want them to hear the truth," she reiterated.

Her father sat back in his chair. "I've paid for this, Grace, with my hard work and days, months, years of my life. It is over and done."

"*Not* for me."

He let his gaze drift around the room. The clock on the mantel measured the moments passing.

Then, with a heavy sigh, MacEachin said, "I told you a lie, lass. I didn't want you to think the worst of me. I was scared back then. Your mother had left, doors were closed to both of us. I saw how it was then for the two of you when I was gone. I knew the story your mother wanted to believe, and I thought we needed a scapegoat to bolster our spirits a wee bit. I didn't think you'd leave."

"I couldn't stay. I was ruined. You were so good and had been so strong, and then mother left and I—" Her voice broke off, but she didn't cry. Instead, her jaw tightened with that resolve Richard admired. "There was nothing for me here."

Jonathon MacEachin's shoulders slumped and then he said, "I know. Georgina told me. I should have done something. A man wants to protect his daughter but I wasn't here. I was afraid if I took up the matter after I returned . . ." He stopped, letting the words hang in the air.

Grace finished them. "They'd transport you again," she said.

"I knew you understood, lass," he said with obvious relief. "You were always a good, clever child."

"How would you know, Father? You weren't around me as a child."

The accusation hit its mark and Richard was glad it had. He'd silently measured her father as a man and found him lacking.

MacEachin looked away. "I'm a good father to my new bairn."

And Grace no longer mattered.

"Does this wife know you are still married to another woman?" she asked, her voice tight.

Her father frowned. "No. Neither does anyone else. I put out that your mother died. I said she left me but had an accident and it was a blessing she never recovered."

"I see," Grace said. "So you rejected your wife and defied the church, even though you live in its shadow. And what of me? How did you explain my leaving?"

"You were a willful child, Grace. No one doubted you didn't have the mettle to strike out on your own. Of course, you were well known in Inverness. Pretty girls always are. Robbie Carlin went down to London and came back to tell us all how you are the rage. The Scottish Songbird. You always had a good voice, Grace. Even when you were a wee thing." He held his hand up to show a child no taller than a toddler. "And I'm glad you are doing well. As you can see, we are bursting at the seams here. It's good you are on your own. Eileen likes having babies."

"But what if *I* needed you, Father?"

His studied the toes of his scuffed boots. "I'm

happy, Grace. I assume your mother is happy. You must see to yourself, lass. You must find your own happiness. I can't do it for you."

With those words, he cut his daughter loose. Beneath the protection of his hand resting over hers, Richard felt her fingers curl into a fist. However, her face betrayed no emotion. She pulled her hand from his and came to her feet. "You are right. I knew that. One thing, Father. You haven't said the words yet. Did you take Dame Mary's money?"

Her father's glance slid to the window, where they could see Richard's father and uncle waiting beside the coach. "I did," he admitted, without looking at her. "Your mother was expensive. She wanted and wanted. *I* wanted her happy. I want all my women happy. And then there was Dame Mary at the end of her life with more money than she could ever spend. The temptation was too great."

Thoughtfully, Grace ran her hand along the grain of the table. And then she said softly, "Good luck to you, Father."

"And to you, Daughter."

She had not turned to Richard, barely looked at him. He waited, willing her to do so. Instead, she walked out of the cottage.

There was a moment of silence. MacEachin gave him a thin smile. "Why are you here?"

"Your daughter thought you were innocent," Richard said, barely able to contain his contempt for the man. "She thought my uncle and father were the guilty ones."

"They *are* guilty. As guilty as I was," her father said. "Dame Mary had a large estate. We all did well."

"But at what cost?" Richard wondered.

"Ask your father and uncle. They have done well. Better than I . . . although I'm happy now. I am what I am. I've paid the price for my actions. Whereas your father and uncle—well, they are satisfied with themselves, but then they always have been." MacEachin's face hardened. "I have a second chance now for happiness. I don't wish Grace ill, but there is no room in my life for her. A songbird. Thank God, Georgina isn't here to know what her daughter has become."

"Or her husband," Richard answered, his dislike of the man complete. He walked out of the cottage.

His uncle and father stood by the horses.

"Well that is that," his uncle said, sounding chipper as Richard approached. "Apparently, Miss MacEachin no longer favors your suit, nephew. She's taken off down the road. Just as well. We need to return to London for that meeting with Hockingdale. Let's not forget how much is at stake."

His father turned to mount with Dawson's help. After he was saddled up and saw Richard hadn't moved, he said, "Son, we need to leave. We are pragmatic men. We take advantage of opportunity. That's what business is."

Richard could have raged out at him. Informed him he was wrong—but why?

Nothing would change.

Except he had. There had been a time when all he would have thought of was the business. It was all he'd had.

"I don't believe I'm returning to London," Richard informed them. "You go on without me."

For the first time in his life, Richard saw his uncle appear shocked. "You can't say that."

"I just did," Richard answered.

"What of Hockingdale?" his father asked. "The ledgers, the businesses? You put them together. No one knows them better than you."

"You'll manage," Richard said cheerfully. "As for myself, I believe from here on out, I'm going to live my life as I wish."

"And what would that be?" his uncle asked.

"Practice law."

"That's senseless," his father answered.

Richard smiled. "Have a safe trip to London. I'll send a letter to Mother with my good-byes."

His father kicked his horse around to block Richard's path. "She won't have a thing to do with you," he predicted.

Richard thought of his mother the last time he'd actually had a conversation with her, before she'd started numbing herself senseless on laudanum. He couldn't judge her harshly. Had he not been in danger of shutting himself off completely from the world? Only his method had been the family business and his loyalty to his father . . . a father who currently was staring at him as if he'd lost his senses. Richard laughed. "Actually, Father, I believe she will understand far more than you could imagine."

He started walking in the direction they'd indicated Grace had taken. She'd gone toward the river and the center of town.

"And what do I tell Banker Montross?" Richard's father demanded. "He'll be furious you jilted his daughter. He may not support the Hockingdale business."

"My uncle is glib," Richard said. "He'll come up with a reason. Or better yet, tell Banker Montross I was wanted for murder. That fact should give any father pause."

"And have you no heart for Abigail?" his father wondered.

"Father, Abigail knew you better than she did me. I'm doing her a favor. Now she is free to find a man she knows and can respect. A man she can love."

He started walking again.

Jonathon MacEachin stood in the cottage doorway. He'd probably heard all. Richard didn't give a damn. The man meant nothing to him and would never be part of his life.

Instead, his focus was on catching Grace.

Richard found her standing on a stone bridge, her head bowed as if she were studying something in the rushing water beneath her. She was a lone, pensive figure amongst the late-afternoon foot traffic.

Gathering his courage, he moved toward her. He knew she could send him packing. She probably would . . . but he had to speak to her. He had to gamble all.

When he drew close, she spoke. "I'm not surprised you followed. I knew you would." She faced him, her eyes shiny with unshed tears. "After all, you stayed with me during that awful interview inside my father's house." She paused, released her breath. "I truly thought him innocent. All these years I believed in him."

Richard shrugged. "It is what you make of it."

"I wasn't expecting a wife," she admitted. "I felt foolish. Did it show?"

"No, you handled yourself well."

"Liar," she said softly.

Richard stepped to stand beside her at the stone railing. "You are right and I'm not a very good one."

She looked out over the river. The wind off the water gently blew her curls around her face and dried the tears.

"What are you thinking?" he asked.

"I'm wondering where I should go from here? What should I do?"

She was so independent. So proud. Her words pulled at his heart.

He held his hand in front of her. She looked down and saw the gold wedding band engraved with leaves and Celtic symbols in his fingers.

"This is yours," he said. "Take it." He pressed the ring into her hand.

"Mine?" she said, accepting the ring in her surprise.

"Yes, yours." He turned and began walking off. It was a gamble. The biggest one of his life.

"What is this for?" she called after him.

"What do you think?" he tossed over his shoulder. He kept walking, praying she would follow.

"Wait. Richard, *wait*."

He paused at the foot of the bridge, and to his everlasting joy, she came to him. She held his ring in her fingers as if it were something precious.

She stopped when they were a foot apart as if unwilling to move closer. "Where is your father and your uncle?"

"On their way back to London."

"And *what* is this ring for?" Her words were defiant, almost angry.

He drew a breath, releasing it before admitting, "I bought it for you. Yesterday. I'd thought that we would marry."

Since she stood on the curve of the bridge, for once they were almost eye to eye. The corners of her lips tightened. She reached out and brushed back a stray bit of his hair. "You don't want to marry me. You could do so much better, Richard." She looked down at the ring. "I'm not the sort of woman a man marries." She raised her eyes to meet his. "You, yourself, said that."

"Grace, I was a pompous ass when I said those words. I love you. I always will. I can't imagine any other woman more perfect for me."

"And your intended?" The words sounded as if she had to force them out.

"It's over. Finished. Abigail doesn't love me and I don't love her. I'm in love with you, Grace. Pure, sweet love, just like the poets sing. And I'm going to break a family tradition right now."

"What tradition is that?" she asked.

"The tradition of not being honest with oneself. You were right. My father and uncle did embezzle the money."

"And they admitted it?"

"They never will. It will always be something due to them. But your father admitted all three of them were in on the scheme. However, none of that is important any longer. I'm not going to live a life of lies. It's not what *I* want."

"What *do* you want?" she asked, almost as if not trusting his answer.

He smiled and took her hand. "I want a wife who is happy to see me when I come home," he said. "One who waits at the door with my children, eager to see me at the end of the day."

"That's a good thing to want," she agreed, the beginnings of a smile coming to her face.

"And I want to take time to enjoy that wife. I don't want to spend my life poring over ledgers. I have all the money I need, Grace. What I don't have is someone willing to help me spend it in a meaningful way."

"And what way would that be?" she wondered, sounding as if she was almost afraid this moment wasn't real.

"I was thinking a small farm. A gentleman's

farm. Some place where my children can have ponies to ride and enjoy clean air and meadow song."

"Would Scotland suit you?" she asked.

"Scotland is lovely," he agreed, "but not Inverness. I will not walk down the street and greet your father civilly. It's wrong to be rigid. Very much like my former self, but I will not wish the man a good day as if there is no history between us. And finally, what I want is a woman who, in spite of all the mistakes I've made, and how notably human I am, would be proud to wear that ring. It's not just a marriage ring, Grace. It's my heart I'm offering. My soul."

At last, tears ran down her cheeks. She could hold them back no more. "I was so angry with you yesterday. I felt betrayed."

"With some cause."

"What of your father? Your uncle? I do not think I could like them overmuch."

"I doubt if they'll visit our farm," he assured her.

"And so what you are saying is that we live our lives for ourselves."

" 'Tis the way of marriage. We create our own family, and you know what, Grace? We won't make the mistakes our parents did."

"How can you be so certain?"

"Because I love you, Grace. I'll always love you. They don't even know what those words mean."

"Here," she said, offering him the ring.

Richard hesitated—and then she raised her left hand.

"Place it on my finger," she said, "and I swear by everything holy, I shall never remove it. My blessed, blessed man, you are everything I've ever desired. I was standing on this bridge wondering why I wasn't more upset with the turn of events, with the lies I'd been given all my life—and then I thought of you, so strong, so wise, and right there by my side even after I'd been cruel. Please put the ring on my finger before you change your mind. I love you, Richard Lynsted, and will do so all the days of my life."

He slid the ring on her finger. It fit perfectly, but then he'd known it would.

She placed her hand in his and together they went that moment in search of a parson. By dark they were married.

Grace wouldn't even take off the ring for the ceremony so he could place it on her finger again and Richard didn't ask her.

Instead, he made her his heart, his soul . . . his wife.